The Doctor from Bombay

Gos Jilani

Chapter 1

"Where have you come from, Sir?" A Customs Officer called him over.

"Bombay."

"I need to search your bags, Sir."

Why did he want to go through his luggage? He had done nothing wrong. Saj shuddered. His heart pounded, and he had sweat beads on his forehead. A shady character had sat next to him on the plane. Did that man plant drugs on him?

"What are these?" The officer pointed to the containers in a plastic bag. He found tropical fruits and a couple of bottles of oil.

Clearing his throat, Saj muttered, "My mother gave them to me. I am a doctor, and these are useful for my health...and I use the oil on my hair. It's a conditioner."

"You can't bring them through. I'll have to confiscate these items."

It was a Sunday afternoon. Saj rubbed his eyes and yawned as he re-packed his bags. He had come off a marathon twelve-hour flight from Bombay. Heathrow

Airport was neat, the floor shiny with no litter, and the walls spotless. Back home, they made little effort to keep the place tidy.

Saj was a handsome man in his late twenties. He tried to straighten the brown jacket he had borrowed from his father. It was old-fashioned and too big for him. A multi-coloured shirt and a bright green tie didn't match.

His eyes darted to every corner of the alien environment. Grabbing his bags, he headed for the exit sign. As he walked around the arrivals area, he noticed a newspaper. Margaret Thatcher's picture stood out on the front page with the headline 'Ten Years of Thatcher 79-89'. Even people in India knew her as the Iron Lady.

Saj searched for his friend. He bumped into people and received angry stares. Half an hour passed but no sign of Dipak. What would he do if his friend didn't turn up?

Someone tapped him on his shoulder. He turned around.

"Dipak. I'm pleased you are here! You got me worried." Saj beamed, and his eyes lit up.

"Relax my friend. We're all accustomed to being late back home. Punctuality isn't our strength."

Dipak was chubby with thinning dark hair and had a moustache too. He stood a foot shorter than Saj with a darker complexion than him. They had been friends since medical school.

"I need to phone home Dipak to let my parents know I've landed safely."

"Don't worry. You can ring later."

"But they will be worried."

4

Dipak walked ahead briskly towards the Train sign as if he never heard him. Saj stayed close to his friend in case he lost him in the crowd.

"How was your flight?" Dipak asked as they struggled to their seats.

Saj yawned. "Exciting, but it feels everything around is moving. It must be the jet-lag." He expected sympathy from his friend but received none.

"You'll be fine to work tomorrow after a good night's sleep."

"Tomorrow?" Saj gasped. His first day as a junior doctor at the Royal Beacon.

He had no choice but to accept what Dipak had arranged for him at the hospital.

"This train is brilliant Dipak, so immaculate and modern. You remember the trains in India? Even the smell is nicer here."

"This is England, my friend."

"They searched my bags in customs. I was scared. They took away my hair tonic. Is it because of my colour?"

"The Customs do it at random and may pick anyone." Dipak smiled, as he read his newspaper.

Saj stared out of the window. Back home builders painted houses with bright colours; each was unique. Here, all looked the same. Why? He wondered.

"It's so green and lush here compared to Bombay. This train is fast and so quiet." Saj chattered with the innocence of a child. Dipak ignored his comments, too engrossed in his paper.

They got off at Harrow Field, a town on the outskirts of London and hired a taxi. The doctors' accommodation was a five minutes' walk from the hospital building. It was August. The sun was shining but dark clouds were forming in the distance.

"Here's your key." Dipak handed it to him. "Your room is on the first floor. You should relax and be ready for the big day."

Saj carried his suitcase upstairs. The room was small with a single bed. It was beautiful compared to his place back home, he thought. He flopped onto the bed, then stretched and yawned a couple of times.

The next he remembered hearing were strange noises which woke him up. He wondered if it was a dream. The room light was on, and he still wore his travel clothes. Rubbing his eyes, he glanced at the clock, 2 am. The noise came from next door. It sounded like banging along with muffled voices. A few minutes later it stopped, and he went back to sleep.

Dragging himself out of bed the next morning, Saj massaged his forehead. The jetlag gave him a headache. A couple of paracetamol tablets he brought from Bombay came in handy. It was his first day in the National Health Service in England, so he had no idea what to expect.

He admired the tall, majestic building of the Royal Beacon as he strolled to the hospital. When he entered, the corridor gleamed. Saj got into the lift. He unconsciously clenched and unclenched his fist as he walked with carefully measured steps into the Medical Ward on the 10th floor.

"I am the new doctor here." Saj hesitated as he introduced himself to a nurse.

"Please come with me."

She left him at the door of the doctors' office. He noted three doctors in white coats busy in conversation. They turned to look at him.

"Erm...I'm Dr Sajindrapalonam. I'm supposed to start work here today."

One of the doctors came forward, smiled, and shook his hand. "I am James."

Another physician with grey hair and glasses was engrossed reading the notes. Saj assumed he must be the senior doctor.

James drew the other doctor's attention after a few minutes. "This is Dr Fitzgerald; he's the consultant. And this is the new doctor, Dr..."

"Dr Sajindrapalonam, please call me Saj," he said with a nervous smile.

"James, he needs to find a white coat," said Dr Fitzgerald.

After those earlier introductions, the consultant did a ward round and examined patients. Saj and the other doctors accompanied him. They discussed the cases and took orders.

The ward looked spotless. Crisp white sheets. Patients had privacy and were treated with dignity and respect. He could see no flies or cockroaches. In hospitals back home, litter would be on the floor and walls and linens would be stained.

On occasions, more than one person would sleep on a single bed, he thought and smiled to himself.

Elderly patients occupied most of the beds, which surprised Saj. Where were the youngsters? Maybe back home, people didn't live long.

Saj sensed that a few patients and staff scrutinised him, so he avoided their gaze. It must be because of his dark skin colour. Soon they would get familiarised, he thought.

The round went on for more than two hours. When it ended, Saj slumped in the chair in the office but soon realised that there was more work to be done.

"Come on. I'll introduce you to the others," James said.

Saj began to relax. James took him to the nurses' office.

"This is Sister Wilkins, and this is Dr Saj, the new physician."

They shook hands. "Welcome to Holmes, hope you'll settle in quickly." She took a bite of cake, a sip of coffee and squeezed her ample figure into the chair.

"Thanks," said Saj. He hoped it would be easy to work with her although she seemed quite stern.

"Would you like to go for lunch?" James asked as they walked back to the office.

"Yes. I am starving."

James must be in his late twenties. He had pale skin with short blonde hair and striking blue eyes. Saj would have loved to have his features.

The canteen buzzed. Saj stared at the meal the dinner lady served. What's this? Boiled vegetables and lettuce were on the menu. How could they cook without spices? They feed these green leaves to cattle back home, he thought.

Copying James in front of him, he had no choice but to order fish and chips. A couple of nurses sat at the table next to them. The smell of the vinegar enticed him, and he used too much. Saj decided to abandon the knife and dig in with the fork hoping James didn't notice his clumsiness. They ate with their hands in Bombay and found it more natural.

"The fish taste nice," Saj said as he took a bite.

James sipped coke from the can. "No curries today. They serve it only on Fridays. I'm not sure you would like it, though." He grinned.

"I don't expect it to be like our curries."

"Do you eat meat Saj?"

"In our religion cows are sacred, so no beef for me. Some people don't consume meat at all. Religion is an important part of our culture."

"I'll eat anything when I'm hungry," James said and chuckled.

"How was your first day?" Dipak asked Saj as they met in the corridor.

"Alright, but there is so much to learn. Everything is so professional here."

A nurse passed them as they walked. "Hi Dipak," she said. He nodded and smiled.

"How are you so popular with the ladies," Saj said.

"They all love me; you need to get on their right side. With time, you'll learn."

Dipak worked as an anaesthetist. He had lived in England for over four years. Although he was plain looking, his pleasant manners impressed all. Saj liked him as he was kind at heart.

"I've organised a get-together tonight at the social club. Do you want to come?" Dipak asked.

"Yes, sure."

The doctors' accommodation was adjacent to the nurses' quarters. The English nurses were all so beautiful. He shuffled from one foot to another and managed little more than a "Hello nice to meet you."

Saj wore black trousers, a white shirt, and a green tie. He thought he would impress everyone at the party.

Ear-splitting music welcomed him at the social club. He recognised a couple of songs by Michael Jackson, which he heard back home. Bollywood and Bhangra music was his favourite.

The room was packed with men and women who chatted and laughed. Saj stood alone holding his breath, his eyes dancing to every corner. He searched around for his friend but couldn't find him.

As he turned around to leave, he saw Dipak right in front of him.

"Where are you off, my friend? Dipak said as he put his arm around Saj's shoulder. He held a can of beer in his other hand.

"I couldn't find you."

"What would you like to drink?" Dipak asked.

"Coke, please."

"Coke? Come on fella, have something strong."

"No alcohol for me." He had to shout as the music deafened. Dipak handed him a glass of Coke.

"Tell me Dipak. The other evening, I could hear noises at night. It came from the room next door, made me worry."

"You are so naïve my friend. Doug, your neighbour, must be having an exciting time, you know," Dipak slurred.

It took Saj quite a while to understand what he meant by "exciting time". He smiled to himself and thought how stupid he must be.

Dipak wobbled on his feet in a jovial mood. How alcohol could affect his behaviour. Back home he wouldn't act in this way, he thought.

"Come on Dipak. Let's dance." A woman in a short red skirt dragged him away.

The ladies looked beautiful and sexy in their skimpy outfits. Girls couldn't imagine dressing in this way in Bombay. He stayed for an hour.

Saj had grown up in a conservative family. His father worked long hours in a factory and earned enough to survive. But was too proud to let his wife take a job. The younger sister studied at college. Father was a stern man. He wanted Saj to become a specialist doctor so he could change the fortune of his family. Doctors were respected and wealthy in Bombay.

He loved his family and knew a lot of responsibility lay on his shoulders. His father sent him to an English medium private school. Education was expensive, more than he could afford, but it was an investment. He was advised by his father to focus on his studies and stay away from any distractions. Hence Saj had few friends in college. He was too timid to talk to his parents about his true feelings.

Chapter 2

Saj felt the heat that morning. Many patients needed his attention. He tried to push his worries aside, took a deep breath and pulled his shoulders back. The nursing staff expected him to know everything related to patient care. It was his first Emergency on call in Holmes Ward.

A couple of nurses hurried to a fifty-year-old patient who was admitted in the last hour. This man had severe chest pain and stopped breathing. He was pale, cold and clammy. After examining him quickly, Saj pondered what to do next.

"I think he needs an intravenous line," a nurse said.

She handed him a cannula. Saj had never seen a needle like this one before. In Bombay hospitals, they used cheaper equipment. He attempted to insert it into the man's forearm, a few times. No luck.

"The veins aren't right. I can't get it in," Saj mumbled. His hand was shaking. The patient looked ghastly.

The nurse stared at Saj as he wiped the sweat from his brow.

One of the senior nurses shouted, "Leanne, could you please call Dr Smith now,"

After a few minutes wait, the other doctor arrived. He grabbed hold of the cannula and inserted it the first time.

"Diamorphine please, and give him oxygen," he instructed the nurse.

Saj stood still at the bedside observing others as they dealt with the emergency. He was envious of the other doctor's confidence. No one needed Saj's help, he was a silent spectator. The doctor injected a drug to ease the pain. The man's colour improved after five minutes. A monitor was put on the patient by a nurse, and the doctor took blood off for tests. He ran an electrocardiogram to check the damage to the heart.

Once the emergency ended, Saj noted a few nurses were whispering as they glanced at him. They must think he was incompetent. What a laughing stock he must be.

"You need to learn the basics. How can you not do such a simple procedure?" Dr Smith frowned and walked away.

"I am sorry," he stuttered avoiding eye contact with him.

Saj sat in the office, staring at the wall, reminiscing the incident. He thought how confident he was in the hospital back home. The doctors here should have shown him how to perform medical procedures. He never had a job in England before, and they knew it. Suddenly he had been thrown in at the deep end. He felt humiliated.

"Are you alright, doctor?" A nurse entered the office and startled him.

"I am fine thanks." Saj forced a smile. He wondered whether she felt sorry for him.

"Could you please come and see this lady. She doesn't look well. Then I'll make you a cup of tea."

They walked down the long corridor towards the patient's side room.

"I'm Leanne, my friend's call me Lea."

"Hello."

"It takes time to find your feet in a new place," she said.

Saj remained silent and kept walking with his head bowed.

"I haven't been working here long. Only finished my nurse training three months back. There have been awkward situations for me, but I can assure you it gets easier." Lea grinned.

Saj looked towards her and gave a half-smile. "I hope it does."

"It will and if you need any help please do ask."

"Thanks."

"Are you from India?"

"Yes. Bombay."

"It must be hard for you being in a strange country on your own."

Saj kept quiet.

"My ancestors have been there. They were in the army. I remember my mum mentioning them. Fascinating country," Lea said.

"It's alright." He sounded unenthusiastic.

"My sister wants to go to your country. She loves travelling."

They arrived at the patient's bedside.

"And this is Mrs Fletcher," Lea said.

The lady in her sixties appeared short of breath and distressed. She sat on the edge of the bed with an oxygen mask on.

"Hello, Mrs Fletcher. I am Dr Saj. I need to examine you."

Lea held the patient's hand while Saj put his stethoscope on her chest and checked her pulse.

"Could you please get me Frusemide?" He asked the nurse while writing the prescription.

She came back with the drug. Saj held his breath and attempted to put in the cannula in her left forearm. He missed the first time but got it in the second.

"Yes, it's in." He sounded excited and administered the drug.

Within a few minutes, her breathing improved. Saj looked up towards Lea, and both smiled.

"Are you feeling better now," he asked the lady.

"Yes, thank you, doctor."

"She'll need a chest X-ray Lea," he said. "And thanks for your advice."

Later that afternoon, he told James what had happened earlier with Dr Smith. James demonstrated some of the required medical procedures and helped Saj understand what the staff expected from him. They had a brief teaching session.

"Ask me anything if you aren't sure." James got up and put his hand on Saj's shoulder.

"I appreciate it." He had found a saviour in James.

Saj didn't get any breaks in the day. He couldn't remember how many cups of tea he drank. By the time he finished dealing with his last patient, he felt exhausted. Rubbing his eyes, he gazed out through the huge glass window. He spotted the first light of the day, realising he had worked nonstop for more than twenty-four hours.

Back in his room at 7 am and still dressed in his work clothes, he lay on his bed and fell asleep. The telephone rang which made him jump. For a moment, he was unsure of his surroundings. He squinted at the clock. It was 9.15 am.

"Where are you?" the ward clerk asked. "The round has already started. They're waiting for you."

"I am on my way."

Saj sat wide-eyed. Realising that there was more work to do, he dashed to join the ward round. The consultant had a scowl on his face. How could they expect the doctor to manage patients without any sleep? Saj wondered.

He stifled his yawns and could hardly keep his eyes open during the round. James helped him write up the notes. How he survived the day, he would never know. Finishing work at 5.30 pm, he made his way to the canteen for dinner.

"How can this be called a curry?" He complained to Dipak who was having his meal. "There are pieces of apples, raisins and god know what else." Saj pointed to the plate as he put it down.

"This is an English curry man. You can forget your own spicy dishes here."

"This taste nothing like our food. I would love to cook myself." Saj took a bite of the naan bread.

"How was your day?" Dipak asked sipping his orange juice.

"Terrible. I want to go to bed."

"Welcome to the NHS."

"Tell me Dipak. Do they mistreat us here because we are coloured?"

"Well. Not always. Some people can be prejudiced."

"How can we work in these conditions. Back home, we did shifts and had enough rest. Why can't they employ more doctors here?"

"Perhaps they are short of medics in England. Therefore, they need foreign graduates. There are too many of us in Bombay."

"People always sound polite and say, 'please and 'thank you' here. We are not accustomed to these words back home." Saj gulped his Coke.

"It's the English culture, my friend. Remember to say these words here in your conversation. We appear more abrupt."

It was a grey Saturday morning. Saj wanted to see the sights and had persuaded Dipak to come too. He didn't feel confident enough to go on his own.

They took an open-top London sightseeing tour bus. The historical buildings fascinated him. He loved to watch people; the way they dressed, their hairstyles and their behaviour.

Saj had only read and seen movies of the Big Ben and Westminster Abbey but couldn't believe all these places were for real. He sat on the top deck of the bus excited like a little boy. The camera he brought from Bombay kept clicking.

The highlight of his tour was Buckingham Palace. He shouted with excitement pointing to the palace. "Dipak. Look. The Queen lives there. I wish my parents were here. They would love it." A few passengers turned around and stared at him.

He had read about the monarchy and the Queen since he was a kid. Back in Bombay, most people could only dream of travelling to London. The high cost of the journey made it impossible.

Saj took numerous pictures; he wanted his parents to see them. Dipak didn't show much interest; he had seen it all before. The sun came out from behind the clouds, but Saj still felt the cold and kept himself wrapped up. Tourists from all over the world thronged central London, all captivated by the famous sights.

As they wandered along, he saw a long queue of people at the bus stop.

"We would push our way in at home. Nobody would care," Saj said.

"People here are more disciplined. Hence the British empire ruled us for a long time."

Dipak stopped outside a bank. Saj had never seen a cash point.

"How can you take money out from the wall. Is there a man behind it?"

Dipak grinned as he counted the cash. "The money is in a digital vault. You can withdraw anytime with a card."

"Fascinating. You don't hear any cars honking, so quiet. Our roads are congested and noisy."

"Drivers follow the rules here otherwise they would be fined. Besides, honking is illegal," Dipak said stepping on to a zebra crossing. "No cows and stray dogs roaming on the roads either."

"Watch out Dipak," Saj screamed. A car was approaching fast towards him. He was amazed, the car braked and stopped a foot away from Dipak.

"Come on. We need to cross. The cars won't wait forever." Dipak waved to him. Saj stared at the cars in disbelief as the two crossed the road. He was impressed. No driver honked. In Bombay, if you tried this you would be killed, he thought and smiled to himself.

He spotted a thin old man sitting on the pavement, as they walked down a busy side street. The unkempt vagrant with a long beard had wrapped himself in a dirty blanket.

Dipak sensed what went through Saj's head. "Homeless people are even in England, not as many as back home."

Saj pointed out. "There is a McDonalds. I am starving." It was past his lunch time.

They ordered chicken burgers and Coke. It was cheaper to take away, so they sat on an empty bench surrounded by pigeons.

"Why did you buy two meals?" Dipak asked.

"One is for that old man. I saw him search in the dustbin for food earlier."

Saj walked to the homeless man and handed him the burger meal. Grabbing the pack, he gazed at him, gave a half-smile, and nodded. Then gulped the food in a flash.

"Take this." Saj handed him a ten pounds note.

The man stared at the cash, hesitated and took it.

"Thanks," he said and gave Saj a salute.

He must have been in the forces, Saj thought.

"I am impressed by your noble gesture," Dipak said.

His friend's comments made Saj proud. "We don't realise how privileged we are," he said.

Dipak wanted to buy a newspaper. An Indian family owned the kiosk which surprised Saj. The ladies were in their traditional baggy tops and trousers and spoke in Punjabi.

"Look," he whispered in Dipak's ear as he pointed to the counter. "Those newspapers on the shelves."

Dipak chuckled. "Do you mean the topless girls on the front page?"

Saj nodded as he glanced around to make sure no one had seen him.

"Yes. These are everywhere. People are more open-minded here. Soon you'll enjoy them," Dipak said and laughed.

"Amazing," said Saj as they stepped out of the store. He opened a packet of crisp as the two strolled along.

"Excuse me." Someone called out from behind in a loud firm tone.

Saj stopped and turned around. A six-foot middle-aged man glared at him and pointed to the pavement.

At first, Saj was confused. Soon he realised what he had done. He had thrown away the empty packet on the street.

"Sorry," Saj said sheepishly and picked up the litter.

Dipak grinned and said, "You ought to be careful here man. This place is not Bombay. You were unlucky to get caught."

"My fault. Now I know now why this country is so clean. I wish we were as strict back home."

"It takes a long time to change our old habits, my friend."

"Is there a temple around here Dipak?"

"No idea."

Saj smiled as he reminisced his trip to London, on Monday morning. He loved it and got to know Dipak better. It was a fantastic experience and a revelation.

"Mr Ridal has come in and needs to be seen by a doctor." One of the nurses, Lucy walked in. Saj thought that she was cute and how her blue eyes sparkled.

This seventy-year-old man had pain in his tummy. But it didn't stop him chatting while Saj examined him. He took blood off for tests and headed to the doctors' room.

As he was about to leave the ward after work, Alex the staff nurse came to him.

"We are having a party at the nurses' hall. Would you like to come?"

Saj felt a lump in his throat. "When is it?" He pretended to sound casual.

"Tonight."

"Sorry. I need to revise for my exams."

"Oh." She lingered in the doorway twiddling her hair. "Why not?" She probed.

He looked at her more closely. She was gorgeous, and for a moment he allowed himself to imagine being at the party with her. But then his father's words rang loud in his ears.

"I'm sorry. I just can't."

That evening Saj was watching the news in his room. There was a knock on the door. He thought it must be Dipak. Alex stood there. She looked pretty in a sexy black dress, different from when she was in her nurses' uniform. The lump returned.

"Are you coming to the party?"

"I have to study."

"You can read later. Come for an hour." She fluttered her eyelashes.

Mesmerised, he found himself saying, "Could you please wait outside while I get changed?" He put on a pair of navy trousers, a pink shirt and sprayed cologne all over.

Alex stayed close to him all evening.

"How come you speak such good English?"

"I studied English since I was at primary school."

"What do you want to drink? "She asked.

"Orange juice please."

"How boring."

"I tried alcohol once but don't like the taste." Saj defended himself.

Alex flicked her long dark hair behind her shoulders. She was in her early twenties and very curvy.

"Steve never wants to go out. He is only interested in football. You're different." She gave him a seductive look. Her eyes sparkled. Steve must be her husband, Saj thought.

"Do you know that a few of the nurses like you?" Alex spoke close to his ear, as the music deafened.

"No." He smiled and blushed.

It became noisier, as more people arrived. The place was overflowing. They all chatted and laughed. Saj wondered why people behaved so erratically after a few drinks. A lady threw up as she rushed to the toilet. He was glad he didn't drink alcohol.

Saj didn't know anyone there. Whitney Houston's track "I Want to Dance with Somebody" came on.

Alex wobbled on her feet. She pulled his arm. "Shall we dance. I love this song."

"But I can't."

"Yes, you can."

Saj had no idea how to dance the English way. Alex was a fantastic dancer and had a superb rhythm. He could only make a few silly Bollywood moves of his own by throwing both arms in the air. That made her laugh.

"Loosen up and move as I am." She held him tight, with her face close to his. He could feel her breasts pressed on his chest. "You are handsome," Alex said as she gazed into his eyes.

Saj forced a smile but wasn't comfortable. What if Alex's husband came, he thought? He danced for a few minutes only to be polite.

"Did you have girlfriends back home?"

"Yeah." He lied, too ashamed to tell the truth. Saj realised that it is the norm for men to have girlfriends here. It would be odd not to. In Bombay, their parents would arrange their marriages.

"I must go," he said.

"It's only midnight." Her speech was slurred.

"I'm really sorry. I must leave. Thanks for the invite."

Saj tried not to feel guilty. He could see sadness on Alex's face as he left. She was fun, and he liked her, but she had a partner. Saj had never experienced any woman throwing herself at him. They had more freedom in this society, and he had enjoyed the attention. There was a bounce in his step and a grin on his face as he walked back to his room.

Chapter 3

After a lengthy consultant round, Saj slumped in the chair in the doctors' office. It had been a week since he attended Alex's party.

"You look tired, James," he said pulling out the patient notes from the trolley.

"Work is non-stop, and the baby keeps me awake at night. Would you like coffee?" James asked.

"Tea, please. Plenty of milk and one sugar."

James always had a smile on his face. Patients loved him because of his kindness. At times, he would take on others' work, he couldn't say no. He had been an excellent help for Saj, and they built a real friendship. Both played pool in the doctors' mess.

"Do you know what I heard." James returned with two mugs. He handed one to Saj and grinned.

"What is it?"

"There is a rumour going around that you and Dipak are...Erm...you know."

"What do you mean?" Saj had a severe look.

"The two of you are an item," James said with a cheeky smile.

"Rubbish. Who told you?"

Saj didn't find it amusing. He realised that he ought to find a girlfriend; otherwise, people will gossip about his sexual inclination.

It was his first full weekend on call. Saj found the long hours arduous. His duty started on a Friday and ended on Monday, without any allocated breaks. Patients with chest, heart, abdominal problems and strokes were admitted. His pager kept beeping all day as he had to cover many wards. Dr Richard Baxter was his senior, but he wouldn't come to help him out.

Saj glanced at the clock. It was 7 pm. His stomach rumbled, so he headed for the canteen. Ordering fish and chips, he looked forward to his meal.

As he sat with his tray, the dreaded call of cardiac arrest sounded on his beeper. Leaving his food, he dashed towards Nightingale ward. He sprinted down the corridor and kept looking for signs for the department. There were a lot of people around due to the visiting hours. He bumped into a man who glared at him, annoyed. After Saj had apologised to the man, he tripped over but kept running. His beeper kept buzzing.

Saj gasped for breath when he arrived on Nightingale. A couple of doctors and nurses gathered around a bed. They attempted to resuscitate the patient. He offered to help, but nobody took any notice of him. They shouted orders. The doctor administered several drugs to this old man and gave adrenaline in the end. It was in vain. Saj was still breathless from his sprint. He sensed a few inhospitable looks from the staff, only for being a minute late. Did they not consider he could be lost being new to the hospital? He wondered.

"Where have you been?" Dr Baxter pulled him to one side.

"I had to run from the canteen and couldn't find the ward." Saj stumbled over his words.

"This isn't good enough. Be careful next time." Baxter wagged a finger at him.

"I'm sorry." Saj looked down and away.

"Where do you come from?"

"Bombay."

"Remember, this isn't Bombay. We work to high standards in this country."

|Saj couldn't defend himself and felt humiliated. Can he not eat one proper meal in peace during the day?

After he had done the paperwork, Saj went back to the canteen. It was closed. He wanted to scream as his stomach churned. At least the vending machine worked. He had no choice but to get a sandwich and returned to the doctors' quarters.

His head was fuzzy when he reached his room, and he collapsed in the chair. Eating the bland sandwich, he felt sorry for himself. Saj thought of his family back home. He missed his mother. Quitting was not an option for him. His parents would be disappointed if he did.

Numerous emergency admissions came in that weekend. Saj managed to get only three hours of sleep and continued to work during the day.

At 3 am on Sunday, the nurse called him to the cardiac unit to see a sixty-year-old lady. Her heart went fast and irregular. She had been admitted with a coronary, a few days before.

The woman appeared pale and drowsy. Her breathing was rapid and shallow, and she struggled to respond to his questions. Saj examined her and read the ECG recording. It showed ventricular arrhythmia. He asked the nurse for Lignocaine to slow down her heart. It didn't work. He tried another drug, but the lady continued to deteriorate. Saj found it hard to keep his eyes open and kept yawning. Staring at the monitor, his mind went completely blank.

Should he call the consultant for advice? He wouldn't be pleased being woken up early on a Sunday morning, he pondered. By the time he came, she would be dead, or should he try a new drug?

It needed a quick and precise decision. Saj went for the second option. Administering the medicine intravenously, he hoped her heart would slow down, but it didn't. He panicked and resuscitated her with the help of the nurses. All attempts failed, and the woman died.

Could he have managed the patient better? He should have telephoned the consultant. But what would he have thought? That Saj must be incompetent, he questioned his judgement.

The lady's husband sat in the waiting room. Saj had to tell him the grim news.

"I'm sorry. We couldn't save your wife." He avoided eye contact with the husband.

The man grabbed Saj tightly. Tears streamed down his eyes on to Saj's white coat, and he held him for a minute.

"You tried your best, doctor. I loved her but never told her often. We planned to go to Marbella next month, to visit our daughter." The man sobbed.

Saj couldn't take it anymore. Wiping his eyes, he walked away and left the nurses behind to console the poor man. He blamed himself for his failure to save the woman. Maybe he could have thought more clearly if he wasn't exhausted.

As Saj wandered down the corridor, he gazed out through the window. Daylight spread on the horizon. It was Sunday and his next working day was about to begin.

It was a Friday, a week later. Saj and Dipak walked to the table with their food trays at lunch. A couple of nurses sat chatting. Both went quiet.

"Ladies. Shall we join you?" Dipak put his tray on the table. "What were you discussing before we came."

"Erm...Nothing," the younger nurse said.

"Rachel said Dr Saj is an excellent doctor. He works hard and is kind to his patients. They all love him." She glanced at the other nurse. "And he is handsome and doesn't have a girlfriend." She giggled.

"No. I didn't say that." Rachel blushed and looked away.

"Yes, you did." The senior nurse grinned.

Saj smiled but kept quiet.

"What about me?" Dipak said. They all laughed.

After a few minutes, the nurses excused themselves and left the table.

"Man, you look like shit. You shouldn't work so hard," Dipak said as he sprinkled salt on his food.

"I can't finish on time, so much to do."

"You leave the ward too late. Nobody will appreciate you."

"I only had a few hours' sleep on my last weekend. This isn't fair." Saj shuffled back in his chair. He told Dipak of the incident in the cardiac unit and how upset he was.

"Don't worry my friend. This happens, and you get accustomed."

"How can I make life and death decisions when I'm shattered?"

Dipak shrugged. "Changing the subject, I am going to a club tonight with a few friends. Do you want to come?"

Saj deliberated for a moment. "My father may call me."

"Don't make excuses. It'll be good for you."

They agreed to meet in the doctors' lounge that evening.

Vogue was an upmarket nightclub. Saj had never been to a discotheque, so he was apprehensive but excited. The streets were crowded on a Saturday night. When they arrived, he saw a queue of young men and women, all stylishly dressed.

After a long wait, they bought their tickets and moved forward. A security man stepped right in front of Saj at the door, which alarmed him. He must be more than six feet, bald with a mean face, and had his arms folded across his chest. Eyeing Saj up and down, he pointed at his feet. "You can't go in."

"What's the problem?" Dipak came to his rescue.

"We have a dress code." The man stared at Saj's trainers.

"Could you please make an exception? We are doctors and come from a long way."

"No, he can't go in, but you can. These are the rules." The bouncer sounded stern.

Saj looked away. He felt that people in the queue were glaring at him, annoyed at the holdup. How embarrassing, he thought and wanted to leave.

"Go and change your shoes. I'll wait at the club," said Dipak.

Saj was glad he made an effort as the club was unique. The deep bass thundered and seemed to pulsate the black walls and ceiling.

Since he had arrived in England, Saj had become more interested in English pop music. He watched Top of the Pops on Thursdays and recorded songs on his cassette recorder from the radio.

Wandering around he observed a mix of young men and women in the club. The girls were beautiful and wore little, the men ogled at them. He finally spotted Dipak with a couple of ladies.

"You are back, splendid. This is my friend Saj." He introduced him.

After a few drinks, Dipak seemed in high spirits. "You need to try beer tonight Saj."

"Are you enjoying yourself?" One of the women asked.

"Yeah. Fantastic music."

"Have you been here before?" she spoke close to his ear. Saj's senses swam in her perfume.

"No, my first time."

People indulging in alcohol conversed and laughed. A lady with long dark hair approached Saj. "Would you like to dance?"

"Erm...Okay." He couldn't believe it.

As he walked to the dance floor, he glanced at Dipak who had a huge grin. Saj had no idea why. Once he had finished with the lady, he found Dipak who had too much to drink. So did both the girls who giggled loudly.

"I think the woman you danced with fancies you. Do you know her?" Dipak asked.

Saj shrugged. "No."

Dipak came near him and whispered, "He is a man dressed as a woman."

"Oh, my God. I never thought it is possible." Saj stared at the woman, his eyes drawn to her neck. Even in the dim light, the bulging Adam's apple must be a giveaway. Saj's face dropped. How could he be so stupid? Why is a man dressed up like that? He winced while Dipak chuckled.

Dipak handed Saj a beer. Why not, he needed to relax. After a while, he became chattier.

Pointing to the glass, Saj said, "This is wonderful."

"I told you."

Saj tried not to drink too much alcohol. His parents would hate him in this state, he thought.

"Shall we go Dipak. It is 1 am." He showed him the time.

"Alright," Dipak said in a faint voice and wobbled on his feet.

The group headed back to the hospital. Saj realised one of the ladies, Lucy was a nurse in his ward.

"Sorry. I didn't recognise you without your clothes, I mean uniform."

"No worries." She chuckled.

Walking back, Lucy held Saj's arm. Dipak went to his room accompanied by the other woman. Saj and Lucy strolled towards the nurses' accommodation in fits of giggles. He meant to say goodbye when she grabbed his hand.

"Do you want to come in for a coffee?" Lucy asked.

"It's too late," he replied after a moment's hesitation.

"You are off tomorrow, come in for ten minutes," she said gazing into his eyes.

"Okay." Saj was in a jovial mood after the drinks.

Lucy's clothes were scattered all around her small room. Perhaps she had been in a rush to go out, he thought.

"Excuse this mess." She gathered her clothes in a hurry from a small worn-out couch. "Take a seat."

Saj sat gingerly on the edge of the sofa, twiddling his fingers. He had never been in female company on his own under such circumstances.

"All the patients speak highly of you," she said. "You are kind to them."

Saj smiled. "You are a good nurse."

"Thanks. Would you like beer or vodka?"

He surprised himself with his reply. "Beer, please."

Lucy came back with the drinks and sat close to him. Saj shuffled, but the seat was narrow.

"I split up with my boyfriend a couple of weeks back." She took a sip. "He was asking for a commitment, but I'm not ready to settle down yet."

She moved even closer. "You are handsome." Her lashes fluttered.

"You are pretty too." He smiled.

Lucy gazed into his eyes, leant forward, and wrapped her arms around his shoulders. Slowly she put her lips on his and kissed him. Saj moved back and gasped, his heart pounding. But he didn't resist Lucy's advances. His parents would never find out what he had been up to. Maybe it's time to leave, he wondered.

Lucy stopped and said, "You have never done this before?"

Saj blushed. "Of course, I have. I'm just tired." He faked a smile.

"Relax and let yourself go."

What the heck, might be fun, he thought.

They kissed again. Lucy held his hand and led him to her bed. Saj held his breath and had no idea what to do or where to start. His hands trembled, and he could hear his heartbeat. With sweaty palms, he slowly unbuttoned his shirt. He took it off and then removed his vest. Lucy gawked at him admiring his muscular physique. Saj had never taken off his clothes in front of anyone.

As Lucy removed her blouse, Saj turned his face away. She took her bra off, and for the first time, he noted her lovely, rounded breasts. He admired her voluptuous figure in the dim light.

"Shall we turn the light off?"

Lucy caressed him passionately ignoring his request.

As she stroked the inside of Saj's legs, his manhood rose ready for action. A tingling sensation crawled all over him which he had never sensed before. Lucy kissed him all over his body and then took off her knickers. Saj didn't know what to do next and froze.

Lucy dragged him on top of her. As they wriggled and canoodled, she held his penis and put it inside her. Within a couple of seconds, Saj let out a loud pleasurable moan. Keeping still for a moment he discovered semen on him. He had climaxed already. Embarrassment stirred in Saj, and he wanted to disappear.

"Sorry, must be the drink. I'm not used to it." He jumped to his feet.

Grabbing a few tissues from the table, he wiped himself down. He rushed to put his clothes back on. Lucy lay in bed with the sheet pulled over her, she had a solemn face. He avoided eye contact with her but soon realised that they didn't use a condom.

"Erm…We didn't take any precaution," he mumbled.

"Don't worry. I'm on the pill," Lucy said as she stared at the ceiling.

"I'd better leave now." He hurried towards the door.

Saj stepped out into the dark corridor. Walking back to his room with his head bowed he relived the event. His first sexual encounter was a disaster. What Lucy must have thought? If his parents came to know, they would disown him. His culture forbade sex before marriage. Saj shuddered, he knew he had broken the rules.

Chapter 4

It was Monday morning. Saj felt more energetic as he had the weekend off. He glanced at Lucy as he strolled around the ward and gave her a half-hearted smile. She appeared long-faced as if she was ignoring him. He was still embarrassed by the other night.

During the round, the consultant examined a frail old man. The patient must be in his early nineties and had several strokes. The night before, he had fallen out of bed and bruised the back of his head. He had been immobile and confused for a long time and stopped eating. The consultant ordered an MRI scan of the head, X-rays, and numerous other blood tests. His action puzzled Saj.

On any other day, he would follow instructions given without questioning. When the doctors returned to the office, he decided to speak his mind. "Dr Smith. What do we plan to achieve with Mr Farrow? He is ninety and has a poor quality of life?"

Dr Smith smiled. "You're absolutely right Saj. I'm not only treating Mr Farrow but his family too."

Saj understood his idea to keep the family happy. The NHS can afford the cost of these tests here, he thought.

"What would you do in Bombay?" Dr Smith enquired.

He thought for a moment, and with a sarcastic smile said, "Most people back home don't live this long." Dr Smith raised his eyebrows.

He felt pleased that he was beginning to interact with colleagues.

Alex walked into the office.

"Mr Farrow's family are here, and they would like to talk to a doctor."

"I'll come in a minute," Saj said.

"What are you doing with the old man?" asked Mr Farrow's son-in-law, who sat with arms folded across his chest.

"After the tests are finished, and if they are normal, he could go home." Saj read his notes.

He frowned. "But he lives on his own."

"Can he not stay with a family member?"

"No, he can't," the daughter said. "We're busy people."

"The other option would be a nursing home." Saj tried to calm down the situation.

"Who the hell is going to pay?" the man said.

"I think the social services would be involved, most likely by disposing of his house."

"What? He wanted to leave the house to us in his Will," the daughter said.

"Okay. We'll talk later." Saj had enough and walked away.

Mr Farrow had two sons and a daughter who all lived nearby. None of them wanted to take care of him. This shocked Saj. In his culture, the family came first. People would kill their own needs and desires. They respected and cared for their family more than themselves, he thought. This patient would live with his children back in Bombay, no questions asked.

Saj slumped in the chair in the office. James walked in.

"How is it going Saj?"

"Not too bad."

"Would you like to come to dinner at my place tonight?" James asked.

"That would be great, thanks." Saj smiled.

"About 7.30 pm. Do you like roast chicken?"

"I do. Believe me, James, I can live without spicy food." Both laughed.

"You know where the married accommodation is?"

"Yeah."

"Emily would love to meet you. She has seen a Bollywood film at a friend's house and loved it. I told her about you."

Saj grinned.

At the end of the day when Saj entered his room, the phone was ringing.

"I called you the other night. The operator told me you were not on call. Where did you go?" His father took Saj by surprise.

"Erm...I went to a doctor friend Baba."

"Be careful." His father sounded suspicious and spoke in a stern manner. "You should be studying hard for your exams, so you can return soon. We need money for Gita's dowry. You have responsibilities for the family. Stay away from women, they are always trouble...wish I listened to your mother and arranged your marriage before you left." His father spoke fast.

"Don't worry...We're doing well in cricket. I'll go to Lords in July to watch them."

His father wouldn't give up. "I don't want you wasting time in bad company."

"How is everyone at home?"

"Good but your mother misses you. I'll finish now. Otherwise, the phone bill will be massive."

"Okay, I'll call you soon." He took a deep breath and sat down slowly on his bed.

Saj knew his family relied on him. He dared not contemplate the consequences of his father knowing the truth about Lucy. His eyes brimmed with tears; he missed his mother.

A knock at the door woke him up. He squinted at the clock; 7 pm. There was no one there when he opened it. The noise came from next door, with the bed shaking. He smiled to himself, got changed and headed out to James for dinner.

Chapter 5

"Mr Willis' relatives are here, they want to chat. You also have four new admissions to see, doctor." A nurse reported.

It was 9 pm the next evening. Saj had just returned from casualty to the ward. He yawned as he studied the notes.

As he was about to examine a lady, another nurse called him away. A man in his forties had an epileptic fit. Saj sedated him and returned to his first patient. He realised he had worked non-stop since morning. Mr Willis' relatives waited patiently.

He couldn't do all the work on his own. If he complained, it would be a sign of weakness, being the doctor from Bombay. He must prove that he was strong, he thought. While his mind wandered all over the place, Lucy entered the doctors' office.

"Would you like a cup of tea?" she asked.

"Thanks." Saj yawned. They had both avoided any conversation, relating to the disastrous night at her place. He thought he needed to break the ice.

"Sorry about the other night." He looked down and away. "I am quite new to all this."

Lucy smiled. "Please don't worry. I like you because you are different."

"Are we still friends?"

"Of course. Let me make your tea," Lucy said and left.

Saj worked on autopilot that day. He managed to carry on and returned to his room at 3 am. He sat on his bed and yawned feeling sorry for himself. His phone buzzed.

"This is the nurse from Heather Ward. One of our patients is complaining of abdominal pain. His observations are okay."

"Could you please give him the prescribed painkillers." He took a few details from the nurse and then fell asleep.

An hour later, the telephone rang again. Saj jumped. For a moment, he didn't know where he was. He grabbed the phone. The patient hadn't improved. Saj's mind went blank, he couldn't think straight. Struggling to keep his eyes open, he suggested a stronger painkiller. He told the nurse he would come down if the pain didn't improve and fell asleep.

Saj slept for half an hour when the emergency beeper buzzed. It was 5.15am. The same patient had now collapsed. Dragging himself out of bed he rubbed his eyes and grabbed his white coat. In the process, he knocked the glass of water off the table, tripped over his shoes and fell on the floor. He got up, rubbed his sore left arm, and dashed out.

A doctor and a couple of nurses had gathered around a patient when he arrived. Frantically they resuscitated him. Saj had never seen this patient before. He joined in with the others. The man survived and was transferred to the intensive care unit.

He peeked at the clock, 7 am. Back to his room he slumped in the chair and reflected on his day. He took a sip of water and felt the room spinning.

Appearing unshaven and shabby he reached Holmes ward at 8 am. His hair was messy as he hadn't showered. He didn't care.

"Dr Saj. Could you please go to the administrator's office as soon as possible?" the clerk asked him. He shrugged his shoulders and headed in that direction.

When he entered the room, he found a couple of men sitting around an enormous table. They all dressed in suits, along with Dr Smith, the consultant. Saj sensed an air of hostility in the room. One of them asked him to take a seat.

"I'm George Stevens, the hospital administrator. Can you tell me what happened to the patient at Heather Ward last night?"

Saj described the whole incidence of the calls. Dr Smith listened to his story for a couple of minutes, then interrupted him.

"That patient had abdominal surgery a few days back. He had internal bleeding and could have died." Dr Smith said, clenching his jaw.

"But nobody mentioned the operation to me. I asked the nurse on the phone." Saj held his breath, his heart beating fast. He was appalled at such aggression from his consultant.

Dr Smith pointed his finger at Saj and frowned. "You should have gone to the ward. You ought to be aware of doctors' duties and patient care. We can take disciplinary action against you. Don't treat my patients in this manner again. This is not Bombay."

Saj listened with patience to his rants, pondering how he should react. The most comfortable option for him would be to keep quiet and accept his mistake.

He took a deep breath and looked into Dr Smith's eyes. "With due respect, I consider myself a conscientious doctor. My patients and staff will vouch for it. Emergency admissions were exceptionally busy. I had only a couple of hours of sleep last night. I admit I must work long days. Is it fair for the patients to be treated by fatigued, sleep-deprived doctors?"

"But if you struggled, surely you should ask for help. Why didn't you?" Mr Stevens asked.

"Most senior doctors, especially consultants hate being disturbed at night. They wouldn't want to lose their sleep. We work seventy-two hours on call. Patients deserve better than what they receive. God knows how many lives alert doctors could have saved." Saj held their gaze.

There was deathly silence in the room. The men glanced at each other nervously.

Mr Stevens turned towards Dr Smith. "Would you like to add anything?"

Dr Smith was speechless for a moment. Clearing his throat, he said in a softer tone, "I think we need to sort out these issues and the concerns raised. I admire the work put in by junior doctors. We must find a solution for long hours."

"You'd better sort it out soon Dr Smith," Mr Stevens said.

They stared at each other, then Mr Stevens said, "Thanks for coming, Dr Saj. We appreciate your hard work. We need to make changes." He shook his hand.

Saj turned around and headed for the door, with a smile on his face. He forgot his tiredness.

"What happened. How did it go?" James asked when Saj got back to the ward.

Saj told details of the meeting. Everyone was impressed. Word quickly spread around the hospital about how he took a firm stand against long working hours. Saj was the hero of the day.

Chapter 6

The alarm blared and woke Saj up at 7 am, on a dark, cold morning. Rolling over, he turned it off. He could hear the rain pelting down with some ferocity and wondered how he slept through the night.

Where was the sun? Saj had not seen a glimpse for weeks. Depressing. In Bombay, people got excited when it rained or got cloudy. It was supposed to be romantic. Really? He wondered.

Thankfully it was quieter than usual in the ward. The clerk told him there would be no consultant round, which made everyone relax. Dr Smith was a stern character and could be quite rude to the staff. The sister liked him, though.

Saj felt relieved. He could catch up with his paperwork, he thought. When he entered the doctors' office, Lucy was waiting for him rather obviously.

After a moment's hesitation, she said, "Can I talk to you for a minute?"

"Yes, Sure. Is everything alright?"

Lucy peeked around. She bit the inside of her lips.

He gazed at her waiting for her reply.

She hesitated. "Erm...I think I'm pregnant," she blurted out.

Saj stared at her and felt his mouth go dry. "What? Are you sure? You can't be?"

"I'm sure."

"But...you told me you were on the pill. How could it happen?" He said and gasped.

"You're a doctor. You should know, there is still a small chance."

There was silence for a few moments while Saj regained his composure.

"I'll talk to you later," Lucy said and breezed out.

"Wait," he said.

Saj dreaded the consequences of what had happened. His heart raced, and his head spun. If his parents found out, they would kill him. He was such a hypocrite, he thought. His family would be ashamed. He had let them all down. But he had to talk to Lucy again.

The phone rang which made him jump. One of the wards wanted him.

He sat in the office in a daze with his head bowed. Who could he talk to? The only person would be Dipak, though he was unreliable. Could he confide in him? He had no other choice.

After he had deliberated for a few minutes, he phoned Dipak. "Are you going to lunch. I need to talk to you about an important matter."

"Everything okay?" Dipak asked.

"I'll tell you later." They agreed to meet in the canteen at 1 pm.

Dipak sat at a table with a couple of nurses. Saj forced a smile as everyone looked up at him.

"Are you not having lunch Saj?"

"I'm not hungry."

He sat and glanced at Dipak. "Can we talk in private."

"Ladies...My friend and I need to chat," Dipak said to the nurses. They had finished their lunch and giggled as they left. The table was in the corner of the room. No one sat close to overhear them.

"What's up? You look like shit as if you've seen a ghost?" Dipak asked.

Saj held his head in his hands and looked down. He was unsure where to start.

Dipak waited and peeped at the time. "Come on Saj. You can talk to me. It can't be that bad. Are your parents okay?"

Saj nodded, too embarrassed to tell Dipak the story. "They are alright."

"I'm due in theatre in fifteen minutes," Dipak said firmly.

"Do you remember that nurse Lucy, who works in my ward?" He spoke in a soft voice.

50

"The blonde girl we met in the club. Did you go back to her room? What happened?"

Saj sat with slumped shoulders as he looked down.

"Oh no... I don't believe it. She's not pregnant?" Dipak gasped.

Saj peeked around to make sure nobody heard. Most people had finished their lunches and gone. He kept quiet and looked away, an admission of guilt.

"How could you be so stupid. Unbelievable!" Dipak said trying to keep his voice down. "Are you sure it's yours?"

"Lucy only told me this morning. I have no idea what to do."

"You must talk to her again and make sure she's right. I need to go man. Come to my place later." He patted Saj on the shoulder as he left.

Saj sat in the canteen all on his own, while the dinner lady cleared up the tables. He stared into space lost in thoughts. It was more acceptable for Lucy to be pregnant here than in his society. People were more liberal in this country, he thought.

At the end of a long, eventful day, Saj got back to his room. He soon dozed off. The phone startled him; it was his mother. Surely, they can't know about Lucy! News travels fast, but this can't be possible, he thought.

"How is everything? I thought of phoning you," he said.

"Your father had a heart attack. He is a little better though we are worried. You should come back soon. Forget about the money. We need you back here, where you belong," his mother said and sobbed.

Tears welled up in his eyes as he listened to his mother. Why did this all happen to him?

"Don't worry. Baba will be okay, but he needs to stop smoking. I must stay here and take my exams. We need the money, can't rely on Baba's income. Did you receive what I sent?"

"Yes, we did."

"I 'll phone you tomorrow to check how he is.".

Saj needed to pull himself together. He hoped Uncle Sina would take care of his father. Perhaps Lucy made a mistake, and he had to talk to her again. He had already missed lunch, so he walked towards the canteen before it shut.

A week went by, and Saj didn't see Lucy. She went on leave, which made it even harder for him. He carried on with his work as usual, though he found it difficult to concentrate. His father's illness and Lucy's pregnancy occupied his mind most of the time.

"Doctor. Do you have a minute?" a patient called out, as he walked to the doctors' office

"Sure. What's the matter, Mr Farrow?"

"Thanks for all your help doc. You are kind. I'm going home tomorrow. This is for you." He handed him a bottle of wine. Mr Farrow, an elderly gentleman, had been in the ward for a month.

"Thank you. You didn't need to do that. Keep the bottle and have a drink on me when you are home?"

"I insist on it. Please take it as it will make me happy. You are a good doctor. You listen to us. Others don't."

"I'll accept it if you insist. Take care of yourself, and don't come back." Saj shook his hand and left. He could give the bottle to Dipak, he thought. The patient's kindness overwhelmed him; it made his day.

A nurse rushed to him. "Dr Saj. Mrs Brown has collapsed and fallen out of bed."

Saj hurried to examine this elderly lady who suffered from cardiac failure. The nurses had managed to put her back to bed after her fall. Her breathing was shallow, she appeared pale and had been sick. Starting CPR, he gave her adrenaline and oxygen as her heart stopped, she didn't improve. Another doctor joined in. Saj shook his head. Time to stop.

He liked Mrs Brown. She chatted with him about her career as a nurse, during the Second World War. Her stories fascinated Saj. Dejectedly he wandered back. He bumped into Dipak in the doctors' mess.

"Do you want to go to the Red Lion tonight?" he asked.

"Um...I'm not sure."

"Come on. I need company. Besides, it will do you a lot of good to socialise."

"Okay."

The Red Lion was a ten-minute walk from the hospital. The pub was a small Victorian building. It had a decent crowd considering it was a weekday. Dipak ordered a beer and asked Saj if he wanted one.

"No, I don't like the taste of it. Remember I tried it before," Saj said, exasperated.

"You must try it a few times before your taste buds get used to it. Give it a chance. It was the same for me."

"I don't want it."

"I'll ask for an extra glass, and you can try mine. It will make you relaxed, and you need it."

"Okay, who cares." He needed to chill out.

Dipak ordered the beer and gave him half a glass. Saj liked it, so he asked for another.

"I told you so," Dipak said.

"This is marvellous," Saj said pointing to the beer. "You're right. Why should I worry? My life is to live up to my parent's expectations. I have no say in any matter. My father never asks me how I feel." He took another sip.

"Enjoy my friend."

"Coming to England is the best thing that happened to me. At least here I can do what I want. I miss my family but felt suffocated back home. " Saj sipped his beer.

"Did you talk to Lucy?" Dipak asked.

"No, she is away for a few days. I think she is back tomorrow, though I am not worried," Saj spoke in an incoherent manner.

"You know Dipak. I think I like English women. I don't want an arranged marriage. How can you spend the rest of your life with a stranger?"

Dipak said, "If only your father could hear you now. Your parents are going to choose your wife anyway."

Saj kept quiet but stared at the girl who sat at the opposite table. She was a cute, busty blonde girl. Wearing a low-cut top, she displayed her cleavage. A lot of attention went her way from the men in the pub.

"Pale skin on women looks beautiful. We would love to have a fair complexion," Saj said in a soft voice.

He couldn't take his eyes off the girl. Saj peeked at his watch as the pub became noisier by the minute. "Eleven. I need to be at work early tomorrow. Shall we make a move?"

Dipak pretended he didn't hear what Saj said and looked away.

"Time to go Dipak. I have an early start tomorrow."

"I'm enjoying myself, man. I don't want to go yet," Dipak slurred.

"We must be careful on the street late at night. It isn't safe."

"You know what your problem is. You worry too much. Okay, you go."

Saj thought for a moment. "I'll stay for one more beer."

Dipak ordered another round of drinks while Saj ogled that girl. Dipak swigged from his glass and chatted with the girl at the bar. Someone tapped Dipak on his shoulder. He turned around. A man in his thirties stood close and stared at him. He stood six feet, burly with short hair, his right arm covered in tattoos like a sleeve.

"Are you the doctor at the hospital?" he asked.

"Yes," Dipak said.

"Can I talk to you outside."

"We can chat here. I don't remember you. Have you been one of my patients?"

"Too noisy here."

"Okay," Dipak put his coat on. "Come on Saj. Let's go." He had already finished his beer.

Saj wobbled on his feet as he stood. Both came out of the pub, with the man behind them.

The strange man stepped in front of Dipak and glared at him.

"You've been screwing my wife," he bellowed.

Dipak stood frozen and speechless for a few seconds.

"Erm...You must be mistaken," Dipak cleared his throat and said, his voice quivered.

The man stared at Dipak, his jaw clenched like a vice, and he prodded his finger at Dipak's throat. "I've been following you."

"It must be someone else...sorry, you have the wrong man," Dipak said.

"What's your problem?" Saj faced the man.

Two more guys appeared from nowhere. They grabbed Saj by his arms and dragged him away. He struggled to break free but couldn't.

Next moment, he saw the chief thug raise his right fist and punch Dipak full in the face. Dipak stumbled backwards, but the man hit him again in his stomach.

"Help, Help," Dipak cried, blood pouring from his nostrils.

"Leave him alone, you bastard," Saj couldn't break free from the two thugs.

"You paki. Stay away from my wife, or I'll kill you," he yelled waving his clenched fist. Then the three disappeared into the night.

Nobody had responded to Dipak's call for help.

Saj rushed towards him. "Are you alright?" Dipak was clutching his stomach and throwing up over the pavement.

"We need to go to the casualty," Saj said.

"No. I'll be fine." Dipak grimaced as he tried to straighten up. "Come on. Let's get out of here."

No one followed them.

Chapter 7

Next morning, Saj was in for another shock as he arrived at work. He saw Mrs Brown, the lady who died the other night chatting to a nurse in the ward.

How was that possible as he had certified her dead? She must be a ghost! He has to stop drinking beer as his heart raced.

"Dr Saj. Good to see you. Please sit down." She put her cup on the table.

"Mrs Brown...What happened?" He finally managed to speak in a shaky voice as he sat on her bed.

She laughed. "Dr Saj. It seems you've seen a ghost."

"What happened?"

"The last I remember, a few people tried to take me away. I didn't want to go," Mrs Brown said decisively with a mischievous smile. "I want to attend my grandson's wedding next month."

Saj said, "Well. I'm really pleased to see you."

He got up and went straight to the nurses' office, "What happened with Mrs Brown?"

"After you left, we shifted her body to a side room. A few hours later when all the lights were turned off, we saw her walk to the toilet. We couldn't believe our eyes. It seems so spooky, but Mrs Brown doesn't remember much. This is a miracle," the nurse said.

Saj shook his head in disbelief, but he secretly felt a bit like a god.

At the end of the doctors' meeting, Saj joined the ward round. Lucy attended to a patient. She came near him, glanced around, and whispered, "I need to talk to you."

"Not now. I'll meet you in the canteen at lunchtime, about half-past twelve," Saj spoke in a soft voice as he wrote in the patient's notes.

Saj kept trying to guess what Lucy had to say. Would she want to keep the baby?

He arrived early. Lucy waited in the corner. His heart pounded, and he gave her a sheepish smile as she moved towards his table in the canteen.

"I'm not pregnant. You are let off."

"Are you sure?" But what about the pregnancy test? You said…"

"It tested positive first, and it can happen if done too early. I repeated it and had a blood test. All came back negative."

"Are you pleased?"

"Yes. I didn't want a baby. I'm too young."

59

"I'm sorry to put you through all this worry," Saj said.

"It wasn't your fault." She blushed.

"Are we still friends?"

"Of course, we are," said Lucy with a grin.

"I'm glad." He felt his muscles relax like a great lump of rock had floated off his shoulders.

At the end of his shift, Saj still felt energised and light-hearted as he tripped back to his room. He rang home.

"Your father is better. The hospital has discharged him."

"Brilliant."

"When do you plan to come back? We all miss you."

"Mama. I need to sit my exam and finish my training."

Saj wanted to share his 3 pieces of fantastic news with Dipak.

"How are you?" asked Saj. He observed the bruise on Dipak's face.

Dipak kept silent.

"How's your tummy. Are you alright?"

"Take a seat. What can I get you?"

"No, I just had dinner."

Dipak got himself a can of lager and took a noisy slurp.

"I am sorry I couldn't help the other night. The beer knocked me out," Saj said.

"It's not your fault."

"What did you tell them at work about your face?"

"I told them I'd had too much to drink, fell and hurt myself." Dipak gulped more lager.

"You need to be careful my friend," Saj said but realised what he had said and grinned. "Listen to me...after what happened with Lucy...though I got excellent news. She's not pregnant. We learnt our lessons."

"Fantastic. It worried me. Both of us have been in a right mess. Women. We're a good pair," said Dipak, and they laughed.

Saj boasted of his godlike qualities of raising people from the dead and shared the good news of his father too.

Dipak attempted a pleased grin but groaned and held his swollen face in his hand.

Saj woke up feeling unwell. His body ached, and he had a sore throat. He made his own diagnosis, an upper respiratory tract infection. At work, he wrote himself a prescription for antibiotics and handed it to the pharmacy.

Later that day, the nurse in charge came to him. "Dr Saj. The pharmacy won't dispense your prescription."

"Why? It's only antibiotics?"

"You can't self-prescribe. You need to go to your GP."

"I'm a doctor, I know what I need."

"This is how it works in this country," the nurse replied.

"In Bombay, I could write my own. Besides, I have to take time off to go to the GP...Anyway never mind." He picked up the patient notes.

"But this isn't Bombay," she said and left the room. Saj didn't appreciate her rude comments.

He needed to register with a GP. He asked around and found one close to him. The doctor had a cancellation, so he managed to get an appointment. Saj asked one of his colleagues to cover him for an hour.

The waiting room at the surgery was packed. Men and women coughed and spluttered. Saj checked the time as he tapped his feet. He wanted the prescription for antibiotics and get the hell out of there.

"Dr Saj...andra...pal..." the receptionist called. Saj got up before she could finish. He pushed through the door and bumped into a nurse rushing along the corridor.

She was gorgeous, and Saj felt quite lightheaded as he helped her pick up the papers from the floor. He smiled.

"Hello," he said.

"Hi. You work at the Royal Beacon, don't you?" she asked.

"Yeah. You look familiar."

"I knew I'd seen you before. I used to be a staff nurse at Holmes ward before I joined here. I am Leanne."

"I do remember now. Saj." They shook hands.

Leanne smiled. "You can't remember all the nurses. There were so many of us."

"And they came and went doing their shifts, and I was still there," he said with a grin.

"I know it's hectic there."

"It's a madhouse."

This is your first visit here, then?"

"And hopefully the last."

She laughed. "We're not that bad here."

"You know what I mean. Do you like this place more than the hospital?"

"Yes, I enjoy my work here. You had better go in. Dr Watson is through that door."

The GP was overweight, bald with an unkempt beard. He must be in his fifties and was dressed casually, no white coat or tie.

"You have an excellent surgery." Saj tried to make conversation.

"Not an easy job to please everyone. Your first visit here, so how can I help you?" the doctor asked.

"I love Sherlock Holmes and Dr Watson. I read those novels back in Bombay," Saj said with a smile, as he sat down.

Dr Watson cleared his throat. He kept a straight face and a business-like approach.

Saj told him about his throat and fever.

He examined his mouth, checked his temperature, and wrote the prescription.

"Take the antibiotics for a week. That should settle it down."

"Thanks."

As he walked past the reception, he saw Leanne leaning against the counter, speaking to the receptionist.

"Thanks!" He waved his prescription as if it were some secret token and immediately felt foolish. They shared a gentle smile.

"I'm going to take a couple of days off."

"You should," she said.

Saj wished he had someone to nurse him! He trudged feverishly home.

Chapter 8

Saj's first emergency that morning was an eighteen-year-old girl. She had overdosed on paracetamol. Thankfully the stomach wash did the trick, but he was distressed when Lisa began sobbing.

"What's the problem. Why did you do this?" Saj asked.

Wiping her eyes, she said, "My mum remarricd, and he's a nasty man. He shouts at me, but when we are alone, he tries to kiss me and touch me. I can't stand it any longer. Mum won't believe me. We had a huge row yesterday, and I couldn't cope. I now realise it was stupid of me, but I had no choice." She sobbed.

"Trying to kill yourself isn't the answer." He handed her a tissue.

"I know." She looked down.

"Your whole life is ahead of you. You can turn it all around. Think about what you want to do with your life. It's the only one you have!"

"I would love to work in a place like this one and help people."

"That's great. When you go home, you must examine life differently. I'll arrange a therapist to come and chat with you."

"Thank you, doctor. You are kind. You are the first person who listened to me."

Saj was struck by her trust in him. He hoped he had helped her.

In the office, James sat writing up patients' notes.

"How are you?" Saj said as he walked into the room.

"Not too bad, been busy...I meant to tell you the good news. Emily is expecting another child."

"Congratulations. Say hi to Emily from me," Saj shook his hand.

"Thanks."

"You do look tired, though. Don't work too hard." Saj said.

James laughed. "Once you have children, your life changes...I can assure you. You wait!"

Thank God, that's not happening now. Saj thought and smiled to himself.

While they chatted, Nick, another doctor entered the office and grumbled to James. "Did you see that stupid man? I told him to give up the booze, but he's at it again. Still, he's an excellent patient with classic liver disease. You can use him for your case presentation. You need to be quick though before this chap snuffs it." He laughed loudly.

Neither Saj or James found him funny. Nick stood taller by a few inches to Saj. His flat nose and physique made him look like a boxer.

"That Mr Santosh in the side room. He hardly speaks any English. It's impossible to take a history from him," said Nick.

"Because he hasn't been in the UK very long," James said and sipped his coffee.

"He has to learn it if he intends to live here," Nick said.

"Give him time Nick."

"He stinks of curry. These people shouldn't come to this country. They benefit from our health service for free, and we pay for it."

"These people work for their money," Saj said putting the notes back in the trolley.

"What work? You mean all the rubbish jobs." Nick pointed his finger towards Saj.

"Yeah, jobs which no one wants to do," Saj replied calmly.

"If I were in charge, I would ban these people from entering the UK," Nick said, his face flushed.

"Thank goodness. You're not," said Saj feeling his blood pressure rising and his hands turning into fists at his side.

Nick glared at Saj and stormed out of the office.

Kim, the physio came in and broke the tension. "Is Mrs Lewis allowed to walk Dr Saj?"

Saj gazed at her for a few moments, as he admired her beauty. "Yes. She has improved, and you can mobilise her."

"Okay. I'll take it slow." Kim left the room.

"You like her, don't you? I saw your face," James said.

Saj blushed and smiled. "She's nice, but I'm sure she'll have a boyfriend already."

Later he saw Kim in the ward with a patient. He was unsure of how to approach her. A beautiful girl like her couldn't be single. A lot of men must chase her. He wondered even if he asked her out, she's bound to say no which wouldn't be good for his reputation.

Saj tried to build up the courage to talk to her. But couldn't take rejection especially in public. If he could speak to her outside the ward. An idea popped into his head.

Intentionally he bumped into her. "How is Mr Rutherford coming on?" Saj asked as he put the stethoscope back in his white coat pocket.

"He is improving and can walk to the toilet and back."

"Splendid. I'm sure Mr Rutherford could go home soon," Saj said. "I meant to ask you. My back hurts, I don't know how I put it out. I need your expert opinion."

Kim seemed surprised and smiled. "I am busy now but come to the department in the afternoon." She left.

After lunch, Saj headed for the physio unit. It was on the ground floor of the hospital. When he got there, he saw Kim examining another patient. He hung about wondering if he were doing the right thing. Whether she would see through his ploy. She finished and asked him to come to a bay.

"Take your shirt off and lie down on the couch," she said.

He didn't know what to expect. "Roll over." She applied pressure with her hands. "Now raise your legs...Does this hurt?" She pressed his back.

"No."

Each touch sent a tingling sensation all over him. Saj loved it and wanted her to carry on.

"Nothing for you to concern. I'll give you a sheet with a few back exercises. You'll be fine."

When Kim had finished, he stood up. His heart raced as he buttoned up his shirt. Now or never, he thought.

"Would you like to go out for a drink?" he said casually.

She gazed at him and thought for a moment. "That would be lovely."

He couldn't believe she agreed. "How about tomorrow evening at the social club, eight?"

"Sure," Kim replied, and they parted ways.

Walking back Saj smiled and did a little air punch. How lucky he had been that Kim accepted his invitation.

Saj dressed smartly in dark chino trousers and a light blue checked shirt. He put on liberal amounts of Calvin Klein aftershave for his date. The social club was situated in the next block of buildings, away from the main hospital. He would go there with Dipak and James. It had a bar and pool table.

Only a few people were present when he arrived. He looked around for Kim. It was already ten past eight. Maybe she's changed her mind, he thought. Feeling let down he turned to leave, and almost bumped into her as she walked in.

"Sorry I'm late, had to drop Simon at his friend's house," Kim said.

"Ah," he said, looking mystified.

"Oh no." She shook her head. "He's my little brother."

"Oh right," Saj said with a smile.

"What would you like to drink?" he asked, as they strolled to the bar.

"White wine, please."

Saj ordered a coke for himself.

"You don't drink alcohol?" Kim said taking a seat.

"I sometimes do." He stammered.

She grinned. "It can't be because you're driving."

Kim was in her late twenties had a beautiful face, short dark hair, and sharp features. Wearing a black skirt, she revealed her curvy figure and her well-toned legs. Saj breathed her pungent perfume.

There was an awkward moment of silence. Both looked at each other and tried to make conversation.

"How has your day been?" she asked as she sipped wine.

"Busy as usual. How long have you been working at the hospital?"

"As a physio for more than a year. It's hectic. I would prefer to work in the community," Kim said. "Where is your family?"

"My parents live in Bombay in India. I also have a younger sister."

"It must be different for you living in this country."

"You can say that. I am getting accustomed to life in England."

"Why do women in your country have a red dot on their forehead?" Kim asked.

"They wear a red vermillion dot near the hair parting to show they are married. They also wear a toe ring indicating their marital status."

"One of my friends is going out with a Sikh guy. He is a nice man, and I have learnt a few things about your culture."

"I'm impressed," Saj said.

"One has to be married in your country before…" She hesitated and smiled.

"Before what? Ah…yes pre-marital sex is considered a taboo in our society."

"Though an Indian may have written the Kamasutra." Kim giggled.

"This will make you laugh. During a housewarming ceremony, a cow is brought inside the newly built house to bless it. Cow's urine is also sprinkled around."

"Jesus!" said Kim.

Saj chuckled and sipped his coke. "What about you?"

"I am close to my family and my brother. I live in a rented apartment not far from here," she added.

They swapped stories about the hospital and the staff.

Kim moved close to Saj and whispered, "You never had back pain, did you?"

Saj blushed and said with a nervous smile, "I did ache." He couldn't lie to her, while he gazed into her beautiful eyes.

"Right."

"You know now. I needed an excuse to ask you out, sorry." Both laughed.

"Would you like another glass?"

"No, I'm driving. I better make a move. Have an early start tomorrow." Kim stood up.

"I enjoyed the evening." She opened the door of her Ford Fiesta.

"I had a splendid time too," Saj said with a smile. A pause. He couldn't think what else to say.

"Good night." She put the car into gear and sped off leaving Saj regretting his lack of experience with women.

Even though it was their first date, they had got on well, he thought.

As he lay in bed alone that night, he thought of her and could still smell her perfume. Why didn't he ask for her number? How stupid. He could have kissed her too. She probably thought he was a waste of time.

Chapter 9

Most evenings, Saj sat on his own in his room. He studied a lot of the time, and when he got bored, watched television, sometimes late-night movies with adult themes. It fascinated him to see naked ladies, which were never shown in Bombay. In his culture, women's clothing must not be too tight or revealing. It would arouse sexual desire in men, which was prohibited. Even kissing wasn't permitted on the screen.

That evening, he didn't have much to do. The phone buzzed. It must be from home, he thought. It was a pleasant surprise to hear from Kim.

"Do you want to go to the movies tonight?" she asked.

"Yes, it will be great." He was excited and didn't even ask which film, he didn't care.

"I'll pick you up in an hour."

He had a quick shower and put on his aftershave to impress her.

Kim was quite a daredevil when it came to driving. Saj had always been a nervous front seat passenger.

"How did you get hold of my phone number?" he asked, as they swayed on a tight bend.

"Ah. I have my ways," Kim said grinning. "I phoned the hospital and told them I was your friend."

"Easy...Oh, I passed my driving test."

"Well done. So, what car will you buy?"

"I don't know yet."

"Perhaps a silver convertible BMW."

"Oh no, I can't afford that."

Kim looked elegant in a short skirt and a sleeveless top. She had a black leather jacket and wore gold earrings and a necklace. Tonight, her perfume was more flowery.

"Which film are we watching?" he asked when they arrived at the hall.

"The latest James Bond," Kim replied.

"But it's a man's movie?"

"I like Pierce Brosnan. He is handsome."

Saj paid for the tickets and bought coke and popcorn. In his culture, men were the breadwinners.

The auditorium was clean and modern, which impressed Saj. The seats felt soft and comfortable. Cinemas in Bombay would have the litter on the floors, walls would be stained, and seats ripped.

Kim wanted to sit right in the back corner away from the crowd. There were plenty of unoccupied seats. The lights dimmed, and the movie started.

Halfway through the film, Kim began to softly stroke his hand. A tingling sensation came all over his body. They glanced at each other and snuggled closer together.

The movie finished, and the lights came on.

"Did you like the film?" Kim blinked to adjust her eyes to the brightness.

"Yeah. I liked the scenes in Paris and Venice. I would love to visit there."

"I went to Paris with my ex-boyfriend last year."

"Oh," said Saj. "What happened?"

"You know the usual," she responded mysteriously.

When they reached his building, Kim turned, stroked his cheek and said, "I find you very attractive, Saj."

Saj gulped and heard himself saying, "Would you like to come up for a drink?"

"Okay."

They walked upstairs holding hands.

"Neat room for a man," Kim said, settling into the sofa.

"I'm a tidy person. And a lady cleans for us once a week."

Kim smiled. "People in the hospital and patients like you. They think you are an excellent doctor."

"Well. It doesn't cost being kind to people," he said. "So, what are your plans for the weekend?"

"I'm out clubbing with my friends on Friday, and then a party on Saturday...How about you?"

"Work as usual. I'm on call. It will be a long weekend," Saj said with a sigh. "What would you like?"

"What do you have?" Kim said.

He thought for a moment. "Beer."

"Cheers."

"Would you like to watch TV?" He settled himself gingerly beside her.

Saj turned on the television. A wildlife documentary was on. His next plan was to kiss her, and he had to make the first move. What if she got offended and rejected his advances? He wouldn't know until he tried, he thought.

Slowly, Saj put his arm around Kim and caressed her. She smiled. A positive sign. He moved his face closer and brushed his lips against hers, and she liked it. Kissing passionately, he stroked her hair. She began to breathe slowly, and she wanted more.

Kim began to unbutton his shirt which aroused Saj. His mind went dizzy with desire. He wanted her more than anything else. After loosening his trousers, he unbuttoned her top. She giggled as he struggled to take off her bra.

"The other way around," she said.

He smiled and blushed. Kim took her blouse off and pulled him towards the bed. They caressed. She undid his trousers and fondled him. This was a first for Saj.

77

"Oh, the big boy is ready," she said and giggled.

Saj grinned feeling more confident.

Kim pushed his trousers off and then pulled her skirt down.

"Shall I turn off the light?" he said.

"I like it with the lights on."

Saj stopped.

"What's the problem?" she asked.

Lucy came into his thoughts. He didn't want to make the same mistake again.

"You don't mind if we use...a condom."

Kim thought for a moment. "But I'm on the pill."

"I would prefer to use it if that is alright with you." Saj sounded apologetic. He was new to all this.

"Fine."

Saj had bought a pack of Durex after the Lucy incident but didn't imagine using it so soon. He struggled to put the condom on. Kim took it off his hand and rolled it on for him. He should have practised it before, he thought.

He kissed her neck and went down to caress her breasts. His hand explored her whole body. She groaned. Kim pulled Saj on top of her, and as he entered her, she cried in ecstasy. She became noisier by the minute, which worried Saj. It would be embarrassing if next door complained.

"Shhh," he spoke in a low voice, and gently put his hand on her mouth.

Kim was in no mood to listen. As they rubbed against each other's bodies, he thrust faster. She moaned with pleasure as she climaxed. And a couple of minutes later he did. Saj rolled over to the side and breathed heavily. He wiped off beads of sweat from his forehead.

Yes. Saj had performed well that time, and now he was a man. He looked across at her and reached for her hand.

After a couple of minutes, Kim got up and took a cigarette out of her handbag.

"I didn't know you smoked." He sounded surprised.

"I sometimes do. Do you mind?"

"No, not at all."

Saj had never smoked, and it was uncomfortable for him. Exhaling the fumes, Kim flicked her ash on the bedside table. He stifled a cough and needed to dispose off the condom. It felt messy down below. He got up and went to the toilet, took it off and washed. His first experience using a sheath was strange. Better be safe than sorry, he thought.

Saj's eyes stung with the smoke. He brought a small plate for her to use as an ashtray, and she stubbed it out finally.

"I'd better go. Early start tomorrow for me. The physio department is short staffed." She started to get dressed.

"Thanks for inviting me. You must give me your telephone number," Saj said.

"I'm usually out in the evenings. You can try maybe to leave a message?" She scribbled on the paper.

Kim opened the door, gave him a long lingering kiss and drifted along the corridor. Saj watched her go and was happy to realise the beginning of a new stage in his life.

Chapter 10

Next morning, Lucy entered the office. Saj tried to focus on a patient's X-Ray in the lightbox.

"Could you please sign these prescriptions? Mrs Fredrick is going home," she said.

She hung around as if she wanted to talk. Saj looked up. "Anything else?"

"Did you know Alex quit her job?"

"No. I didn't."

"She used to like you."

Saj shrugged his shoulders. "Why did she leave?"

"Rumours are that she had a fling with a doctor. Hence she resigned." Lucy hung about waiting for his response.

"Don't look at me," he said with a cheeky smile.

Saj remembered the assault on Dipak. Oh shit, He must be Alex's husband, must be the reason she left, he thought.

"I'm back with my boyfriend. He is more understanding now."

"Great. Good luck."

Lucy smiled and left the room.

A few minutes later, the office phone rang. Saj picked it up.

"How are you?" Kim crooned.

"I'm fine. Busy."

"How was it for you?"

Saj blushed. He glanced around to make sure no one listened. "I can't talk now, it was good."

"I enjoyed it as well, " Kim said.

"I'll speak to you another time." Saj got worried as he put the phone down. What if someone listened to their chat? Maybe the telephone operator? He escaped to the ward.

"Casualty wants you urgently Dr Saj," a nurse reported.

Saj left his patient and hurried down the long corridor. When he arrived, a doctor and a couple of nurses were busy around a bed.

"Dr Saj is here," one of the nurses announced, as he approached. Saj was a bright, confident and experienced doctor now. Other physicians valued his opinion.

As he got close, he gasped and let out an "Oh No" under his breath. It was the same girl who came in a few weeks back with overdose. Lisa had promised not to do it again.

The girl lay there unconscious, her breathing was shallow. She was pale and clammy. Her blood pressure was unrecordable, with nothing showing on the heart rate monitor. Saj administered a drug to treat the paracetamol overdose and injected adrenaline.

"Come on Lisa. You have to live." He attempted to resuscitate her and felt sorry for what she went through. The staff continued CPR and Saj wouldn't stop. She had no heartbeat and stopped breathing.

"Her pupils are fixed and dilated," the other doctor said.

Saj carried on and gave her intracardiac adrenaline. The doctor and the nurse exchanged glances. She had gone.

"I think it's time to stop, Saj."

He stared at the young girl for some time. Then he turned around and walked away in a daze. Desperately he tried to hold back his tears.

How could she do this again? She was only eighteen and had her whole life ahead of her. Maybe he should have done more when she came last time. Did the psychiatrist and the social worker follow her up? Saj walked past the girl's mother with his head bowed. The poor woman sobbed, being comforted by a nurse. "It's my fault she's dead," her mother said.

Saj carried on and went outside the hospital. The rain had stopped, though the sun struggled to come out from behind the clouds. He needed fresh air to clear his head. It wasn't professional being too attached to patients. He couldn't do more than he did, he thought.

Back in his room after work, Saj was still upset about the girl's death. Opening a bottle of beer, he sank onto the couch.

The phone broke the silence. He let it ring, then picked up a letter from the table from his parents. They had sent him photographs of one of his cousin's wedding. He guessed this was a hint from his mother. She had been looking at girls as his bride. Saj sighed. It had been over a year since he had come to England, and so much had happened in his life, he thought.

One afternoon. Saj walked towards Richdale ward. Holmes had no empty beds as the admissions had been hectic. He met James in the corridor.

"You look tired," Saj said.

"The baby keeps me up."

"Are we still on for tennis next week?"

"Oh...yes, that should be okay. See you later."

There was a tennis court on the hospital grounds. Saj could just about play, but he enjoyed James's company.

Saj was reading the patient's notes in the doctor's office in Richdale when Nick entered.

"Hey, Nick," he glanced at him and smiled.

Nick had never been popular with patients or staff. He had a reputation for being arrogant and loud. But didn't care what others thought of him.

"Have you taken over Mrs Evans'? She should be your patient," Nick said with a frown.

"None of the nurses asked me. And besides our ward is full."

Nick glared at Saj, his face red. "She needs to go to Holmes Ward."

Writing the patient's notes, Saj said, "This is the consultant's order, not mine. I am only following instructions."

Nick moved close to Saj and prodded his finger at him. "Mrs Evans is your patient. I will have nothing to do with her from today."

Saj looked coldly at this unreasonable man. "I'll check with Dr Smith and let you know."

Nick lost his cool. He grabbed Saj by the collar and forced him against the wall. "You should bloody go back to Bombay where you belong. Open a curry place."

Saj had enough of Nick's nastiness. He grabbed the hand holding his collar. Then he twisted his arm hard and pushed him back. Nick groaned in pain as he fell to the floor. The notes he carried in his other hand went flying. Saj's strength surprised him.

"Don't ever touch me again. You bully! I'm more civilised than you are." Saj glared and pointed his finger at him. "Mrs Evans will stay here."

Nick grunted and made weird noises, as he got off the floor. He held his right arm and grimaced. It must hurt. Both stared at each other for a moment

"You lot should go back." Nick rushed to gather the papers spread on the floor.

"And who would fill the medical posts here which you lot are not interested in doing. The NHS would collapse," said Saj with a sarcastic smile."

One of the ward nurses came into the room. Perhaps she had heard the argument.

"Mrs Evans needs her drug sheet written up," she said to Nick.

Nick looked at Saj and mumbled. He stood still for a moment and then hurried out of the office with the nurse behind him.

Saj sat down, took a deep breath, and carried on writing his notes. Mrs Evans could stay in this ward.

Chapter 11

Saj stared at himself in the mirror. He remembered what Kim had said about his looks. Having a moustache for such a long time, it became a part of him. Back in Bombay, most men had one, and it was their tradition. They believed you need to have a moustache to be a real 'man'. Kids couldn't wait to grow one. Silly! What the hell, why not?

Saj chuckled at his new image and couldn't believe how different he looked. He decided to surprise Dipak with a visit.

"What have you done. Looks funny?" Dipak said as he shook his head and laughed.

"I wanted a change," Saj said with a smile. "Funny, some men at home think the bigger and bushier your moustache, the more macho you are."

"This is a myth, man. Rubbish. They pretend to be tough."

"Most Englishman don't have moustaches."

"Perhaps you are enjoying female company too much?" Dipak grinned.

"Following your footsteps. No seriously, I do get lonely. Sometimes I miss home. There is only so much revision you can do."

Dipak had his clothes spread all around his room. Empty bottles of wine and cans of beer sat on the table.

"How are you doing?" Saj asked.

"You know me. I live my life for the day. Enjoy myself. Who knows about the future?" Dipak replied.

"But...you must be careful."

"Well. If you had a childhood like mine, you would think differently."

"What happened?"

"It's a long story. Do you want to hear?"

"Yes, I do."

"My father left when I was only five. I can hardly remember him. My mother worked hard all day in a shop to feed me. We had no money. She met a man and married him. He was generous enough to spend on my education, only to please my mother. I didn't get on well with him," Dipak said.

"As years went by, he abused and mistreated my mother. I was miserable. I decided that the day I became a doctor, I would leave home." He sipped beer.

At no time, had Dipak talked about his life before. Saj listened patiently as he passed a bottle of beer to him. Saj realised how lucky he had been. Dipak had had a sad upbringing. Poor chap, he thought.

"My father is very firm with us. I can never talk to him or express how I feel. Maybe he doesn't mean it," Saj said. "But it makes life hard for me." His expression dulled as he stared at his glass.

"But now you are a grown-up adult."

"How are you so sought after by ladies?" Saj tried to lighten the mood.

"You have to treat them well and spend money on them."

Saj told him about the incident with Nick, and how he had fought back.

"Awesome, man. You stood firm against him. He's a bully."

"His words shocked me Dipak. We'll never be accepted in this country if everyone has a similar opinion."

"Most people here are not like Nick. They accept us. You may find a few odd ones who think they are a far superior race. But they are in small numbers."

"I hope so."

"We can take it too personally. You must forget about these idiots. If anyone is nasty to us in Bombay, we're not so sensitive."

"You're right. How long have you been here?" Saj asked as he sipped wine.

"Almost four years now."

"I don't understand. We have dark skin and would love to be paler. People here like darker complexion. They hope to gain a tan and go under the sunbed."

We're never happy with our colour whatever we are,"
Dipak said, and both laughed.

It was a Sunday afternoon. As always, the weekend on call
had been hectic for Saj, without much sleep. He sat in the
office sipping coffee. He didn't even like coffee but saw
other English doctors drink it as a stimulant. In Bombay,
people drank tea.

"You look, terrible doctor," a nurse said, as she entered
the room.

"Thanks." Saj yawned. He looked scruffy, he hadn't
shaved or brushed his hair.

"Sorry, you have a lot of new admissions."

"I know." He yawned again.

By the time Saj finished, the clock had displayed two in
the morning. Hoping to get a few hours' sleep, he lay down
on the bed fully clothed and fell asleep.

His bleep made the dreadful cardiac arrest tone. Saj
jumped out of bed in a daze. Gathering his thoughts, he took
a sip of water and darted for the ward. He was surprised that
the call was from the long stay place. Only terminally ill
patients were kept there, and most were not suitable for
resuscitation.

Saj took the stairs two at a time. When he arrived, the
nurses were standing around someone on the floor. One was
kneeling shouting, "No! No! No!" A patient must have fallen
out of bed, he thought. Saj pushed his way through. He froze.
It was James lying on the floor.

"Oh, my God. What happened?" Saj shouted, his voice quivered.

"We called him to see a patient, then we heard a loud bang...he's not breathing," the nurse spoke fast.

Saj trembled. His mind went blank, his heart pounded. This can't be real. For a second, he thought this must be a prank. Any moment, James would stand and laugh.

"Call Dr Smith and the anaesthetist. Hurry," Saj yelled.

He immediately started the cardiac massage as the nurse hurried and brought the crash trolley. Saj couldn't feel any pulse.

"Come on James. You can get through this." Saj continued with the resuscitation.

"We'll use the defibrillator, please stand back."

They shocked him twice, but still no heartbeat. The monitor displayed asystole.

"We were supposed to play tennis next week. Do you remember? You must live for Emily and the kids. Come on James. Please help me out like you always did," Saj mumbled as his eyes welled up.

"Where are the others?" He shouted.

At last the other doctors arrived. James was intubated and defibrillated again without success. Saj asked for intracardiac adrenaline as a last resort. He took the long needle and stabbed James in the heart.

"Come on James. Can we take him to intensive care? We're wasting time," he said to the anaesthetist, as he wiped sweat from his forehead.

"We need to stabilise him here," he replied.

The team continued with resuscitation for another fifteen minutes. James stopped breathing, his heart monitor showed a straight line. His colour had drained away.

The anaesthetist said, "The pupils are fixed and dilated. I think we have done all we can."

Saj quickly wiped his eyes. James appeared calm, the way he had always been. The nurses stood silent, tears flowing down their cheeks. Saj realised that he had lost one of his best friends.

Wearily he walked back to his room feeling numb. Was this real or a nightmare? James didn't deserve this. He had wanted to be a GP. Emily and the kids would be devastated.

Opening a can of beer, he slumped and stared at the wall. He kept beer only for guests but felt he needed it. He felt numb. At 6.30am his phone rang. The nurse informed him that Emily was in the ward. How would he face her?

Saj had to drag himself in. He saw Emily from a distance. She sat in the doctors' office and waved her arms as a nurse attempted to console her. Emily gazed at Saj as if hoping for a miracle as tears spilt down her cheeks. They hugged for a minute, as she sobbed on his shoulder.

"I'm so sorry Emily," his lips quivered as he spoke. "I tried my best. I've never felt so helpless in my life. He was like a brother to me. James has always been there for me when I needed help. He needed me only once...I couldn't help him. I failed him." Saj wiped his eyes and looked away.

This was one of the worst experiences in Saj's life. There was no way to ease Emily's pain.

A thought crossed his mind. He needed to talk to the hospital manager. It was 9 am. The secretary tried to stop him. "They're in a meeting doctor," she said.

He barged in. People sat around a table as they chatted.

"Excuse me. We're busy," one of the men said.

Saj pointed his finger as he glared at the men. "I knew this was going to happen. I warned you. We can't work without sleep. You've now killed a young doctor."

"Now calm down Dr Saj," the manager said.

"It's alright for you guys. You sleep soundly and come to your offices refreshed." Saj clenched his fist. "If James had not worked without a break, he may still be alive."

The manager stood up and said, "Doctor...you're upset, and we're sad too but..."

"What would you know! If only you guys knew what is it like out there? You're all responsible for James' death. This is criminal. You are putting the lives of our patients at risk as well. A sleep-deprived doctor can no way be at his best."

"We understand but…"

"How can you lot sleep at night...better than us obviously...this will be out in the media, so be prepared. I don't give a shit anymore. I resign." He stormed out of the office before they could respond.

The news about James's death had spread like wildfire. All the staff were devastated. Later in the day, the hospital crawled with reporters. They were informed that the administration would release a statement soon. But the Press wanted first-hand information, so they hassled the doctors and nurses. Saj tried to keep his mind occupied. Someone knocked on the office door.

"Excuse me, Doctor. Could I speak to you." said a well-dressed man, as he entered the room. He was accompanied by another guy who carried a few cameras around his neck.

"I'm John Pott, the chief reporter from the National News, and this is Mark."

Saj pretended to write the notes as if he didn't hear him.

"We're sorry what happened to Dr Hunt. We understand you were with him at the end."

Saj kept silent.

"Could you please give me more details of the incidence. Your side of the story."

Was this his opportunity to tell the world how doctors were abused? Then he changed his mind. He couldn't trust the media.

"You'll know more when the hospital issues their statement. Nothing more to say." He carried on reading the notes.

"But doc... You were the first-hand witness."

"I'll tell the enquiry board if they ask me."

"Doc. We'll pay you for any information you give us."

By now, Saj had enough. He glared at the reporter and shouted, "I don't need your bloody money. Get out of here, and don't ever come back."

The reporters were shaken." Okay Okay. We'll get more info elsewhere." They hurried out.

That evening, Saj had bought a bottle of whisky to try and poured out a glass. He kept seeing James's face. He vividly remembered their first meeting in the ward and smiled at the memory. What a nice guy.

James's death made television news the next day. It was all over the newspapers too. Long hours for junior doctors, had been criticised and debated nationally. This incident stirred the whole issue. A lot of conflicting statements came out. Lies were told to the media about the cause of his death. Saj knew the exact circumstances but decided to keep quiet.

The statement from the hospital authorities read. "We are shocked and saddened by Dr Hunt's sudden demise. He was a conscientious and likeable doctor, and our heartfelt condolences are with his family. An enquiry committee is considering the matter, once they receive the coroner's report."

James's death tormented Saj, and he had sleepless nights. He started drinking most evenings, hoping it would relax him. Dipak had gone back to India on holiday, he didn't know who to confide in. It was difficult for him to focus on work, the next few days. He missed James and found it hard to believe he was no longer there. The hospital administrator had persuaded him not to resign, so he stayed, for now.

Chapter 12

Six weeks had passed since James' funeral. Saj concentrated on his studies, his Royal College exam was due soon. His parents hoped he could return to Bombay and practise as a specialist. He needed to pass the first time.

Saj hadn't heard from Kim for a while. She had given him her address, and he thought he would surprise her. He got the taxi to stop at a shop. He was no expert in wine, so he asked for the finest one.

Kim had told him she shared an apartment with a couple of friends. It was located on the second floor of a block of flats. He pressed the doorbell an waited. The building was not well lit. A young woman opened the door.

"Hi. Does Kim live here?"

The woman looked him up and down. "Come in," she said. "Down the corridor, then take a right, her room is the last one. I'm not sure whether she's in."

He walked down the poorly lit hallway. Old boots, a shabby small table and carrier bags cluttered the corridor. Kim's door was half open, the light turned on. He slowly pushed it. "Surprise!"

Kim lay naked on the bed kissing another woman.

"What the hell are you doing here?" She screamed

"I…I just thought. Oh, God!"

Still clutching the bottle of wine, he backed out of the room.

"Wait." She hurried after him, with a sheet wrapped around her and grabbed his arm as he was nearing the front door. "I'm sorry. I should've told you before," she said.

"Told me what!"

She hesitated. "I'm also interested in women."

"I don't believe what I've just seen." He shook his head.

"Please Saj, come and sit down." She held his arm.

Saj resisted, but she pulled him to the small sitting room. He sat with reluctance on the worn-out couch looking away.

"I'm very fond of you Saj." Her voice trembled. "Over the last few years, I had a couple of boyfriends. They all let me down. Cheated on me. In the last few months, I developed feelings for women."

"But how can you like women. I don't understand."

"Maybe I always have, though didn't realise it. Now I don't know what I am... I like men as well. I am fond of you."

"I don't believe it," Saj said.

"Don't tell anyone, please. No one else knows."

"Only because I had the privilege to witness it."

"I don't want my parents or my brother to find out. They would be devastated."

Saj didn't know what to make of it all.

"Some men like all this," she said with a nervous smile.

"I have to go." He got up, thinking England held many secrets.

"Will I see you again?"

"Yes, in the ward. Goodbye."

After returning to the hospital, Saj headed for the social club. He met Dipak there. They had plenty to catch up on. So much had happened since Dipak went on holiday. He ordered them both a beer.

"So how is your love life?" Saj asked.

"Well. You know me!"

"You don't want to know my story. You won't believe it."

"Come on, tell me more?"

Saj told Dipak the incidence of Kim being in bed with another woman.

"Are you joking?" Dipak asked as he sipped his beer.

"I'm serious."

Dipak shook his head in disbelief. "Why these surprises happen to you?"

"I was shocked. I really liked Kim," Saj glanced around to make sure no one was listening. "How do women have sex with each other? You know what I mean. Women have nothing to put in."

"You are naïve my friend. They use artificial penis and toys and rub their private parts." Dipak showed his expertise with pride.

"How do you know all this?"

"Call it being a man of the world."

"Of course, nothing like this happens in Bombay," said Saj.

"You don't know that. Everything is so secretive back home because of our culture. And fear of what society would think of us," Dipak said. "We're not allowed to talk about it. Here most of it is out in the open."

The following evening after work Saj sat in his room reading a journal, but he couldn't settle. He decided to take the bus into town and see a film.

The roads were busy. There were quite a few people on board the bus, but no one spoke to him. Saj got off at the town centre, the Odeon was the right opposite. A Bond film, "The Living Daylight" started in ten minutes. During the movie, he stared at the screen, but his mind drifted far away. The film ended. He didn't take in any of it.

The bus back seemed to take ages. Saj glanced at his watch. Midnight. He wrapped the scarf around his neck and put his hands in his pockets as it had got cold. He checked behind to make sure no one followed him. A couple of homeless men were asleep on the pavement.

Saj heard some shouting up ahead. When he got closer, he spotted two men. They held the third man by his arm and dragged him down kicking him, shouting "Bastard. Take that." Both wore hooded jackets. Saj could vaguely see their faces. They were of Asian origin, and the third man was white. He was astonished. It was Nick.

He walked towards the men. "What's up?"

"Fuck off, or you're next."

Nick was shaking on the ground. "Please take the money. Just don't hurt me," he bleated.

The other guy squared up to Saj and said, "Give me your wallet."

He tried to grab Saj by his neck, but Saj kicked him in the stomach. The thug fell and moaned in agony. His friend left Nick and jabbed at Saj, but he was too quick for him. He moved sideways, punched him in his solar plexus and kicked him to the ground. The first man had got up and attempted to grapple Saj who kicked him between his legs. The man screamed in pain. During all this time, Nick had got to his feet but just watched.

"Get out of here, or I'll kick your head in and call the police," Saj shouted.

"Ah. We'll come back for you later. You are a fucking bastard. You are a traitor to your kind," one of them yelled as both ran off.

Saj was breathing heavy. He held his right hand which hurt.

"Are you alright? Did they take anything?" he asked Nick.

"No, you got here before they could," he stuttered.

"Come on, let's make a move."

They walked fast towards the hospital.

"How did you do that?" Nick said.

Saj smiled. "Well. My Tae Kwon Do training came in handy tonight. I held a black belt back in Bombay."

"It was bloody awesome."

"Don't think I wasn't scared, I was," Saj said with a smile.

"Thank you mate."

"No problem. I would do it for anyone."

They walked on. Nick paused at his block.

"I'm really sorry for all the things I said. I was wrong." Nick's voice quivered. He put his hand out, and Saj shook it.

"Would you like to come in for coffee?" Nick hesitantly asked.

"Okay."

His room was like Dipak's on the same block, but a lot tidier.

"Please sit down," Nick said pointing to the chair.

"Thanks."

"I sincerely apologise for the nasty things I said," Nick said in a quiet voice, biting his nails as he sat on his bed. "Will you forgive me?"

"Of course. It's all forgotten."

"You know Saj. I come from a poor background. We lived on a council estate, my mum and me. I was bullied at school by a gang of…. you know different sort of kids."

"You mean coloured?"

"I was in the minority at school. The teachers turned a blind eye. I used to get beaten up. Never any good at fighting back. Since then I disliked coloured people. I know you can't judge everyone the same way, but I did," Nick said his head bowed.

"I understand. I would have been the same."

Nick looked up. "Thanks for what you did tonight. I am grateful." He paused, then said, "I wonder what I would have done in your shoes."

"You would have done the same and helped me." Saj smiled.

Chapter 13

A few weeks passed. On a Monday morning after a weekend off, Saj felt more energetic. He sat at the office viewing X-rays and writing notes.

A nurse entered with a cup of tea for him.

"Thanks." He looked up and smiled.

"Dr Saj. We're having a night out tomorrow. It's one of the girl's birthday. Would you like to come?"

Saj had nothing better to do. "Yeah. Where are we going?"

"All of us are meeting in Tagali, an Italian restaurant. Later we plan to go to Bookers."

Saj got ready for the evening, putting on a beige chino and a navy shirt with a dark casual jacket. He also remembered to wear his leather shoes this time.

Sitting in his new car, he smiled, feeling proud. Tagali was situated in an affluent part of town, an upmarket restaurant. Saj managed to find a seat with the others in the party. The lights were dimmed, and the ambience chilled.

As he sat, he heard a voice. "Are you better now?"

Saj turned around. The nurse from the GP surgery sat next to him.

"I remember you. Leanne?"

"You've got an excellent memory." She smiled. "How are you?"

"Yes, I'm fine, thank you...how come you're here?"

"Am I not supposed to be here," she said grinning.

"No, I didn't mean that." He took a sip of water.

"Do you mean why am I here?" she said. "Well. I know Elaine from when I worked in the hospital."

"Ah, I now remember you telling me."

Saj thought Leanne was gorgeous. She must be in her mid-twenties. Her dark shoulder length hair and brown eyes made her porcelain skin stand out. She wore a long black dress which fitted her figure well.

"Amazing. I never expected to see you again," Saj said.

"Small world." She smiled.

"How is your Dr Watson? I mentioned Sherlock Holmes to him, he didn't find it amusing."

Leanne chuckled. "He's not that bad once you get to know him. He has a dry sense of humour."

"Sometimes doctors aren't good patients," Saj said.

"You can say the same about nurses."

The waitress came to take the order. Saj ordered a simple vegetarian pizza, he didn't have any idea of Italian food. Leanne asked for a fancy pasta dish.

"How long have you worked in the doctor's surgery?" he asked.

"Must be more than a year. I love it, quite different from the hospital."

"Good to like your job."

"If you don't mind me asking, where are you from?"

"Bombay, where I qualified as a doctor."

"Oh, I remember you telling me. What is it like in Bombay?"

"Okay. Life can be difficult out there."

"I have limited knowledge, but families are important in your place, aren't they?"

"Yes, they are. Religion and family are a vital part of Indian culture," said Saj. "From an early age, a child is taught the importance of household. And the role he is expected to play."

Leanne listened to him with attention and kept constant eye contact with Saj.

"Our culture places a lot of significance to society. Everything you do, from schooling, the way you dress, even getting married. They all reflect the type of person you are."

"Sounds interesting. Do you have a family?"

"Yes, back in Bombay…I mean my parents and younger sister. I came to England to take specialist exams and earn some money."

"In your society, families tend to live together."

"You're right. We have joint family systems. Parents, male children and their spouses and grandchildren all reside in the same house."

"I have a brother and a sister. My brother lives in London. We don't see much of him." Leanne sipped wine.

Saj couldn't believe the size of the pizza when the food arrived. Perhaps he ordered the family size, he thought. It was huge for one person, but the smell was enticing. He laughed so did Leanne.

"Do you have arranged marriages back home?" she asked, as she nibbled the garlic bread.

Saj smiled. "Yes. These are common in rural regions. Love marriages are more prevalent in cities." He took a bite of the pizza preferring to eat it with his hand.

"This pasta tastes nice. Would you like to try some of it?"

"No thanks. I must finish mine…You are quite knowledgeable about other cultures. I'm impressed." Saj gazed into her eyes.

She smiled. "I hope we are not ignoring others."

Saj looked up. "They are all busy eating."

The pizza was delicious, he could eat only half of it. He didn't like wasting food, so he offered the rest to Leanne. But she had too much food herself.

Saj enjoyed Leanne's company. He liked the fact she took an interest in him.

"Are you coming to Bookers?" he asked.

"I don't go to nightclubs much," Leanne said.

"Come on, it will be a laugh. You have to watch me on the dance floor."

"Alright."

The nightclub was close to the restaurant. Saj left his car, and they all decided to walk. They had to queue for half an hour to get in. He didn't mind the wait, it gave him an opportunity to chat with Leanne.

"Would you like a drink Leanne?" he asked, as they strolled to the bar.

"Coke, please...And you can call me Lea."

Saj ordered two Cokes. He enjoyed the music, they played techno and electronic. The crowd packed the dance floor. He tapped his feet and nodded his head with the music. He seemed ready though hesitant to ask Lea to join him.

"Do you come here often?" Lea spoke close to Saj's ears.

"No, but you should see my Bollywood dance. It will make you laugh."

"Show me."

"No, I can't. This is not the right music. I'll show you another time."

"Another time?" She laughed.

The DJ played "Rhythm is a dancer."

"Do you want to dance? This is a great song."

"Okay."

He took her hand and lead her to the centre of the dance floor. She was not at all self-conscious.

"You're a fantastic dancer," he spoke loud over the beat.

"You're not too bad yourself," she said with a smile.

Lea giggled when Saj displayed a few silly moves by throwing both arms in the air. The DJ slowed down the tempo, and put on Whitney Houston's, 'I Will Always Love You.' They looked at each other, smiled and shrugged and he led her off the floor. Other couples embraced and moved slowly to the music. Saj reproached himself for missing such a great opportunity.

He bought another drink, they chatted and laughed. They were wholly absorbed in each other.

One of the girls came around. She grinned and said to Lea, "Oh, so you are here. We haven't seen you all night." She then glanced at Saj.

Lea smiled and said to her friend, "See you later."

"Your friend is cheeky," he said.

"It's getting late. I think I'd better leave soon," Lea said looking at her watch.

"I'll come with you."

"You don't need to, I can call a taxi."

"No, I'm tired as well, must be the dancing."

Both said goodbye to a couple of ladies from the group and headed for the exit. They collected their coats from the cloakroom and left the club. People still made their way in as it started to drizzle.

"I can drop you home. We can walk to my car," he said.

"Are you sure?"

"I'm positive, no problem."

They hurried back to the car park, relieved to be out of the rain.

Lea gave him directions to her house. It took half an hour to reach the private road with luxury detached homes. Saj had never been to that area before. He pulled up outside Lea's front gate.

"This is my parents' house," Lea said.

The house was massive with a well-lit gravel drive in the front. A Mercedes and a BMW were parked. Saj felt embarrassed about his Ford. They sat in the car for a few minutes chatting. He noticed one of the bedroom lights came on.

"I had a great time tonight. I would have been bored if you weren't there," Saj said noticing how bright and clear her eyes were.

"I enjoyed myself too, thanks."

"Will I see you again?" he asked.

"But not at the surgery." She said and smiled. Saj loved her sense of humour.

"I'll call you."

"This is my phone number." Lea wrote it down on a paper which she took out of her handbag.

They said goodnight, and Lea got out.

Saj sat in the car on his own for a few minutes. He watched Lea go in and relived the whole evening. She was lovely. He felt so comfortable with her as if he had known her for a long time. Smiling to himself, he started the car and drove off.

He still thought about Lea as he lay in bed. She came from a wealthy family. He was poor. He wondered what Lea and her parents would think?

Chapter 14

The television was on, but Saj sat at the table engrossed in the British Medical Journal. The phone rang.

"How are you, Baba?"

"I am better. I am back to work now."

"Wonderful news."

"How are your studies going. When do you plan to return?"

"I'll see how it works out." He didn't want to give anything away. "Did you receive the money I sent you?"

"Yes, we did, but the expenses are so high. You need to send more. We are buying household goods for Gita's wedding."

"How are Mama and Gita?"

"They're okay, but they miss you a lot. They want you to come back."

Saj loved his family, but at no time did they consider his wishes. He wondered maybe it was his fault because he never talked about his feelings. After every phone call from home, he was down in the dumps.

He sat in silence. The telephone rang again.

"How are you?" Kim asked.

"Alright," he replied.

"I was wondering…would you like to go out for a drink?"

A moment. "I have plans tonight. But sorry, I can't go out with you anymore. We can still be friends."

"I would like that," Kim said.

"Best of luck. I'll see you in the ward."

That evening, he had arranged to visit Emily. He hadn't seen her for a while.

"How are you?" Saj asked as he sat on the couch.

"Some days I'm okay, others I'm not." Emily sounded glum. "I wish it would go away. James talked so much about you. He loved you."

"How is your boy taking it? Where are the kids?"

"Martin is at a friend's birthday party. I didn't want to stay. The baby is asleep," she said. "He still doesn't realise his dad is gone." She said rather too brightly, sniffed and turned her head away.

"I passed my driving test and bought my first car."

"Fantastic. What car did you get?"

"Nothing fancy. It's a Ford, but I like it. My friend Dipak wanted me to buy a classy car to impress people. That doesn't interest me. I prefer a comfortable and reliable one."

Emily smiled.

"How is your job? Are you back to work?" Saj asked.

"Yeah...Oh, I forgot to offer you a drink. What would you like? I can open a bottle of wine."

"Sure, I'm beginning to like wine."

Emily poured two glasses and handed one to him.

Saj gestured to the four empty bottles on the table. "Has your family visited?"

Emily blushed. "My parents have been around a few times, and my brother too."

"Are you going out?"

"Not much...don't feel like it."

A pause.

"We were to play a tennis match that day. The loser was meant to take everyone out to Jai's restaurant." Saj looked down.

"I know. James told me," she said wiping her eyes.

Why did I say that? He thought. Now she's upset again.

He put his arm around Emily to comfort her. She drew closer, sobbing. And then she was kissing him and dragging at his clothes, breathing heavily. Saj managed to pull back and held her at arm's length.

"No, Emily. You are distressed and vulnerable now."

She sat with her head bowed. "Sorry. I always liked you." Her voice trembled.

"But...for God's sake, James was one of my best friends. You're still in shock...I must go."

"I apologise. Are we still friends?" Tears rolled down her face and left track marks on her cheeks.

He smiled. "Of course, we are."

Saj said goodbye and left shaking his head in disbelief. He felt it would be awkward to meet with her again but did not want to abandon a friend.

Chapter 15

It was Saturday. Saj was invited to attend a Diwali party at
one of Dipak's friends. Diwali is also called the Festival of
Lights, one of the most important religious festivals in India.
Back home, he enjoyed them with his parents. They all used
to dress up in their best garments and had fun. He missed his
family and friends that day.

Saj wore a traditional Indian costume. A purple loose long
shirt with golden embroidered patterns, which came down to
his knees. He put on dark blue trousers and a navy jacket.

He was unsure what English people would make of his
Indian clothes. Did he look silly?

Dipak lived in the building adjacent to his. Saj walked up
the stairs to the second floor. As he turned towards the
corridor which led to Dipak's room, a woman went past and
smiled at him. "Lovely costume," she said.

"Who is that girl?" he asked with a cheeky smile, as he
entered Dipak's room.

"She works in the laboratory here." Dipak poured a glass
of wine.

Saj chuckled.

"What happened to the nurse you were going out with?"

"I finished with her. She wanted commitment, talked about marriage and children...Beer?"

"Coke please."

"Boring, enjoy yourself, man." He gave him a can.

Saj opened the can of coke.

"How is life treating you?" Dipak took a sip.

"I do hope the administrators change our hours. It's too much."

"Me too."

"I feel guilty buying things for myself. I need to save more for my sister's wedding," Saj said. "I do send them money. Baba isn't happy that I don't phone them every week. He says I shouldn't waste my time going out. He thinks I'm still his shy little boy. I'm worried he might arrange my wedding in Bombay."

"Hmm." Dipak sipped wine.

"I'm not ready for it; I don't want an arranged marriage." Saj rubbed his face.

"You have changed Saj. I agree we deserve a choice. We shouldn't be forced to wed a stranger. It is our life, not our parents."

"Would you marry an English girl here?" Saj asked.

"I'm not the marrying type. I want to enjoy life which is what I'm doing."

"You are right."

"I think we better make a move; we'll be late. Jai wouldn't be too pleased. He would miss me at the party." Dipak stood.

Jai owned a chain of restaurants. Dipak had met him while he dined one of his girlfriends, a couple of years back. They had been good friends ever since.

Dipak dressed smartly in a stylish dark blue suit, too embarrassed to wear Indian clothing. He kept up with the latest fashion with designer wear.

"I wish you had told me you were wearing an English suit," said Saj.

"Don't worry man. Traditional clothes appear good on you."

"I went to town and bought clothes for myself. You advised me to get rid of most I brought from Bombay."

They sat in Dipak's flash black Mercedes.

"How can you afford this car? Must be expensive?" Saj examined the luxurious interior and beige leather seats.

"People here judge you by the clothes you wear, and the car you drive. For us being foreigners, it is even more important."

"You can't live beyond your means?" Saj said.

Dipak grinned. "Credit cards are your best friend."

"I'm taking driving lessons."

"Can you afford a car?"

"I'll need to save up."

Saj didn't feel safe as he sat in the front seat. Dipak drove erratically and never forgot any of his bad habits, driving on the crazy roads in Bombay. He would speed and then brake sharply, always shout, and swear at the other drivers.

Jai had an enormous detached house with a well-kept front garden. A red sports Mercedes and a navy Jaguar were parked in the drive. His restaurant business must be thriving, Saj thought.

Dipak pressed the bell on the large oak door. "Welcome," Jai said and embraced Dipak. He must be in his thirties, podgy with dark hair. Like most Indians, he also had a thick moustache. Jai wore a long bright red embroidered jacket.

"This is Saj. We work together."

"Dipak told me a lot about you," Jai said smiling. They shook hands.

Beautiful artwork made of shimmering cloth decorated the entire house. The place had a festive atmosphere with coloured lights everywhere. Numerous traditional candles gave the rooms a pleasant ambience, and their enchanting fragrance filled the house. Classical music played in the background.

Guests were dressed in bright, colourful Indian attire. Laughter and chatter rose in the rooms. Children ran around screaming, all excited with a few mothers chasing them. This large gathering of his countrymen in England fascinated Saj. He spotted only one white English couple in the crowd. They appeared strange wearing Indian clothes. Saj noted Dipak in his suit and smiled.

Jai introduced both to his family and friends. Saj was shy to mingle early on.

"Wow. This place is awesome." The English man looked around. He stood next to Saj.

"Yeah. It is," Saj said, as he turned and shook his hand. "I'm Saj."

"Dave. I am Jai's neighbour. Never been to anything similar before," he said. "Is this a religious celebration? Must be massive back in India."

"Yes. Diwali is a five-day festival of lights we celebrate back home. It coincides with the Hindu New Year and celebrates the triumph of light over darkness."

"What is its significance?" Dave asked.

"The story told is the legend of Lord Rama and his wife, Sita. They returned from exile after they defeated the demon king Ravana back in the 15th century. The lights represent the victory of good over evil," Saj said.

"Fascinating. What else do you do at Diwali in India?" Dave asked as he took a sip of his mango milkshake.

"We share sweets and exchange gifts. People clean their homes and wear new clothes. They decorate buildings with fancy lights and enjoy a feast of delicious meals."

"Sounds like our Christmas. We eat and drink, don't we? I can't wait to try the fantastic spicy food here," Dave said with a smile.

"And of course, massive fireworks display, in the end, is traditional."

"Thanks, Saj for the information. My wife loves these dresses and costumes. I'll talk to you later." Dave left. It surprised Saj how English people took an interest in his culture.

Saj stared into his glass and thought of home. He missed his family. It was the first time he had celebrated Diwali on his own. The celebrations started with their prayer to God by a couple of priests. They dressed in their traditional clothing. They had many Gods and chanted as part of the rituals.

After the prayers had ended, Jai spoke. "Ladies and gentlemen, we are now going to have a cultural show."

Three professional lady dancers, wearing red and blue colourful glittery costumes, danced to classical music which Saj enjoyed. It was followed by a dance from six children of varying ages. Dressed in western garments, they performed modern dances to the tune of Michael Jackson. The kids were all part of Jai's family. One of his friends sang a couple of Bollywood songs.

Dinner was a feast. Saj had never seen such a variety of rich, savoury dishes in one place. Five different types of rice, more than ten curries, kebabs, naan bread, parathas, papadoms and much more. Numerous sweets and drinks, including alcohol, were laid on the tables.

Saj enjoyed the delicious home-cooked meal as he hadn't eaten spicy dishes for quite a while. Dipak loved his food and gorged as if there was no tomorrow. People overindulged in both cuisine and alcohol Saj. Most guests ate rice and curries with their hand as they did back in Bombay.

Dipak knew what Saj was thinking. He whispered in his ear, "This is a desi party, not our canteen. I wish I could eat with my hand in the hospital." They both chuckled.

"Plenty of food still left. Please help yourself." Jai came over to Saj and Dipak.

"It's delicious," Saj said.

"Come, I'll introduce you to a few friends," Jai said, as they walked to a middle-aged man. He dressed in an expensive double-breasted beige coloured suit and red tie. He held a glass of whisky in his hand.

"This is Dinesh," Jai said glancing at the man.

"Danny," the man said as they shook hands.

"These are my friends Dipak and Saj."

As they walked away, Jai grinned. "He likes to call himself Danny. The man owns a chain of corner shops. A few of us pretend to be more English, than the English themselves."

It amused Saj how some people wished to lose their Indian identity and culture. They wanted to blend in with the locals. It must be about self-esteem, he thought. He wondered how he would feel in say, a year. How would he have changed?

The guests went out to the garden soon after dinner. The security lights revealed a massive lawn with a patio and chairs. Thankfully no rain. People took turns to set off the fireworks. The sky glowed spectacularly. Everyone seemed excited especially the children who ran and screamed with delight. For the moment, Saj forgot all his hardships at work and home.

When the fireworks finished, people moved back indoors. The party kicked off in style with a disco. A professional DJ played Bollywood tunes, while bright coloured lights and lasers dazzled. Most of the guests joined in, with traditional classical dancing at first. Later they showed their moves to Bollywood and Bhangra pop music.

Dipak was in a jovial mood after a few drinks. He got up to dance. It was tempting for Saj to drink alcohol but decided against it. He wanted to stay sober after his last experience. The music blared, and the lights sparkled.

Saj moved his head with the beat, as guests danced. From nowhere, a young lady appeared. She had beautiful long dark hair and a twinkle in her eyes.

"Would you like to dance?" she asked.

"I am not a good dancer."

"Come on. I'll show you." She wouldn't take no for an answer.

Saj got up.

She wriggled her hips and displayed her fantastic rhythmical moves to the music. Saj tried to show his own silly moves. She giggled.

"You are a good dancer," Saj said.

"Thanks. I have been to dance school since I was ten." She smiled enticingly.

"I need a drink," she said after they danced for a couple of minutes.

They helped themselves to mango milkshakes.

"I'm Kavita, and you are?"

"Call me Saj." They shook hands.

"Jai is my older brother. What do you do Saj?"

"I am a doctor."

"Ahh." She smiled.

"Kavita. I want you to meet someone." An elderly lady held her arm and took her away.

"See you later," Saj said as she left.

Meanwhile, Dipak wobbled on his feet. He pranced like crazy trying to grab the ladies to dance with him. He hopped by throwing his arms and legs around, without any rhythm. His behaviour embarrassed Saj, but he didn't know what to do.

"Are you okay?" Saj asked.

"I feel fantastic. What a party," Dipak spoke in an incoherent manner.

The disco continued until midnight; then they turned the music down.

Dipak said, "Jai, the fun has only begun, carry on, man."

Saj noticed a few guests muttering and raising their eyebrows, as they stared at Dipak. The music suddenly stopped. Saj walked to him and whispered, "Time to go, my friend."

"I'm enjoying myself, man. I don't want to go!"

Saj realised how too much alcohol could change people's demeanour. At no time, had he seen Dipak act this way before. Perhaps this is the reason no one in his family drinks in Bombay. The crowd dispersed from the dance floor. Saj had to literally drag Dipak away, and make him sit down for a breather.

Jai came to Dipak. "Are you alright?"

"I'm great, man. Fantastic party, I am getting warmed up."

Sweat poured off Dipak. Saj fetched him a glass of water. He could hear Jai apologise to his friends about Dipak's behaviour. Gradually, the whole atmosphere calmed down.

"I'm sorry man," Dipak said in a faint voice.

"Don't worry," Jai said.

Dipak searched his jacket pockets for his car keys.

"You are in no fit state to drive. I'll call a taxi." Saj sounded stern. He had had enough of Dipak making a fool of himself.

Jai ordered the cab. It was 1 am, and most of the guests had gone home. Dipak apologised again as they shook hands and left.

Chapter 16

Saj was desperate to talk to Lea the next evening. He was nervous about ringing in case her parents answered. Sitting on his couch, he conjured a reason to call her. He could tell her about his move to the rented flat.

He had felt suffocated living in the hospital accommodation. An advert for a one-bedroom flat had been displayed on the notice board at work. It was only five minutes away. The apartment had essential amenities, and he liked it. He had saved enough and put money aside for his sister's wedding.

His heart raced as he picked up the phone. What if Lea doesn't want to see him again? Maybe they are having dinner, he would disturb them.

Saj cleared his throat and dialled before he changed his mind. To his surprise, the phone line sounded dead. Had Lea given him the wrong number? He carefully redialled, and this time it rang. The phone kept ringing. Maybe they're not in. He was just about to put the phone down.

"Hello," a lady answered.

It must be her mother.

"Oh...Can I speak to Leanne please?"

"Could you hold on for a second? I'll see if she is in." She sounded very "English" and posh.

Lea took her time. Maybe she didn't want to talk to him, he thought.

"Hi," she said.

"This is Saj. How are you?"

"I'm fine. This is a pleasant surprise."

"I hope I didn't disturb you."

"No, not at all."

"I'm moving to my flat next week. I'll let you know my new phone number later," Saj said.

"Where is it?"

"Not far from here, it will be fun living away from the hospital."

"Yes. You'll enjoy it."

"Have you ever seen a Bollywood film?"

"No, though I'd love to. I like the colours and costumes, and the way women dress up."

"There is a special show this Saturday evening. I wondered if you want to go? And before you worry about the language, it has English subtitles," Saj said and laughed.

"Okay."

Saj was delighted. They chatted for a while.

"I'll see you. Shall I pick you up at 7?"

"Sure. Bye."

On Saturday evening, Saj parked his car on the road outside her house and waited for her. Lea saw him from her window and came down.

"Hi, how are you?" she asked with a smile, as she opened the door and sat in the passenger seat.

"I'm great thanks. Shall we go?" He started the car and drove off.

"The movie is for the Asian community," Saj said as he headed for the Odeon. "It has been a long time since I have seen a Bollywood film. Hope you'll like it."

"I'm sure it will be fine. It can't be any worse than some of the films I've watched," Lea said with a grin.

Lea was dressed casually in jeans and a long-sleeved top, with a short jacket. The fragrance of her perfume was magical. In a hurry to be on time, Saj had forgotten to put on his aftershave.

They arrived at the cinema, and as expected it was quiet. Saj got the tickets and Lea bought coke and popcorn.

It was a typical romantic Bollywood movie full of songs and dances. The story about a boy and a girl who fall in love. They faced opposition from their families and a villain. As they watched, he took Lea's hand in his. She didn't mind. A few funny scenes made her laugh out loud.

"What did you think?" he asked, as the lights came on at the end.

"Yes. I liked it."

"I am surprised. It could have been shorter."

"The girls were so beautiful. Their dresses were eye-catching."

"Girls are always more attractive than men. Bollywood films are a fantasy world. The hero fights off ten villains barehanded, without a scratch on him. Real life is completely different in India. "

Lea laughed.

"Did you notice that men and women never kissed on the lips?"

"Yes, you are right," she said.

Saj chuckled. "It's because of our culture."

"Strange."

They realised everyone had left the auditorium, while they chatted. Both got up and hurried towards the exit.

"I hope we are not locked in," she said.

It was a cold, clear night, as they walked to the car park.

"So, how do you speak such good English?" Lea asked.

Saj smiled. "I studied in a private school. We were taught most subjects in English. We read Charles Dickens and Shakespeare, would you believe it?"

"I am impressed."

"My favourites were Great Expectation, David Copperfield and Oliver Twist."

"Wow," she said.

"We're quite a conservative and close family. My father's major priority was to provide us with the best education. But it was expensive on his salary, so he struggled."

"Family is important in your culture. I know this from the Asian patients who come to our surgery."

"There are good and bad aspects of everything," Saj said. "My father wanted me to be a famous doctor, whatever it took. He has high hopes for me. I'm the one who will eventually support the family...Enough of me...what about you?"

"Well. We're somewhat close. My older brother Toby lives in London. Nicole, my younger sister, is at home" she said. "We have our differences at times, though we do get along. Women rule in our house. Mummy is the head of the house. Daddy will do anything to keep the peace."

Saj smiled. "It's the other way around in my family. My father is the boss, my mother agrees with whatever he says most of the time."

They drove to Lea's house. He had intended to park on the road as he had done before.

"You can drive in," she said. "Thanks for tonight. I enjoyed the film. It was different."

"I'm glad. I thought you might be bored."

"Would you like to come in for a coffee?"

"I think I better go." Meeting her parents intimidated him.

"Come on. It's only ten."

"Okay." Now is this a good idea, he wondered.

Shrubs and trees filled the substantial front garden. Saj's small Ford seemed out of place on the circular drive as it stood next to the Mercedes and Lea's Toyota Corolla. She walked to the door, Saj followed her. As she opened it, he was taken aback by the splendour of the house. His feet sunk into the thick red carpets. The furnishing and the decor were exquisite. Lea took him to the lounge.

"Take a seat. I'll see who's in," she said. "Would you like tea?"

"Yes please."

Lea left the room, and he sat down and grasped his hands together. The four huge couches smelled of real leather. Classy artwork hung on the wall although Saj had no knowledge of art. Beautiful chandeliers were suspended from the ceiling, but to his surprise, there was no television.

The house impressed Saj. He heard someone walk behind him. He turned around and saw a young lady coming towards him.

He stood up.

"I'm Nicole."

"I'm Saj," he said with a nervous smile, and they shook hands. "You must be Lea's sister."

"I am. Lea told me all about you...Please take a seat," she said.

Nicole was an attractive young woman in her late teens, although Saj never got it right when it came to guessing women's age.

Lea walked in pushing a trolley with tea, biscuits, and cakes, which Saj liked. The tea was in a big pot accompanied by china cups and saucers. He had thought that in this society, they only offered drinks to visitors. In Bombay, guests would be served snacks and food, whatever the time of the day. It was their traditional hospitality. Guests were treated like Gods in their culture.

"Mummy and Daddy have gone out to a dinner party. They won't be back until midnight," Lea said meaningfully.

Saj breathed an inner sigh of relief.

"This is a lovely house."

"It's too big for us."

The phone rang. Nicole got up to answer it and left the room.

"Your sister is nice."

Lea grinned. "Ah, you don't know her. She can be quite wild."

After they finished their tea, Saj glanced at the time. "I think I'll go now. I enjoyed the evening." He wanted to leave before her parents returned.

"Me too."

"Here is my telephone number for the flat. I'll move in a week." He passed her the slip of paper.

"You must be excited."

"Yes. It will be good to forget about work when I'm finished at 5."

They walked outside to his car holding hands. Then Saj gently kissed her. He was aware her sister might be watching them from inside the house, so he made it quick. He got in the car, waved, and drove off.

When Lea went back in the house, Nicole waited for her.

"He's handsome," Nicole said, with a cheeky grin.

Lea smiled and said, "We're just friends."

"Oh yes...and you want me to believe that!"

Lea kept silent.

"I'm not sure what Mummy will think of him, though. You know what she's like. She is so old-fashioned, and Saj is...different."

"You mean, he's coloured."

"I like him. Mummy is from the older generation," said Nicole.

"I'm tired. I'm going to bed now. Good night."

Chapter 17

Not long after Saj moved into his new flat, he took his
specialist exams. It was a long, arduous day full of
assessments. He did well but couldn't answer the last
question, so he thought he would fail. The next week was a
nervy period for him, he kept himself occupied with work.
What if he failed? His father expected him to pass. It would
be a disaster and an embarrassment.

A couple of weeks later, he received a letter from the
Royal College. Saj held his breath, his hands shook as he
opened the envelope. His eyes lit up, he couldn't believe it.
"Yes!" he punched the air with delight. Grabbing the phone,
he dialled his mother.

"I passed," Saj said in a loud voice.

His mother cried. "I'm so proud of you," she said. Then
her tone altered, and she became quiet.

"What's the matter, Mama?"

"Your father is unwell again. He is off work now. The
doctor has put him on new medicines. You should come
back home, now you passed."

"Mama, I want to gain experience and earn more. You know how poorly doctors are paid in Bombay...and we need money for Gita's wedding."

"You ought to think of your family first. I'll talk to you again." She hung up.

Pouring himself a glass of wine, he sat on the couch, his shoulders slumped, deep in thought. His eyes brimmed with tears and he wiped them. He felt that his moment of happiness had changed to sadness.

He called Dipak. "I passed," Saj said.

They went to the social club to celebrate.

"Fantastic news. I am so pleased for you." Saj thought Dipak was missing his spark.

"What's up?"

"Nothing."

"Now come on. You can tell me."

"Well, nothing important...this girl who works in the path lab. I like her." Dipak took a sip.

"And... what happened?"

"Well...for whatever reason, she doesn't want to see me anymore." Dipak sat with his head bowed.

Saj never knew Dipak to be upset about women. His motto in life, 'There are plenty more fish in the sea.'

"Don't worry. You'll find someone else."

Dipak shrugged his shoulders and took another sip.

They had a few drinks. Saj tried his best to cheer him up, but it was hard work.

Saj was thrilled about Lea. She was intelligent and smart with a brilliant sense of humour. In her opinions and behaviour, she seemed conservative, and he loved that. He was aware of their class difference.

He received a note one day from Lea. It read, "I miss you. Lea xxx"

Saj got on the phone to her. "I got your note. I miss you a lot too. Sorry I've not been in touch. Exams. But I passed!"

"Well done. It will mean a lot to your parents."

"I would like to cook you a meal one evening. Then you can see my new flat too. When are you free?"

"I'm busy for the next few days," she said.

"Next Friday? I am not on call."

"Okay."

"I'm not a great cook. Do you eat spicy food?"

"Yes, I'm sure it will be delicious."

"I have to go back to the ward. See you on Friday." His heart was racing as he put down the receiver.

Saj walked to Holmes planning the dishes he would cook to impress Lea when Nick met him.

"The health authorities are changing our work hours," Nick said.

"Shifts will be better."

"You took a stand against this nonsense Saj."

"But it won't bring James back though."

"It was tragic. No, it won't. But something good has come from James death, and he would be proud of that."

The office phone rang, an urgent call from casualty.

"Catch you later," Nick said

Saj saw a boy in his teens. He held the left side of his chest in pain. The boy was restless, could hardly breathe and his face was turning blue. Saj listened to his chest. There was no breath sounds on one side. He made a diagnosis of pneumothorax. It needed immediate action. Otherwise, the boy would die. He explained it to his mother.

Saj inserted a big needle in his chest and attached it to a drain. A gush of air came out. The boy's breathing settled and his colour improved. He turned towards Saj, forced a smile, and nodded his head behind the oxygen mask. Saj felt relieved, his call was right. He advised the nurses to arrange a chest X-ray and transfer him to the recovery ward. Later, the boy's mother came to him.

"Oh, doctor. You performed a miracle. How can I thank you? He's my only child, my life. I thought I had lost him," the mother said as she wiped her eyes.

Saj gave her a gentle hug and smiled. "I only did my job. He'll be fine."

"Thank you. We are grateful." She shook his hand and left.

It was moments like this, which made it worthwhile being a doctor, he thought and smiled to himself.

Lea was coming for dinner that evening. Saj wanted to impress her. He tidied up and bought a bouquet of mixed flowers, and a plug-in rose air freshener. He thought that she might find the curry smell unpleasant.

Saj had watched his mother cook when he was a kid. Experimenting with different spices, he cooked vegetables and chicken, served with rice. He hoped Lea would like his food. She would think he was a modern man, even though he wasn't.

There was a knock on the door.

"How are you? Do come in." He smiled and kissed her.

"I'm all right."

Lea was elegantly dressed in a long dark skirt and a full-sleeved top with her hair pinned up.

"You look beautiful," Saj said with a smile.

"Thanks. This is a lovely flat." Lea looked around.

"It's not too bad." The flat had one small bedroom and a lounge, with a little kitchen attached. It came furnished. He thought that the kitchen in Lea's house seemed more spacious than his whole place.

"Please take a seat," he said, pointing to the small grey couch.

"It looks neat. I'm impressed." She had no idea Saj had put in extra effort to tidy the place. What he couldn't clean up, he had dumped in the wardrobe.

"Would you like a drink? There is a limited choice. How about white wine?" He suggested before she answered.

"Yeah."

Saj poured a glass for Lea and one for himself.

"Tell me about your family." Saj took a sip.

"Daddy works in the city. He is the CEO of an investment bank. My brother, Toby, is in banking for another corporation; he lives in Hampstead."

"The stock exchange and the market collapsed recently," he said.

"I don't understand much about shares and stocks. It goes up and down," Lea said and laughed. "Mummy owned a marketing company which she sold. She does charity work which keeps her occupied. What about your family?"

Saj hesitated for a moment. "My father works in a factory, and my mother is a housewife. My younger sister is in college. We're middle-class. Not wealthy like yours," he said with a wry smile.

"There's nothing wrong with that. We have our own issues, money can't solve."

"I'll check the food, hope you'll like it." Saj went to the kitchen.

"I'm sure it will be good. I'll tell you if it isn't."

He laid the plates and the cutlery on the small table.

"Smells wonderful. Do you want any help?"

"No thanks," he shouted from the kitchen.

Lea sat at the table with difficulty, it was cramped. Saj left the cutlery in a pile on one side. She looked at it and giggled.

"You can tell I'm not used to all this," he said and chuckled. "As long as you like the food."

They started the meal, and to his surprise, Lea liked it. She ate both chicken and vegetables. "This is delicious."

"It's one of my mother's recipes, with my experimentation." He laughed.

"Your experiment was successful," she said and smiled.

"Are you being honest, or only polite?"

"I'm not a big fan of spicy food. But this is good, not too hot either."

"This is authentic curry. What we eat back home, different than what is served in restaurants here. I put fewer spices for you."

"Thanks."

Saj was relieved. "If I am honest, I don't find the food here appetising. It's too bland."

"That's why so many Indian, Italian and other restaurants are in business."

"Maybe I should open a curry house." Saj laughed and poured more wine.

After dinner, they sat on the couch. It was small, so both squeezed in quite tight.

"Thanks for the meal. It tasted better than restaurant food and definitely healthier," Lea said.

Saj smiled. "I don't add any butter or cream to my cooking."

They drank more wine, and he enjoyed her company.

"One of my friend's mother comes to your surgery. She said you are very kind," Saj said.

"I try my best to be helpful. Most patients are worried about coming to the doctors."

"Not all nurses are compassionate, though."

"People give compliments to you as well in the hospital."

"And who gives you this news?"

"Well, I have my sources," Lea said with a cheeky smile.

"And what do your sources say?"

"That you are sensitive and kind to patients. You are a gifted doctor, and everyone likes you."

"We should have a mutual admiration club." He laughed.

Saj gazed at her eyes and moved a strand of hair off her face. "You are beautiful."

Lea smiled, held his hand, and kissed it. She appeared comfortable in his company. Saj leant forward and pressed his lips to hers. He put his arm around her and became more passionate and intense. Suddenly Lea hesitated and pulled away.

"I hope I haven't upset you," he said.

Lea bit her lip, shook her head and looked down. Then sniffed back some tears.

"What's the matter?" He embraced her gently.

She took a deep breath, wiped her eyes and gazed at Saj.

After a momentary silence, she said, "I never told this to anyone except mummy."

"Told what? You're making me worried."

Lea sat with her head bowed and avoided eye contact.

"Last summer we had a big party at our house. It was my parent's wedding anniversary. About midnight I came out to get fresh air. It was a warm, pleasant evening, so I went for a stroll in the garden." She paused.

"And?"

"There was this man, a family friend of ours. He followed me outside and grabbed me from behind. He was drunk and started kissing me. I tried to push him away, but he was strong. He pulled me to the ground and attempted to unbutton my top."

"I'll kill the bastard." Saj clenched his fist.

"I was scared and froze for a minute. I couldn't scream."

"Maybe nobody would have heard you with all the partying and music. What happened?"

"The noise and the headlights of a car leaving distracted the man for a moment. I scratched him and poked his eye. He screamed as he clutched his face."

"That's my Lea."

"I ran fast towards the house. Nobody noticed, most were drunk. I went straight upstairs to my room and locked the door. My heart was beating fast, I gasped for air as I sat on my bed." She sobbed and wiped her tears.

"Where is he now. I'll kill him. Why didn't you report him?"

"I wanted to forget about the incidence."

"Where is he now?"

"He joined the forces and has been posted abroad."

"I'm so sorry. You were brave. I am very proud of you Lea." Saj leaned forward and drew her towards him.

"Nothing happened that night Saj."

He poured another glass for Lea and held her hand.

"Sorry," she said.

"It's okay." Saj stroked her hair and then kissed her on the neck. She closed her eyes.

He stopped and moved back.

"What's the matter?" Lea asked.

"Nothing."

"What?"

"You are beautiful...I'm getting turned on," he said and smiled.

"Okay." She smiled back.

They canoodled with even more vigour. Saj pulled away. He knew Lea was someone special and wished to proceed gently with her.

She paused. "I've not had many boyfriends."

He wanted to say, me neither but he didn't.

"We don't have to do anything." Saj resisted the arousal he felt. He stood up and got a glass of water.

The phone rang.

"Hello, Baba. I meant to phone you," Saj said and took a deep breath.

"We haven't heard from you for over a week. You have forgotten your family," his father sounded annoyed.

"I've been busy. Do you mind if I phone you in an hour?"

Saj appeared solemn after he got off the phone. He took a sip of water. Calls from home always meant more pressure for him. When was he coming back home? That would be the first question asked.

"Is everything okay?" Lea asked.

"Yeah. It was my father." He took another sip and sat next to her.

She looked at her watch and got up. "I need to go."

"Do you have to?"

"Mummy doesn't know I am here, she gets worried. I really enjoyed the evening, the food was great," Lea said putting her coat on.

"When will I see you again?" he asked as she headed for the door.

Lea smiled. "I'll give you a ring."

They stood at the door hugged and said goodbye.

After she had left, Saj wondered whether he was falling for her. The flat seemed empty without her. He didn't want to think much about his future back in India.

A couple of days later Saj called home again.

"How are you?" he asked his father.

"I'm improving though still not back at work. The doctor has prescribed a few new drugs."

It was excellent news for Saj. "How is everyone?"

"They're alright. Gita is taking her exams."

"Baba. I need to go out. I'll ring you soon." Saj wanted to get off the phone before his father asked him to return home.

He sat with a glass of wine contemplating his family in Bombay and Lea. The phone interrupted his thoughts.

"Hello, Saj. I miss you," Lea said

"I've been thinking about you at work. I miss you too Lea. When will I see you again?"

"Are you free next Saturday evening?"

"Yeah."

"Would you like to come for tea with us?"

"It will be lovely...Will your parents be around?" He sounded hesitant.

"Yes, they might be but don't worry," Lea said and chuckled.

"I'm not worried." He lied.

Chapter 18

Dressed in his navy suit, Saj hoped to impress Lea's parents that evening. What if they didn't like him? They were wealthy and upper class. He belonged to a poor family, he thought.

His mouth was parched as he parked on her drive. Saj sat in the car for a couple of minutes and took a few deep breaths. Someone might be watching, he thought, so he got out. It started to drizzle. He rang the bell and waited. Come on, he needed to get hold of himself. For God's sake, he was a professional, a lifesaver!

"Come in," Lea said with a smile as she opened the door.

Saj glanced around, as he searched for her parents.

"How are you?" she said.

"I'm great thanks."

The moment he sat down, a middle-aged lady walked into the room. He stood up.

"I'm Margaret."

"I'm Saj," he said with a nervous smile.

He put his hand forward to shake hers, but she moved away. Perhaps she hadn't seen.

"Do sit down," she said.

Both Saj and Lea sat on the couch. Margaret looked elegant like Lea. A lady in her fifties, she had a slim physique with short greying hair and wore glasses.

"So, Lea tells me you are a doctor in the hospital," Margaret asked.

"Yes." Saj nodded.

"Did Lea tell you, she planned to be a doctor. She changed her mind. We hoped Lea would meet a nice Englishman."

He glanced at Lea who shook her head and forced a smile.

"Nicole wants to study medicine. She intends to travel the world and do charity work. This is a phase a lot of this generation go through...Which part of India are you from?" she asked.

"Bombay."

"Oh...My father got posted in Delhi in the British army. He told us interesting stories about the place."

Saj relaxed. At least they were building rapport, he thought.

"There's a lot of poverty there," Margaret said.

"I agree, but there are affluent areas as well."

"Is Saj your real name?"

He seemed confused for a second. Then he realised what Margaret meant.

"My name is Sajindrapalonam, People prefer a shorter version." He forced a smile.

"I know a GP. His name is Jasander Singh, he calls himself Jack. Strange."

Lea appeared uncomfortable with her mother's inquisition. "Would you like a drink Saj?"

"Tea please."

Lea didn't move. Saj knew she didn't want to leave him on his own with her mother.

"Saj is very popular in the hospital, Mummy. They all love him."

"Good, though there are people who could make life difficult for you," said Margaret.

Which is what she was doing at that moment, Saj thought.

"Are you going to go back to Bombay. You have arranged marriages there, don't you?"

Saj didn't reply. "This is a lovely house," he said looking around. He thought flattery would help.

"This is one of the most expensive properties in this locality. We also have a villa in Spain," Margaret said.

As they chatted, a man entered the room. Saj felt relieved. Now he would be off the hook from her mother's interrogation.

"I'm Christopher, call me Chris," he said with a warm smile and shook Saj's hand.

Saj stood and responded with a smile. "I'm Saj."

"Please do sit down," Chris said.

Christopher stood almost six feet, with a slight belly.

"Lea told us about you. How's the job?" Chris asked.

"Good but busy. I took my Royal College specialist exams and got through." Saj thought they would be impressed.

"Well done," Chris said.

"Thanks."

Nicole brought a trolley with tea, coffee, and cakes. Lea handed Saj a cup.

Saj liked her father, he made him welcome.

"I need to do some work," Margaret said and left the room.

After half an hour Saj glanced at the time. "I better go. Pleased to meet you Chris, Nicole. Bye." Lea followed him out.

The rain had stopped, as they stood next to his car.

"I'm sorry about Mummy. She's always like that."

"Your dad is a nice man."

They smiled and kissed goodbye.

Back at Lea's house, a heated discussion ensued. Margaret came down after Saj left. She made her feelings known.

"Mummy. You were very rude to him." Lea frowned.

"He comes from a different background darling. What would our friends say?"

"Who cares what they think. Ours is a new generation. If they're racist, that's their problem, not mine."

"He seems a fine young man," her father cut in.

"How do you know, Chris? You have only just met him."

"Stop judging him, Mummy," Lea shrieked.

"I'm off to bed." Margaret left the room.

"I didn't expect her to be so rude. Saj was a guest. I should've never invited him."

"Don't worry darling. You know your mother," Chris said. "She will come around in the end."

"I hope so," Lea said.

The next evening Lea came to Saj's flat.

"I'm sorry about Mummy's behaviour." Lea shuffled on the couch. "She was out of order. She shouldn't insult a guest."

"Your mother hates me," said Saj.

"Mummy is ignorant. My grandfather served in the army, so she feels part of that colonial regime and the British empire."

"I think she needs to open her eyes and see clearly."

"It's not all her fault. She believes in what she has been told about India," Lea said.

"Margaret ought to realise the world has changed. There is good and bad everywhere."

"I know, but some of your people don't blend in well here."

"What do you mean?" Saj said.

"It's the way some of them live and dress," Lea said avoiding eye contact.

"This is a free country. The Asian people can live how they please as long as they are not breaking the law."

"Mummy judges your culture by what she observes here."

"So, she turns a blind eye to all the ills in this society. I can name a few." Saj noticed that the conversation was getting heated.

"Go on then."

"Let's not argue. I'm sorry." He smiled.

"Me too."

"Your father's a gentleman."

"I wish Daddy would stick up for himself."

"Come on. Give us a cuddle." He wrapped his arms around and hugged her.

Lea gazed at him and went quiet.

"What is it?" he asked as he stroked her hair.

She paused.

"What are you thinking? Come on. You can tell me."

After a long silence, Lea said, "I think..." and she stopped. He glanced inquiringly at her.

"I love you," Lea said in a soft voice.

Saj smiled. He had never experienced real love before. He loved his family but at no time expressed his emotions in words. People didn't speak openly about affection in his culture. It was all unsaid love. Wow, he thought.

"Sorry, not sure why I said that. I'm emotional." Lea looked away.

Saj held her tightly. He knew that Lea was unique. "I love you too," he said.

Lea smiled.

An hour passed. Glancing at the watch, Lea said, "I don't' want to, but I have to go."

"Sorry. I never offered you a drink," Saj said as he stood.

"Not to worry."

"I'll give you a ring when your mother is out." He grinned. Lea forced a smile as she left.

Chapter 19

Saj read the Times on his lunch break in the doctors' mess.

"We will be doing shift work soon," a doctor said taking a bite of his sandwich.

"It will be good for us," Saj remarked as he focused on the newspaper.

"Have you heard that the Coroner's Report for James was death by natural causes."

"Hmm."

"Saj, are you sending any Valentine cards this year?"

"Ah, What's that?"

"Saint Valentine, you know?"

"Sorry I don't," he said and smiled scratching his head.

"You don't celebrate it in Bombay, do you? Meant to show your love for someone. You send her cards, flowers or chocolates, take them out for a meal."

"When is it?" Saj asked.

"On the 14th."

"Next week?"

Saj bought a Valentine card and phoned Lea.

"I just called to say I love you," he said.

"Oh! You're like Stevie Wonder," she chuckled.

"Who's that?"

"The famous American singer."

"Never heard of him." Saj laughed.

"This was before your time."

"Do you want to go for dinner next Friday?"

"Valentine's day?"

"I know." He pretended as if he always knew.

"It would be wonderful."

"Jai's curry place?" Saj asked.

"Great," she said.

"I already miss you."

"I miss you too."

Saj phoned Lea every night at about 11 pm to say goodnight.

As arranged, Lea came to the flat on Friday evening. Saj was ready to go.

"You look gorgeous," he said.

"Thanks." She smiled and kissed him.

"I've got something for you." He went to the kitchen and brought out a bunch of red roses and Valentine's card and handed them to Lea.

"They're beautiful. Thank you." She smelled the flowers. His friend advised him to buy red roses. In fact, this was the first time Saj had bought flowers for anyone.

"If I did that I would sneeze." He laughed when she smelled the roses.

"And this is for you." Lea gave him a big box of Cadbury's chocolates with a card.

"Thank you. But you'll have to share the chocolates with me."

Jai's restaurant was busy when they arrived. Indian classical instrumental music played in the background. Many scented candles were lit all around the room, and the soft lights created a romantic atmosphere.

"What would you like to order?" he asked Lea, who was reading the menu.

"I'll go for my usual chicken tikka masala."

Saj smiled. "Never understood why this is the most popular dish in this country."

"Maybe because the curry is creamy and mild."

"I never tried it until I came to this country."

"You eat different types of spicy food back home?"

"That's right. It varies from the north to the south of India. There is a large variety of cuisines which differ in spices and the ways they are cooked. This gives them a distinct aroma and flavours."

They ordered their food and a bottle of wine.

"Do you have strict customs and beliefs in your culture?" Lea asked.

"There are a few, but you don't want to know."

"I do." She smiled.

"Honour killing is one of the most shocking rituals. It is more prevalent in rural society. The families ensure that a person does not marry outside his caste, religion and social status. Many communities are extremely strict about these matters."

"What happens if a person rebel?"

"If someone goes against their rules, they may be disowned, or worse, killed, for bringing dishonour on the family."

"Jesus, that's terrible." She took a sip of water.

"But this custom isn't widespread."

"How is your family in Bombay?"

"They're alright...How's your work?" Saj didn't want to talk about his parents.

"Hectic. All the staff are under tremendous pressure because few are off sick."

The waiter came and piled the knives and forks on one side of the table. Lea glanced at Saj and giggled.

"It's funny the way the waiter arranged the cutlery on the table," she said with a smile.

"I bet it brought back memories for you." He sniggered.

After returning to his flat, they sat in the sitting room and had tea.

"You seem quiet. Everything okay?" Saj asked.

"Well...I am not sure whether I should talk to you about the matter."

"Try me."

"You know Dr Watson at the surgery."

"Sherlock Holmes and Dr Watson."

"Please be serious Saj."

"Sorry, go ahead. I'm listening carefully."

"He's not right."

"What do you mean?"

"Watson's behaviour in the last few months seems odd. His mood has been erratic. He doesn't concentrate on his work. He's made silly mistakes, and..." Lea paused.

"And?"

"I noticed a few controlled drugs were missing. I can't explain it. Maybe Watson has taken them."

"Sounds alarming. So, what are you going to do?"

"I don't know."

"Is there a senior nurse you can confide in?"

"I need to."

"Do you want me to talk to Watson?" Saj asked.

"No. It would complicate matters. Anyway, thanks for listening, it worried me."

"Come here." Saj hugged her.

She kissed him. "I have to go now. Mummy gets concerned if I'm late. Thanks for a lovely evening and the flowers," Lea said as she put on her coat.

"My pleasure. I enjoyed it."

Lea paused. "You play tennis, don't you?"

"I can wallop the ball sometimes out of the court. I'm not brilliant." He chuckled.

"Me neither though it doesn't matter. We can play at the club Mummy goes to, say on Saturday afternoon. I'll give you a ring."

"Your mother won't be there?"

"No. My parents are away to Spain for the weekend." Lea shook her head and smiled.

Saj walked her to the door. They looked at each other and hugged again.

"I love you Saj."

"I love you too."

Chapter 20

It was a Saturday morning. Saj was ironing his clothes. His mother used to take care of him and did all his chores in Bombay. The telephone rang.

"Hello Saj, it's Lea."

"Hi. How are you? I was thinking about you while ironing."

"What were you thinking?"

"I just miss you."

"Miss you too. Do you do your own ironing?" Lea laughed.

"And washing as well. Someone has to do it, though I hate it. I enjoyed our game. You're good at tennis."

"Thanks. You have a natural talent though. I'm glad you had a good time there."

"I'd like to go again, so I can improve. I want to take a few lessons."

"That's a great idea. I have some good news. Remember the issue with Dr Watson. I spoke to my senior colleague, and now she will deal with it."

"That's great. You must be relieved."

"Yes, I am."

"I'm glad you called. There's a Freddie Mercury Tribute Concert at Wembley Stadium next Saturday. Would you like to go?" Saj asked. "I have tickets."

"Yes, I would love to," Lea said.

"I like some of the Queen songs, especially 'I Want to Break Free.'

"He was terrific. Poor Freddie. He died in 1991."

"Yeah. It was only last year. Really sad. Love you, Lea."

"I love you too."

The following Saturday, Saj drove to Lea's house.

"You look lovely." Saj kissed her. She blushed and smiled.

The sun was shining in a clear blue sky. A chilly breeze made the atmosphere cooler as they drove towards Wembley. Saj had never been there before. A queue of cars crawled along the road leading to the stadium. They had to wait for more than an hour to get in.

Saj looked around. "Wow. Unbelievable. Look at the size of the crowd."

"Exciting. The stage is huge," Lea said.

They cheered and danced, holding hands like teenagers. Saj knew only a few of the acts but still loved the music.

Both were exhausted when the concert finished. It had been a long day. The worst was yet to come. It took them more than two hours to get out of the car park. By the time they drove out of the stadium, it was midnight.

"Did you enjoy it?" Saj asked.

"Yes. It was incredible, thanks." Lea leant over and kissed him on the cheek.

"Never seen such a massive crowd."

"Saj. Can we stop somewhere to eat? I'm hungry."

"Most likely only a fast food place will be open at this time of the night."

The roads were quieter as they came out of central London.

"I can see a McDonalds. We could go there," Saj said.

"Okay."

He parked, and they got out of the car. As they approached the restaurant, he saw a few young men standing around the entrance. Saj and Lea hurried past them. The place was empty bar a couple of people waiting for their orders.

"What would you like Lea?"

"I'll have a Big Mac meal."

Saj ordered two meals.

"Maybe we should take it away." He was wary of the odd characters at the restaurant door.

"Good idea."

While they waited, the men walked in. There were four of them, scruffy, wearing hooded tops. One of them had a black skull tattooed on his right hand. Lea bit her nails and held Saj's hand tight avoiding eye contact with the men. Saj kept her close to him.

"Have you heard the song...Black or white," one of them shouted.

"These fucking Pakis come here and take our jobs," another man said.

"And our women too."

Saj clenched his fists. Lea breathed deeply.

"Come on Saj. Let's go. I'm not hungry."

"No. It should be ready any minute. You take my car keys and wait in the car, lock it from inside. I'll come out if they follow you." He gave her the keys.

"No, I'm not leaving you here."

"You go, Lea, please," he said sternly.

Lea gazed at Saj for a few moments. She then walked slowly towards the door with her head bowed.

"Where are you going, darling?" One of the villains stood in her way.

"Let her go. She has nothing to do with this," Saj said in a loud voice.

Saj knew these guys meant trouble. He hoped he could take them on. But there were so many of them. A young couple who were waiting for their order got up and left. They must have sensed trouble.

The taller man attempted to grab Lea. Saj rushed at him and punched him in the stomach. The thug groaned in pain and staggered back.

"Run Lea... Run."

"I'm not leaving you." She yelled.

The other man attacked. Saj blocked his punch, grabbed his arm, twisted it, and kicked him in the stomach. The other two men stepped forward. One of them hit Saj in the face which left him in a daze for a moment. Then the other punched him in the solar plexus. Saj fell backwards on the floor, his mouth bleeding. One of them straddled him, while the other kicked him in the head. Saj tried to cover his face with his arms.

"Leave him alone. Can anyone help," Lea screamed. The young man behind the counter had disappeared.

Saj acted like a wounded tiger. He struggled, got up, and kicked one of them in his chest. The man groaned in pain. The other two jumped on him. They held him down while another thug punched him in the stomach.

"Stop that now." Someone roared from behind. "Step away."

A big, burly man with shaven head stood with one of his mates, who was as big as him. He had tattoos on the side of his neck.

The young thugs gawked at the big man and his friend for a moment. They glanced at each other. The leader of the gang moved back, away from Saj. The others followed.

"The two of you should leave now," the burly man said to Saj.

Lea trembled as she went over to Saj and helped him back to his feet. He wiped the blood off his face with his torn shirt sleeve. Clenching his jaw, he glared at the thugs as he stumbled past them.

"One against four. Pitiful!" Lea said to one of them.

She held his arm, and they walked towards the restaurant door. As they passed the burly man, Saj looked at him and said, "Thanks." The man nodded.

Lea got in the driving seat and started the car. He sat gingerly on the passenger side.

"You're bleeding. We need to go to casualty," Lea said as she drove.

"I'm fine. There is a box of tissues on the back seat."

Lea stopped the car on the roadside. She mopped the blood off his face and held his hand.

"I'm sorry. We shouldn't have gone in." She sobbed.

"We didn't know."

"You were brave Saj." She kissed his hand.

"It scared me, but I had no choice. I was worried about you. Those bastards wanted trouble."

"I love you Saj."

"I love you too Lea." They hugged.

"Ah, my mouth hurts." He grimaced.

Lea phoned him the next morning while he was having breakfast.

"How are you?" she asked.

"Still a little sore but I'm okay. I've taken painkillers."

"You were so brave Saj."

"Or stupid." He chuckled.

"You must think so badly of us."

"Well. This can happen anywhere. These scums are present in every society in the world."

"I'll come in the evening and cook you a nice pasta dish. I'll bring a bottle of wine. It will be a change for you."

"That will be lovely."

"I love you so much."

"I love you too Lea." He put the phone down.

The phone rang again a minute later. Saj hurried to pick it up thinking it was Lea.

"We all miss you Saju. It was your cousin Rana's wedding last week. Everyone was asking about you," his mother said.

"I miss you all Mama."

"We got the money you sent. When are you coming back?"

"I'll talk to you later. I have to go now."

Saj slumped on the couch lost in thoughts. What was he going to do?

The following Friday, Saj phoned Lea's surgery during his lunch break. He didn't feel confident enough to call her at home, in case her mother answered.

"Is everything okay?" Lea sounded concerned.

"Yeah. Do you want to meet in town tomorrow afternoon? I need to shop, then we could have tea."

"I'm busy then. How is Saturday lunchtime for you?"

"That sounds fine. It's my weekend off."

"By the way, I plan to purchase a mobile phone soon. These have just come out and are amazing things. You'll find it easier to ring me, and not worry about Mummy," Lea said and laughed.

"I can't afford one now. These phones are expensive though incredible invention," said Saj.

They met in one of the chain restaurants for lunch.

"How are you. Have you recovered?"

"I'm fine. It's slightly tender around this area." Saj felt the left side of his lower chest."

"Poor Saj." Lea kissed him. "What did you buy?" She peeked at his shopping bags.

"Only toiletries and a shirt."

"Can I see it?"

Saj took the shirt out of the bag. "This is for work."

"This colour suits you."

After they had finished lunch, he said, "Shall we walk to the park. It's a beautiful day."

It was early afternoon. Saj could feel the warmth of the first spring sun on his face, as they walked holding hands.

"One point I realised since I came to England. You need to appreciate sunny days and make the most of it."

"I can imagine the cold weather must be worse for you, coming from a tropical climate," Lea said as they crossed the road.

"In Bombay, it can be sweltering and uncomfortable in summer. Therefore, people like winter. The grass is always green on the other side. But you still need the sun."

Daffodils and tulips were abundant along with blue forget me not. Saj could hear the birds chirping, preparing their nests and welcoming the late arrival of spring. Many people were out basking in the sunshine. Saj and Lea held hands as they strolled around. He spotted an empty bench in a secluded spot. "Shall we sit down here?" he said.

Saj appeared sombre and thoughtful. After a few minutes of silence, they gathered their thoughts.

"Do you want to say anything Saj?"

He gently squeezed Lea's hand and looked into her eyes.

"You are sad, and it's worrying me. What's the matter?"

"I need to tell you more about myself."

"You aren't married, are you?" A higher note of concern entered her voice.

"No." He forced a smile. "My parents expect a lot from me. I'm always under pressure to please them. They want me to arrange for my sister's wedding. It's our tradition."

Lea listened to him intently and stroked his hand.

"I haven't told my parents about you yet. I would like to, but...they wouldn't approve of it, I know." Saj sat with his head bowed.

As he spoke, the sun disappeared behind the clouds. A cool breeze blew, so Saj put his jacket back on.

"In your culture, people are close to their parents which is nice," she said. "You are responsible for them when they are old. Here, that's not always the case."

"Maybe. But for us, there is too much pressure to please your family. What society will think if you don't?"

"When we get older here, you end up in an old people's home. Most kids don't want to be burdened by their parents." Lea said.

"We should care for them. But we have our lives as well. We make too many sacrifices back home," said Saj.

"Your parents are lucky to have a son like you. We rarely see or hear from Toby. He's so involved with his own life."

Saj kept quiet deep in thought. "I'm unsure what I'm supposed to do Lea. I love you, but I'm not yet ready to tell them about you."

Both said nothing for a long while. "I understand." She looked down, biting her nails.

He put his arm around her, and they embraced for a few minutes. He wasn't accustomed to public display of affection but felt like it. This would be frowned upon by people in Bombay.

The clouds covered the sun, making it darker. There was a light sprinkle of rain, blowing in on the breeze.

"I think we should go before it starts to pour down," he said.

"You don't like getting wet, do you?"

"No," he said with a forced smile.

They briskly walked back holding hands. Both didn't say much as the rain came down harder. Hurrying to their cars, they reached Lea's first and kissed goodbye. Saj dashed away as it poured down.

Chapter 21

Saj received an invitation to the Diploma Award Ceremony in London three weeks later. The prestigious Royal College of Physicians would hold the event. Some of the most famous doctors and professors in the country would be there.

He was thrilled when he read the letter which was dated May 10, 1992. Most doctors in Bombay could only dream of such an achievement. His parents, alas, wouldn't be present to witness it. The invitation included a plus one. Saj rung Lea on her new mobile number and invited her to the ceremony. She agreed to go.

On the day of the ceremony, Saj wore his navy suit with a blue tie. Lea was in a long black dress.

"You look dashing," she said.

"Thanks. You're beautiful."

The event was to commence at 7 pm followed by dinner. Saj drove to London which took him an hour. Lea appeared subdued during the journey, which was understandable. Unsettled matters concerned both, and neither knew what the future held for them.

The Royal College building had a hundred years' history related to the medical profession. Most doctors came with their families, and they all sat in their designated seats. Saj thought of his parents; he wished they were there too.

After a couple of speeches, the award ceremony commenced.

"Dr...Sajan...pal...nam." The lady announced on stage.

Lea and Saj looked at each other. He went up and received his diploma from the President of the College. Proud of his achievement, he saw Lea from the stage, and they both forced a smile.

The photographer took pictures of him and Lea. While others chatted before the dinner, Saj held her hand in silence. He knew she was confused.

"We should enjoy the moment, and not think about the future," he said.

She gazed at him. "That's all we can do now. Show me the certificate."

Saj handed it to her. "Your parents would be proud if they were here."

Dinner was a banquet full of variety and flavours.

After dinner, Saj went to chat with the senior doctors and professors. They congratulated him on his success. He made sure he didn't leave Lea on her own for too long. When he returned, she was sitting down and looked pale.

"What's the matter?" Saj appeared concerned.

"No... Nothing. I felt light-headed. I'll be okay in a few minutes."

"Has this happened before?" He held her hand.

"Once or twice, but it goes away quickly."

"Does it come on when you're stressed?"

"Maybe. Don't worry. I'm alright." She forced a smile.

Saj knew things weren't right between them.

"You rest for five minutes. Would you like a drink?"

"Water please."

He fetched her a glass and sat with her.

"I'm fine. We can go whenever you want," Lea said.

"I'll bring the car to the entrance." It was raining heavily. Saj ran to the car park and got drenched. He brought the car back, Lea got in, and they drove off.

Saj was concerned. He loved her. What would the future hold for them? He thought. They drove in silence.

"Are you alright?" he asked.

"Yeah...be careful, it's difficult to see in this rain."

Saj reached a junction and kept going.

"Oops." He realised he should have stopped.

"Watch out!" Lea screamed.

A van raced towards them. Saj braked sharply, and the car screeched to a halt. Luckily no car was behind him.

Lea was shaken and breathing heavy. Saj sat motionless for a minute, his heart beating fast. He contemplated what could have happened, his mind distracted by all the issues.

"Are you okay? Sorry. I lost concentration for a moment."

"I'm alright."

Saj started the car, and they drove back home in silence. The rain had died down by now. It was half an hour before they got back to his flat. Lea seemed still shaken.

"What can I get you?" he asked.

"A cup of tea please."

He took digestive biscuits out.

"I'm sorry you didn't enjoy the evening," he said.

Lea kept quiet.

"Is the funny head gone now?"

Lea nodded and put her arms around Saj. Both knew what the other thought. He stroked her hair, and they began kissing intensely. Then Lea stopped. She pushed him away quite roughly and stood up.

"We should take it easy," she said.

"I agree."

A buzzing noise confused Saj. He looked around.

"My phone," Lea said. "Hi, Mummy...Yes, I'll be home soon...I'll be careful, Bye."

"Is your mother aware you're here?"

Lea paused and shook her head. "No. I'd better go now." She moved towards the door.

They kissed goodbye. Saj gazed sadly at the closed door for some time, trying to reconcile his thoughts.

Saj sat in his flat reading a medical journal, but his mind drifted elsewhere. A couple of weeks had passed, and his feelings for Lea had grown. He didn't want to give her up for some old custom in India. That evening he visited Dipak to discuss matters. But soon realised Dipak was down in the dumps.

"What's up?" Saj asked.

"Sharon broke up with me," he said in a faint voice.

For the first time, Dipak made it evident that he could fall in love. At no time, had he admitted to deep feelings for any woman. Saj tried to lighten up the mood as best as he could, but it was hard work.

He left as soon as he could and opened a bottle of red wine when he returned to his flat. 'Only Fools and Horses' was on TV. Great! It would cheer him up. Saj loved the characters, especially Del Boy and Rodney. He thought the two were hilarious. Sometimes he found it difficult to understand the English accent. He had to listen carefully by turning the volume up. Since he had finished his exams, he had more spare time. So, he watched TV and Bollywood films on video.

The phone…

"Hello, Mama. What's up?"

"Your Baba is in hospital in a private ward. I am worried."

"Oh, my God." He gasped.

"You should come back now Saju. We need you here."

"Please Mama, don't cry."

"You don't care about us. You used to be an obedient son. What happened? You changed," she said. "Must be all the luxury you can't give up. We brought you up and sacrificed our lives. Your father is ill, and you are not bothered." She wouldn't stop.

"Believe me, I do care."

"All our relations are astonished that you're not here...we're embarrassed. We always make excuses for you."

Saj kept quiet.

"Remember, you'll always be a foreigner in England. Your family and friends are here. People will never accept you there," she said. "How can you stay away from your mother? You have finished your exam now, no more excuses."

"Please don't cry." His eyes brimmed with tears. Saj tried not to break down, so he moved the phone away from him. He couldn't tell his mother about Lea, especially with his father being in hospital. They'll be devastated.

"Are you still there?"

"All right. I'll come as soon as I can, I have to hand my notice," Saj blurted out and hung up.

What if his father died? He would never forgive himself if that happened, he thought. His father worked hard all his life and looked after his family. As far as he could remember growing up, he never took any holidays. Now his family needed him more than ever. He must return to Bombay.

But how could he abandon Lea? They loved each other. Saj wished to spend the rest of his life with her. His parents would never accept her. She wouldn't want to live in Bombay either. Life was chaotic back there, so much poverty and the pollution and heat were intense. The language would be a massive barrier for her.

Saj opened a can of lager and took a sip. God was punishing him because he neglected his parents and lied to them. Since he met Lea, life was good in England. He enjoyed the freedom and his work here. But his parents needed him. He was the only doctor in the family, and that meant a lot to them.

What should he do? He swigged his drink.

Chapter 22

Saj woke up on the couch the next morning. Rubbing his eyes, he yawned loudly. He looked around. A few empty cans lay on the table. He held his head with his hands, oh it hurt, and he was nauseous. His neck and arms were stiff as he stretched them. Slowly he got up, walked to the kitchen, and gulped a glass of water with a couple of paracetamol. That was his breakfast!

The ward seemed quiet that day. Saj sat in the office with a cup of coffee when a nurse entered.

"You look, terrible doctor. Are you okay?"

"Erm...I had a bad night."

"Poor doctor...Mr Parker wants to have a word with you."

"Sure." he forced a smile.

Saj couldn't concentrate at work over the next few days. He remained subdued and did his best to pretend things were alright. Hoping alcohol would relax him he drank too much, but it made him worse. He lay in bed awake, deliberating about his parents, Lea and his future. It was decision time, he knew he couldn't run away forever.

Who could he confide in? Dipak had his own issues and was depressed. It seemed that Saj had lost interest in everything.

One day he met Nick in the corridor. "You look awful? Nick said.

"I got a few issues on my mind."

"I know we had our differences, but if I can be of any help, please ask me."

"Thanks, Nick. I will." Saj headed for the ward.

He took a few steps stopped and turned around.

"Actually Nick. Do you have a minute?"

"Sure. What's up, man?" Nick stopped.

"Shall we go to the doctors' mess."

Fortunately for Saj, it was empty.

He sat and explained the whole situation regarding his parents and Lea.

"Sorry, Saj. This is a bloody mess."

"Thanks," he said with a sarcastic smile.

"What do you want to do?" Nick asked.

"I'm so torn between my parents and Lea. I love Lea. Eventually one will get hurt," Saj said his lips quivered as he took a sip of water.

"I know in your culture you have to respect and obey your parents. The family is important, but it's your life. You need to think about yourself."

"If anything happens to my father I will never forgive myself. I feel so guilty. He has done so much for me. I'll always be grateful to him."

"I understand that Saj, but your parents wouldn't like you to be miserable. You must talk to them about Lea. Be brave. If they love you, they will consider your happiness."

Saj kept quiet for a few moments. "It's easy said than done. You don't know my father. He is stubborn. "

Nick's beeper went off. He took it out of his coat pocket.

"Sorry. Need to dash Saj. The ward wants me."

"Thanks, Nick."

"For what?"

"For listening."

"I wish I could do more. But if you need me for anything man let me know. Good luck."

They shook hands and parted.

Saj slumped in the chair in the doctors' office and could hardly keep his eyes open. The room spun around, and his body ached. A decent night's sleep was what he needed, he thought. He could ask his GP for sleeping tablets though he knew Lea would be there. It would be unprofessional and would go on his medical records. In Bombay, he could just walk into a chemist and write his own prescription. Doctors were held in high esteem. No questions asked. What should he do?

There are lots on the ward trolley, he thought. He could just take a couple. Where would he find the key? What if he got found out? He would be thrown out. Desperation took over, and he made up his mind.

Saj was on call that day. He sat in the office and watched the nurse do the drug round and waited for an opportunity for her to be distracted. One of the patients called, and she left the trolley unmanned. The ward was short staffed that evening.

Saj held his breath as his heart raced. Pretending to see a patient he got up. The medicine trolley stood in the middle of the ward. Glancing both ways his hand trembled as he picked out a few pills. Then strolled back to the doctors' mess. He felt ashamed as he put the pills in his pocket and closed his eyes for a couple of minutes.

Five minutes later, his beeper went off which startled him.

Had they found out? What would happen to the good old Dr Saj, he wondered. What would Lea think about him? For a moment, he hesitated but had to answer the call. He cleared his throat, his muscles felt tight.

"This is...Dr. Saj." His voice quivered as he dialled back. It went all silent at the other end for a moment. As he waited, he held his breath, his heart pounding.

"Sorry to keep you waiting doctor. It's hectic in the ward. Could you please come over and see this lady? She doesn't look well," the nurse said.

"I'll be right there." He felt relieved. God must be on his side, he thought.

Saj took a tablet that night and managed to get a few hours' sleep. It made him drowsy the next morning. He didn't want to take pills regularly in case he became addicted.

Back in his flat that evening, Saj looked through the window and contemplated his future. A week had passed. Only a few people were on the street. A couple of cars drove past. It was raining, and people preferred to stay indoors. He loved to observe people; the way they dressed, their fashion sense and behaviour fascinated him.

Saj knew it was decision time for him. Any moment his mother would phone him. He had no choice, but to sacrifice his own happiness for his parents. He couldn't ignore his duty to his family. His ailing father needed him back in Bombay. But what about Lea? He loved her so much.

The phone. Saj left it ringing for a while, and it stopped. He thought it must be his mother. After a minute it rang again. But it was Lea.

"Are you okay, you took a long time to answer," she said.

"Sorry, I was busy in the kitchen."

"A friend of mine is having a garden party for her thirtieth, this Saturday. Would you like to come?"

Should he tell Lea now his decision to go back home? It would break her heart. Not over the phone, he thought. There was a pause.

"Hello, are you there?" she said.

"Sorry, Lea. I don't feel like partying now."

"Oh, come on. It will get you out of your flat. Besides, we haven't been out for ages."

That was the problem. Saj didn't want to mislead and hurt Lea. He loved her so much, he thought. What should he do?

"Saj, you didn't answer. Is everything alright?"

"Yes. I'd love to come."

"Great! I'll pick you up at seven," Lea said.

They chatted a little longer. Saj loved the sound of Lea's voice and adored her. She was the last person he wanted to hurt.

Saj had planned to cook a vegetable curry for dinner, but he had lost his appetite. He would have to tell her very soon.

Chapter 23

D-day had arrived. After the ward round in the morning, Saj headed to the Medical Personnel Department. He met Jack in the corridor, who worked in obstetrics.

"Hey, Saj. Excellent news. Our on-call hours are being reduced. We'll be working shifts in a couple of months, all due to you," he said.

"Great," Saj said with an ironic smile and carried on.

"I'll invite you to my wedding. It's in October. Make sure you come."

"Congratulations."

"We'll have to go out for a drink," Jack said.

Saj nodded.

At the Personnel Office, he stood near the door having second thoughts.

"Sam...I need to give you my notice to resign," he said in a faint voice.

"That's a shame Saj. Why?"

He paused for a moment and held his breath. "Family reasons."

"I hope everything is okay."

Saj shrugged. "My father isn't well in Bombay."

" Sorry. I know in your culture, family comes first," she said. "My younger sister was married to an Indian guy. It didn't work out for them. Too much pressure from parents. Unfortunately, it's a problem with mixed marriages."

"Yes, it can be." Saj looked away.

"We'll all be sorry to see you leave. You fought for doctors' rights."

"I'll be sad too." He could only force a smile.

After a brief pause, she handed him a couple of forms. "You'll need to fill these in."

Saj read them for a minute. "I'll do it now." He was worried he might change his mind. He felt sick and tired of all the indecision.

When he walked back to the ward, a nurse came up to him.

"Dr Smith has been around, he looked unhappy. You didn't attend the medical meeting today."

"Oh shit. I forgot." Saj knew his personal life was beginning to affect his work.

How would he break the news to Lea? They were going to her friend's party on Saturday night. He would have to tell her then.

The dreaded day had finally arrived. It was Saturday. Saj couldn't bear the thought he might not see Lea again. He was in no mood for fun but forced himself to get ready. It seemed Lea wanted to be with him whatever happened. Maybe she sensed what was coming her way.

There was a knock on the door.

"You look beautiful in this dress," he said.

"Thanks."

"Please take a seat. I won't be a minute. Would you like a drink?"

"No, I'm fine."

Saj hoped she wouldn't notice the cans and bottles in the corner of the room.

"Do you think this looks right?" He emerged from his bedroom in a navy shirt and chinos, with a black jacket on top.

"You look handsome."

"I'm ready, let's go."

There was an air of sadness between them. Neither talked much as Lea drove. Finally, she said, "If you think our house is big, wait until you see my friend's."

"Hmm."

Saj knew he had to speak to Lea and get everything out in the open.

They arrived at a large Edwardian house and entered through a big gate. It had a long driveway surrounded by shrubs and trees. There were numerous cars, and the place was floodlit. In the back garden, there was a huge marquee.

As they walked towards the reception, someone called from behind.

"Lea...so you are here. I thought you wouldn't come?" It was her friend Stacy.

"Happy Birthday Stacy." Lea smiled and kissed her on the cheeks. She handed her a neatly wrapped gift.

"Thanks. You didn't sound right on the phone. Is everything okay?"

"Yeah." Lea blushed. Then she turned towards Saj and introduced him. "Sorry...this is my...friend, Saj."

"Hi." He shook her hand. "Pleasure to meet you, Stacy."

"Lea...at no time you have mentioned Saj before," Stacy said with a grin.

Lea looked down and away. "Sorry."

"The bar is over there if you guys would like a drink. I'm glad you came," Stacy said and left.

Lea and Saj ordered champagne. Both seemed quieter and not their usual selves as they sat and looked around avoiding too much eye contact.

It was quite noisy, but Lea tried to make conversation.

"Stacy's parents are well connected. They know a lot of high-profile people, politicians, celebrities," she said, pointing out a famous TV couple.

"Hmm." Saj nodded. He was miles away.

The buffet was served, fresh whole salmon, cherry tomatoes on their vines, salads and meats. Saj had never seen so many dishes before, but he didn't feel hungry.

Later, the lights dimmed, and the disco started. The DJ played techno songs. For the first time, Saj didn't enjoy the music.

"Would you like to dance?" Lea asked.

"Okay." He slowly got up.

Saj realised Lea also missed her sparkle. The DJ slowed down the tempo and played, "Nothing Compares to You". It was one of Saj's favourite songs. He looked into Lea's eyes. Then he held her hand and pulled her closer, and they danced. There was so much sadness in his eyes.

"I'm so sorry," he whispered in her ears, his lips quivered.

Saj was unsure whether she heard him as the music was loud. He held her tight. He loved Lea so much.

The DJ played a couple of love songs, "I Will Always Love You", and "Love Is All Around". It made the mood even worse. They held each other tight as they danced. The music and the atmosphere suited the night. Both were totally lost in each other, oblivious to their surroundings. Neither of them wanted to let go. Maybe this was their last dance together, he thought.

If only circumstances were different for them. If only Saj could consider his own happiness first, and not his parents, he wondered.

The songs changed to a faster tempo. Saj and Lea continued to dance, holding each other close. They didn't listen to the music. Some of the guests left the floor. At one stage, they were the only ones' dancing. Eventually, Lea realised and pointed it out.

It was midnight. Champagne was still flowing, and men and women chatted and laughed. Everyone was having a fabulous time. Saj wished he was one of them.

"Do you want to stay longer?" he asked.

"No, we can go, if I can find Stacy." Lea looked around but couldn't find her in the crowd. "We'll go. I'll phone her later."

Neither spoke as Lea drove back home. When they arrived at his flat, they sat in the car in silence for a few minutes.

"What is it Saj? Is it me? Don't you love me anymore?"

"I love you so much, but I need to talk to you. Do you want to come up?"

"It's getting late. But if it's important. I hate to see you like this. You look so miserable."

Saj poured a glass of red wine.

"Would you like one?"

"No thanks."

He went quiet for a minute but knew he had to be truthful.

"Lea, my darling." He held both her hands. They were icy cold. "You remember I told you about my parents in Bombay. My father is ill, he's been in the hospital." Saj tried to break the news gently. "I'm the only son in the family, the only doctor. In our culture, sons have a duty. Otherwise, society thinks ill of you. My mother wants me to come back and look after my father...That's what I'm expected to do."

"You are a good son."

"I've resigned from my job."

Lea stared at him and gasped.

Snatching away her hands, she said, "So...are you not coming back? You resigned without even discussing it with me?"

Saj kept silent and couldn't bear to look at her.

"What can I do Lea? I thought I would not resign if I spoke to you. I love my parents, and I love you. Either way, someone will get hurt. I must sacrifice my happiness. But we don't deserve this." He wiped his eyes.

After a pause, Lea said, "Your parents must be so proud of you." She sobbed. "So, this is goodbye?"

Saj found it hard to handle, he got up and poured more wine.

"You have to do what you think is right. No more wine for me. I'm driving." She took a tissue out of her handbag and wiped her eyes. "So, when do you leave?"

"In six weeks."

"Six weeks!"

"I need to go," she said, getting up.

"Why don't you stay longer?"

"No, I'll be too late."

"Will you be alright to drive?"

"It's only twenty minutes from here."

"I'll give you a ring when you are back home."

Saj walked her to the door and tried to embrace her, but she manoeuvred away from him and ran away down the corridor.

"Lea," he cried after her. "I'm so sorry. I had no choice."

Chapter 24

During his last weeks in England, Saj worked on autopilot. When he told others, he planned to return to Bombay, they were sad. Everyone in the hospital liked him. He was fed up trying to explain why he had to go back. He wished he could hide away.

Saj booked his flight. His mother had been overjoyed when he told her.

"Wonderful. I'll tell everybody the exciting news. Can you bring me chocolate and biscuits? I have heard they make good ones. And something for the relatives. They will love to get presents from England."

"Alright."

"Are you okay?" she asked.

"I'm all right." Saj wished he could tell her his anguish but couldn't.

The next couple of weeks were a blur. Saj kept in contact with Lea by phone, but it was dreadful for both. She was angry and sad. He never knew which emotion would be uppermost.

One evening Lea felt she had to explain the situation to her family.

"Saj is going back to Bombay," she said. "His father is ill. In their culture, he is duty-bound to care for him. They don't have a proper NHS, not like England."

"I've never been comfortable with him for some reason," Margaret said.

"It's because he's not white. I guess you are happy now. You're only concerned what your "friends" think." Lea frowned.

"That's not true. I knew Saj would go back to Bombay. I didn't want you to get hurt."

"Huh. You were so rude to Ihim? Since that first day, he has been reluctant to phone or visit me at home. You must be pleased he's going back."

"Darling, I want what's best for you."

Wiping her eyes, Lea said, "What would you know? I love Saj. He is kind and caring, I'll miss him so much."

"You'll be alright without him," Margaret said.

"Now come on, let's not argue," Christopher said. "When is he leaving?"

Lea kept silent.

Her sister Nicole said, "He seemed nice. I really liked him."

After they had finished the conversation, her parents left the room. Lea phoned Saj. She already missed him.

"How are you?" She spoke in a soft voice.

"Depressed. You are always with me." Saj sounded miserable. "How was your day?"

"Not good," she said.

"I'm sorry. Not long now."

After a short pause, Lea said, "I want to come to the airport."

"Is that a good idea...I mean..."

"Yes. I insist."

"Okay...I think about you all the time." Saj choked with emotion.

Lea sobbed. A lot of tears were shed on the phone. Finally, they ended their conversation.

During the next few days, Saj sorted out his financial matters. He kept some money in his Barclay bank account, in case he needed it. Lea was going to drive him to the airport. He didn't want to contemplate, how he would say goodbye to her.

The fateful day arrived. Saj bought a few boxes of chocolates for his family. Turning around, he stared at his flat for the last time and then loaded his luggage into Lea's car. It was a gloomy day, with light rain in the air.

"Do you have everything, passport, ticket?" she asked sitting down in the driver seat.

Saj nodded as he closed the door.

Both sat in the car. Lea had a road atlas open, for directions to Heathrow. They drove in total silence for a long time. The rain got heavier.

"We got plenty of time, no rush," Saj said. He had always been a nervous front seat passenger.

She joined the motorway. The roads appeared quiet, it was off-peak. When they arrived at Heathrow, Lea carried on to the short stay car park. Saj took his luggage out of the car.

"I'll carry your other bag."

"Are you sure?" Back in Bombay women were not supposed to lift any heavy stuff. Men wouldn't let them.

"Thanks."

The airport terminal brought back memories for Saj. How different he was now.

The departure lounge was crowded. Saj stared at the flight screen for the British Airways check-in desk and headed in that direction. Lea walked along with him in a daze without saying a word. He wanted time to stand still forever so he could stay with her. But that wouldn't happen. Perhaps she shouldn't have come with him.

Saj queued up at the check-in desk and asked Lea to wait for him. They avoided eye contact. Both tried to hide how they felt. He checked in his baggage. The weight was within the allowed limit which pleased him.

When he returned to the spot where he left Lea, she wasn't there. She had vanished. He looked around and waited. Perhaps she had gone to the toilet. Fifteen minutes passed, still no sign of her. Lea had gone.

Reality hit him hard as his eyes brimmed and panic flooded his body. Lea couldn't face saying goodbye, so she decided to run away. She must be heartbroken. He sprinted to the entrance but stopped. It would only make it worse, he thought and turned around.

Wiping his eyes, Saj made his way slowly towards security.

Lea dashed to her car at the airport car park. She dropped the car keys as she tried to open the door. Did she make the right decision by running away from him? She loved him so much and couldn't bear to see him leave. He's not coming back, she'll never see his handsome face again, she thought. Resting her head on the steering wheel, Lea sobbed hysterically.

Chapter 25

The BA plane landed at Bombay airport. Saj felt the heat and humidity as he exited the aircraft. He was in a trance as he walked to the passport desk, thinking of Lea. Everything had changed for him so fast.

Saj showed his passport to the officer at the immigration desk. He glanced at his photo, then looked up and stared at him, with a stern face.

"That's me in the picture. Now my hair is shorter, and I shaved my moustache," Saj said.

"Where are you coming from?"

"England. I'm a doctor." Saj knew doctors were respected here.

The officer's behaviour changed. He smiled.

"Oh, Doctor Sahib. You look smarter now," he said. "How is it in England? I would like to visit, but my salary is meagre."

"Different." Saj was in no mood to chat.

"Will you go back?"

"I don't know." Saj looked away. Under different circumstances, Saj would have been friendlier.

There was a queue building behind him.

One man said, "Why is he taking so long?"

"Keep quiet," the officer said. He knew he had the authority and was in no hurry.

Saj eventually managed to get away and headed to the luggage collection. On his way down, he saw a young English couple. They smiled as they talked and held one another's hand. The woman reminded him of Lea. He already yearned for her. Is she missing him as well? The sadness in her eyes at Heathrow told him all.

He had to wait half an hour for his luggage to arrive. One of his suitcases was partially open, the other ripped on one side. Saj was in no mood to complain. He took his bags and put them on a trolley. A huge crowd waited outside in the airport lounge. The noise was deafening, and the heat and smell in the air hit him. People embraced and seemed delighted as their loved ones arrived.

Saj searched for his father in the crowd but couldn't find him. Some people came to him and offered a taxi service, he declined. Have they forgotten, or got the day mixed up?

Someone tapped him on his shoulder. He turned around, his father stood with a big smile on his face. Wearing traditional clothes, long baggy shirt with trousers, he was over fifty but looked good for his age. They embraced each other.

"I thought no one was here," said Saj.

"We couldn't find you in the crowd, besides you look different," his father said.

"How are you now?"

"Yes, much better with the new drug."

They walked to his mother. She had a broad grin on her face when she saw Saj. He touched his parent's feet, as a mark of respect, almost forgetting his traditions since he had been away. Gita, his sister was also there. All spoke loudly and asked him numerous questions at the same time, thrilled to see him.

"Come on. We'll go to the car," his father said.

Saj yawned and found it difficult to take it all in. The long flight had been exhausting. His father put the luggage in the boot of his old Nissan Sunny with difficulty, sweating profusely.

"The weather is warm," Saj said.

"It is cooler at night. You'll get accustomed to it again," his father said, as he drove off.

His mother and sister wouldn't stop chatting. They told him so much about the family and everything that had happened. Saj wished for peace and silence.

The streets were noisy with car horns blaring and a lot of motorbikes weaving perilously between the cars. They all drove in a crazy manner and altered lanes at will.

"You're quiet," his mother said.

"I'm tired. It was a long flight."

"You'll have plenty of rest and healthy food to eat. Not like in England. I'll cook your favourite dishes." Saj kept silent. What could he say?

"Our relatives will be here tomorrow. They want to see you," his mother said.

"You look better than I imagined Baba," he said turning to his father.

"The doctors have discharged me. I am okay now."

A motorbike turned right and sped across in front of the car.

"Watch out," Saj shouted. His father braked but the car hit the motorcycle, and the boy fell off.

Saj and his father got out of the car. To their surprise, the boy was unscratched.

"Stupid boy. You should know where you're going," his father said with a frown,

This boy must be about fourteen. He was obviously shaken, but he apologised, started his bike and left. They got back in the car and carried on their journey. It took them more than an hour to get home.

When Saj got out of the car, he stared at their home. This was a middle-class estate, but his house appeared shabby. The white paint outside had faded, some of it flaked off and needed decorating. The house had three bedrooms, and his room remained untouched. His parents couldn't afford to spend money on refurbishments.

Once Saj had changed, they sat down to eat dinner. He looked around the table for cutlery. But soon remembered he had to eat with his hand.

"I've prepared a few traditional spicy dishes for you. You must have missed our food," Saj's mother said. She was an excellent cook.

"Hmm." Surprisingly he wasn't hungry. He tried a few dishes, only to keep her happy.

"Saju. You need to eat more. You have lost weight; don't you think?" she glanced at his father for approval.

His mother would always encourage him to eat more and put on weight. In their society, weight gain was a sign of good health. If you are slim, you are unhealthy.

"You must be tired, go to bed early." his father said. "Tomorrow is a busy day, we have guests coming to see you."

His parents had already started to take over his life, he thought. He had no say in these matters. Maybe because at no time did he speak up for himself.

Saj's room was small, with a single bed in the corner and a desk and chair. A few of his old medical books were still scattered as he had left them. It had no windows, except for a small ventilator at the top. The white paint had peeled off the walls. There was only one room with windows in the house which belonged to his parents. Gita also had a small place like his.

He turned the ceiling fan on and mopped sweat from his forehead. Then he lay on his bed thinking about Lea and his life in England, only a few hours back. Why did she run away at the airport? He wished he was with her.

Gita walked in. Saj jumped and wiped his eyes.

"Are you okay. Have you been crying?" She sat next to him.

"No. I got something in my eyes. It must be the dust." He pretended to rub them.

Gita was an attractive young lady in her early twenties with a few features similar to Saj. Her long dark hair was tied back in a ponytail. Her big brown eyes stood out on a slim face.

"Nice you are back Saju. I thought you would never return," she said.

Saj kept silent and looked away.

"We'll talk tomorrow...I'm tired," he said, as he lay on his bed.

"Okay, I'll go now."

Saj felt the room was spinning. Perhaps the jet-lag was catching up, he thought. After a few minutes, he fell asleep.

The next morning Saj woke up early. He changed but soon realised he had put on a shirt and trousers out of habit. He discovered his mother had left his traditional clothes on the side table. There was a cotton, light green baggy long top and loose trousers. He put them on and joined others at breakfast. The family members spoke loudly in an animated manner, and all at the same time. This was normal for them, entirely different from English culture.

He sat at the table, and his mother served him parathas and fried eggs. Saj had missed this food in England.

"We're so pleased you're back," his mother said.

Saj nodded, while he ate his fried bread.

"Your uncle Sana and his family are coming today," his mother said as she sipped her tea.

Saj pretended he didn't hear her.

"Baba. You shouldn't eat fried food," he glanced at his father.

"I'm alright. This isn't much," his father said.

"Doctors advised him to be careful what he eats, though he never listens. You must tell him," his mother said. "Gita is in her final year at university. We need to find a boy for her."

"Mama. Do we have to talk about it now?" Gita said.

"But what about Aran?" Saj thought she was already settled.

"We broke off the engagement. The boy's family expected too much money and jewellery, and..."

"And a car," his father said.

Saj turned to Gita. "Maybe if you find a nice young man, you should let us know."

"No. We'll arrange it," his mother said.

He wondered what his parents had in store for him. Lea! Lea!

After breakfast, he unpacked his bags. He had brought a few gifts for the family and handed them out. Boxes of chocolates and necklaces for the ladies, and a watch for his father. At the airport, he bought a Times to read on the plane. His father grabbed the paper from him when he spotted it.

That afternoon, his uncle visited with his daughter.

"Do you remember Ruma?" his mother asked.

"Erm...Oh Yes. I do. You look different," he said to Ruma.

"She would be, she is older," his mother said and laughed.

Ruma blushed. Saj used to like her, and now she had grown up to be a pretty young woman.

"You look different too." She bit her inner lips.

Ruma was short, curvy with long dark hair, and wore jeans and a baggy top.

"Shall we go and sit outside?" She asked Saj.

"Sure." There were a patio and a small garden at the back.

The sun was shining, without a hint of any clouds in the sky.

"It's warm," Saj said, as he unbuttoned his shirt.

"You'll get accustomed to the heat again."

"I hope so."

"How was it in England?"

"Good, very different." He mopped the sweat from his forehead with his shirt sleeve.

"I remember you chased me with a spider in your hand. I got scared," Ruma said.

"Ha ha." Saj laughed for the first time.

Then he thought of Lea, and his mood changed.

"How do you feel being back?"

He paused for a moment and thought. "Alright...I have to get accustomed to it."

"There is a new movie in the cinema. Sajan Khan is the hero. Shall we go one day?" she asked.

"Okay." He didn't sound particularly keen. "What are you studying?"

"I'm in my final year of medical school."

There was a pause in the conversation.

"I know girls are beautiful in England. They have blonde hair and pale white skin." Ruma said as if she read his mind.

"Yes. Some are blonde." Saj squinted his eyes in the bright sun. "Some have brown, red or even black hair. Funnily enough, people there like to have a tan. They sit in the sun a lot when it is out."

"And we try to make our skin paler, even if we have to bleach it," she said. They both laughed.

At that moment, his mother came out. "You two are getting on well," she said with a grin. "Come inside. We are having tea."

"Can't we have it out here, Mama?" Saj enjoyed the sunshine. He had been deprived of the sunny weather for too long, he thought.

"No...It's too hot outside. Besides your skin will go dark in the sun," she said. Both had to go indoors.

Tea was served with fresh samosas, onion bhajis and Bombay mix. Saj found the snacks delicious.

That night Saj lay awake in bed. He thought about Lea, how she was, and he missed her so much. He also reflected on his day with Ruma.

Chapter 26

Over the next few days, his parents took him to visit friends
and family. Everyone was delighted to see Saj. His mother
wouldn't stop praising him to others which made him feel
embarrassed.

Ruma was an intelligent girl, Saj liked her, but Lea
occupied his mind all the time. He wished he was with her.
How would he tell his parents about Lea? He had thought the
plan was for Gita's marriage first, but it seemed his parents
had other ideas.

One morning, Ruma phoned, and they arranged to meet in
the town to watch a new Bollywood movie. The two met in a
cafe close to the cinema. She looked cute in her colourful
traditional shalwar kameez while Saj wore jeans and a shirt.
They had tea and biscuits.

"You are handsome," she said.

Saj returned the compliment with a smile. "You look
lovely as well."

The cinema was a pretty run down place. Saj recollected
his first trip to the cinema with Lea in England when they
watched a Bollywood movie.

He didn't show much interest in the film and couldn't wait for it to finish. On a few occasions during the movie, when Ruma smiled at him, he forced a smile back.

He tried to please everyone he came across. By getting out, Saj thought his mind would be distracted. But it didn't work. Lea was always with him. He missed her a lot, though he dared not tell anyone.

It was soon the time for Holi, the Festival of Colours celebration. Saj had loved Holi since he was a kid. This was a fun time with friends and family and the day marked the arrival of spring. People threw coloured powder and water at each other.

That day Saj and Gita dressed in their scruffy clothes for the Holi. They went to a friend's house in the morning. People overflowed onto the roadway. There was a carnival atmosphere, and everyone was having fun. Men, women, and children of all ages screamed and laughed. Saj grabbed hold of the red and blue colours and threw them on Gita. She shrieked and sprinkled the powder back on him which made his hair yellow.

Saj spotted Ruma in the crowd. She saw him approach, immediately guessed his intentions and ran for her life. He chased her, smearing her with yellow, blue, and green coloured powder and water. This was the first time Saj had laughed since he returned to Bombay.

"Ahh...I'll get you back," Ruma shrieked. She took the red powder and smeared his hair and face, they both giggled.

The sun was at its glory in a cloudless sky. Strangers blasted each other with colours, nothing and nobody was off limits. The air was filled with bright red, blue, green, and yellow colours. The wind blew it all around. Bollywood songs provided a great atmosphere and people danced.

Saj was having a fantastic time. Ruma offered him a traditional Holi drink. Bhang is added, which is derived from cannabis and is intoxicating. He had a couple of glasses and felt out of this world. He forgot all his worries.

Men and women screamed with joy and lovers held hands. Ruma danced to cool Bollywood tunes, and her delightful seductive moves impressed Saj. He lost his inhibitions and joined her in the crowd. Gazing into his eyes, she held his hands, while they danced.

"I really like you," Ruma said.

"I like you too. You're fun," Saj said with a smile.

It got dark, and Saj searched for Gita. He found her giggling with her friends. The music had stopped, and people drifted off and headed home.

Walking back Gita said with a cheeky smile, "Ruma is fond of you."

When Saj returned home, he lay on his bed and reflected on his day. He had a brilliant Holi. For the first time, he didn't think much about Lea. Ruma was a terrific girl. She was full of life and great fun. Saj knew she was fond of him, but he didn't want to encourage or mislead her.

The next morning, his mother came to him. "This letter is for you. It must be from your hospital." It had an English stamp on it.

Saj took the letter and went to his room, closing the door behind him. He had a gut feeling that it was from Lea. He was bewildered how she had got his address, but it soon became more manifest.

Dear Saj

I'm sorry that I ran away at the airport. I couldn't bear to see you leave. I love you and miss you so much. I haven't been able to concentrate at work. I don't mean to worry you, but I have no one else to talk to. I can understand your predicament, that your family comes first. Please don't worry about me. I'll feel better as time passes. Take care of yourself.

Love

Lea

PS. I got your address from Dipak, as I was desperate to contact you. Sorry.

As he read the letter, his eyes filled up with tears and rolled relentlessly down his cheeks.

His parents had gone out to visit relatives that evening. Saj sat in his room with paperwork. He was hoping that keeping busy would distract him. Gita came in.

"Can I ask you something?" she said and sat on the chair.

"Yes sure."

"Are you pleased to be back home?"

Saj pretended to be busy with his papers and didn't answer.

"What's the matter? You aren't right."

"I'm disorientated." He carried on with his paperwork.

"You've been here three weeks. I know there's something wrong. Please look at me."

Saj kept quiet, he couldn't bear to look at her.

"Come on Saju...Please tell me. You know, we have no secrets. I won't tell Mama or Baba."

He was afraid to tell Gita the truth.

"Ruma likes you a lot? I heard Mama talk to Baba...."

"What did she say?"

"They discussed your wedding to Ruma."

"What!" He gasped. "They have told me nothing. I only like her as a friend."

"Please tell me what's the matter," she said.

He avoided eye contact with Gita. "I love someone else."

"Who is she? Did you meet her recently?"

"She isn't here."

After a moments hesitation, Gita asked, "Is she...white...English?"

Saj kept silent.

"Oh, my God, I don't believe it. I knew something was wrong." She stared with wide eyes, breathing deeply.

There was a pause.

"How will you tell them? They wouldn't ever dream you would take such a decision. It will break their hearts. They want Ruma as your bride." Gita spoke fast. "And what about Ruma. She has her heart set on you. Oh, God. This is a mess." She stood up.

Gita came back with two glasses of water and handed one to Saj.

They sat in silence for a minute.

"What am I supposed to do Gita?"

She stared at him.

"It will hurt people either way. I know it will be a shock to them." Saj sipped from his glass.

"What is she like?"

"She is lovely, funny, pretty, intelligent and very kind. She is a nurse. Her name is Lea. You'd like her."

Saj handed her the letter from Lea. "Here. She wrote to me."

"She does love you," Gita said after she read it.

He nodded.

Saj knew he had to tell Ruma about Lea. He hoped he hadn't misled her. To him, Holi was fun, but to her, the flirting was more serious. She deserved better, but so did Lea, he thought.

It was a Saturday. Saj thought Ruma's father would be at work. The man owned three clothes shops, and it was always a busy day for him. Ruma's mother had died ten years back from tuberculosis. As she was the only child, her father spoilt her.

The sun blazed down. Saj walked the short distance to her house. On his way, he saw children playing cricket in a side street. They shouted and screamed and enjoyed themselves. The roads were chaotic as usual, full of cars, motorbikes, three-wheeled rickshaws. No pedestrian crossings, it was the law of the jungle. He remembered how organised it was in England. A stray dog ran in the middle of the road. It almost got killed by a car. Saj mopped sweat from his face with a handkerchief and took a sip of bottled water. The heat was intense.

Ruma lived in a big detached house on a peaceful street. Saj could hear a dog barking behind the gate. He stopped, the dog looked mean. Her father came out.

"Hello Uncle," Saj greeted him.

"I am off to work. Come in. I'm sure Ruma will be pleased," he said with a smile.

Great! He's in on it as well, Saj thought.

Her father opened the gate for him, said goodbye and left.

The house was well furnished and splendidly decorated. Saj waited in the lounge.

"This is a surprise. How are you?" Ruma said.

"I thought I would visit my cousin."

"Ah…We're only distant cousins."

"So, no college today?"

"Today is Saturday, there is no college. You forget everything," she said and chuckled. "I enjoyed Holi. I had a bad headache the next day, must be the drinks."

"It was good," Saj said, as he shuffled on the couch.

"I meant to ask you. One of my friends is having a party, and I thought...."

"Ruma. We're cousins, aren't we?"

"Yes, we are though I like you a lot. Papa spoke to your parents about us," she said with a smile.

"I like you as well, but..."

"But what?"

"As a friend only."

"I thought it was more than that. We had great fun the other day at Holi," Ruma said.

"Yes, as a friend. Please understand."

"What's wrong with me?"

"Nothing, you are a pretty girl; most men would love to marry you."

"But not you," she said, her voice quivered.

"I had no idea you loved me," Saj said

"I was too shy to tell you," Ruma replied as she looked down.

"Maybe then I wouldn't have played around with you. It's my fault, I gave you the wrong signals."

"You were just friendly. I think you felt sorry for me because my mother had passed away," she said wiping her eyes.

"No. That's not true. I like you a lot as a friend. Please don't cry."

Saj was desperate to escape from this mess and needed to tell her about Lea. He paused for a moment.

"Could you please keep a secret. Nobody knows yet," said Saj.

She nodded, pleased to share a confidence with him.

He took a deep breath. "I'm grateful to you, but...I love someone else."

Ruma looked up towards him. "Who is she?"

"You don't know her."

"Is she in this country?"

"No,"

"Do your parents know?"

"No. I'll tell them when the time comes."

There was an uncomfortable silence. Saj and Ruma sat opposite each other, and both were glum-faced. Saj was aware he had hurt her. That was the story of his life, he thought.

"I'm so sorry Ruma. I've to go now. I told Mama I would take her to the market." He stood up.

Wiping her eyes, Ruma got up and walked him to the door.

"I'm really sorry if I gave you the wrong impression, it wasn't intentional. You deserve someone better," Saj said.

He felt some relief as he walked out into the warm sunshine.

Chapter 27

Saj's father had gone back to work full-time. He had been under the impression back in England, that he was very sick. His mother had started a part-time job at a clothes shop. He felt they had not been honest with him. Saj had plenty of free time to himself. It provided him with an opportunity to plan his next step. He was determined to tell his parents about Lea.

At lunchtime, he sat in front of the television watching a soap. The phone buzzed which made him jump.

"Saj."

"How are you Ruma?"

"Saj...Saj...I love you," she spoke in a faint inarticulate voice. A few moments later, he heard a crash. The line got disconnected. He tried her number, an engaged tone. He waited for a couple of minutes and dialled again – nothing.

He ran towards Ruma's house, his heart pounding. What if she had done something silly? He wouldn't forgive himself, he thought. Saj arrived at her door within ten minutes. To his surprise, it was open. He barged in, still breathing heavily from his sprint, and surveyed the house. No one was in the lounge or dining room downstairs. He could hear the dog bark from the back garden.

Saj hurried upstairs. As he pushed Ruma's bedroom door, his worst fear had come true. She lay on the floor unconscious, with the phone next to her. Two bottles of pills were beside her.

"What the bloody hell have you done?" he gasped.

Ruma lay motionless. He checked her pulse. It was rapid and feeble, her breathing shallow. Saj couldn't rely on any emergency service here. Running downstairs, he went out on the street looking for a taxi. Perhaps God was on his side because he spotted one. He waved, and it stopped. Saj carefully carried Ruma downstairs. The driver helped him put her into the cab. They managed to lay her down on the back seat.

"Take me to the emergency department and be quick!"

They set off. The taxi driver drove fast, cutting through the traffic at speed. Saj kept a close eye on Ruma. He rechecked her pulse; it was rapid and weak.

"Come on please hurry. I'll pay you extra if you go faster," Saj said to the driver.

"Don't worry about the money. I'll try my best."

They came to a set of traffic lights. The driver glanced both ways and sped through the red light.

"Watch out," Saj screamed pointing to a vehicle.

One of the oncoming cars had to brake sharply and missed them by a whisker. Saj closed his eyes and held his breath. It took a quarter of an hour to reach the emergency unit, and the taxi stopped at the casualty entrance.

"Here's your fare." Saj handed him the cash.

"I don't want the money, sir. Let's take the lady in."

Saj left the cash on the driver's seat.

The man dashed in and returned with a stretcher. They put Ruma on it and took her in.

"Thank you so much."

"Do you want me to do anything else?"

"No. You've helped enough." Saj offered him more cash, but he refused to take it.

"I'll pray to God for her." The man drove off.

The driver's kind gesture overwhelmed Saj. He was a poor man, but it wasn't all about money here, he thought.

"Nurse," Saj shouted. She hurried over to him.

The nurse fetched the doctor. He quickly examined Ruma. The doctor asked the nurse to take the patient to the emergency room.

"I'm a doctor myself. She took a cocktail of pills." His voice trembled as he handed him the bottles. "It must be half an hour back. I think she'll need a stomach wash as soon as possible."

The doctor examined the bottles and frowned. After taking more information, he proceeded to treat her. Saj waited outside the treatment room, pacing up and down the corridor. What if she died? The consequences for the whole family would be unimaginable. He felt responsible and prayed for her recovery.

An hour later, the doctor came out.

"She should be okay. We managed to take most of the tablets out," the doctor said. "You brought her here in time. She has woken up but will need rest. We're going to admit her overnight for observation."

"Thanks. Can I see her?" Saj took a deep breath and mopped the sweat from his brows.

"She'll be transferred to the ward soon."

During all this hectic activity, Saj had no time to inform anyone. He called Ruma's father first. Then phoned home to tell his mother about the incident. An hour later, he headed for the ward. It was up two flights of stairs and packed with patients. The place appeared run down with stained walls and litter on the floor.

Saj spotted a couple of men sleeping on the ground, next to the patients' beds. They were relatives, who couldn't find anywhere to stay. Three women and a child sat on the floor, having their meal. A woman breastfed her baby. He shouldn't compare it with English hospital, he thought. Government hospitals in Bombay were poorly managed, due to lack of resources and corruption. Wealthy people went to private clinics. But this was his country, and he was proud of it.

He asked at reception about Ruma. She ignored him and pretended to be busy. When he insisted, she looked at her records and pointed him. He was relieved to see Ruma sitting up in bed.

"How are you?" he asked.

She kept silent, looking the other way.

"I'll ask them to shift you to a private room," he said checking her observations. They were normal now.

"Sorry...I am so ashamed, don't know why I did it."

"It's okay." He sat on a chair next to her bed. "I'll make sure they take good care of you here."

Wiping her eyes, she said, "Please don't be concerned about me...she is one lucky girl. You should go for her. I'll be fine."

Saj appreciated what she said. "I'm sorry. You'll have many admirers, but we'll always be friends."

"Papa told me a long time ago, you and I would be married. He had talked to your parents about us. I thought...we were meant for each other, even though it happened way back. We had this understanding between us."

"I'm sorry they misled. you."

"No fault of yours."

"Oh, my God...What happened?" Saj heard a loud voice behind him. Her father rushed to her.

"Nothing Papa...I had a severe migraine this morning. I took a few strong tablets which made me ill," she said. "Must be allergic to them. I'm fine now. Fortunately, Saj was visiting." She avoided eye contact with her father.

"Are you alright Ruma?" He then glanced at Saj and said, "Thanks for your help."

The hospital served dinner while he was there. Saj stared at the food with disgust. Back in England, some patients complained about the poor quality of NHS cuisine. They should try the food at Bombay hospital! Perhaps they would stop moaning, he thought and smiled.

Saj excused himself, said goodbye and left Ruma with her father. What a day full of drama? But thankfully it was over. He didn't want to contemplate how badly it could have ended. At the hospital gate, he waved for a taxi and headed home.

"What exactly happened with Ruma?" his mother asked Saj, the next day, as the family sat in the lounge having tea and snacks.

"She took tablets for a headache and reacted to it...then I took her to the hospital."

"Ruma is a beautiful girl, she likes you a lot," his mother said.

He kept quiet and focused on the TV.

"We discussed that the two of you would be suited," his father said sipping his tea.

"But she is my cousin. She is only a friend to me." Saj shuffled back on the couch uneasily.

"She's only a distant cousin. We think you two would make a good couple. I spoke to your uncle a week ago."

"I thought the plan was for Gita to marry first?" Saj said.

"Ruma will receive many proposals soon. You don't wait to miss out," his mother said.

"And she being the only daughter, you would acquire money and gifts as dowry," his father remarked.

Now or never, Saj thought. His heart beating fast, he took a deep breath, paused, and said, "I can't marry Ruma."

"Why? She is a beautiful girl, and they are a wealthy family," his mother said.

"I don't mean to upset you, but..."

"But what?" His father frowned.

"I like someone else."

"What. Where did you meet this girl?"

"I met her in England, while I worked in the hospital."

"Is she a gori?" she asked.

Saj paused held his breath and looked away. "Yes, she is white."

The next he heard was his mother cry out.

His father pointed his finger at his wife. "You spoiled him."

"I knew something was wrong since you returned. You hid the truth from us." His mother mopped her tears.

The father glared at him. "How could you do this to us? We brought you up and paid for your education. Is this how you repay us?"

"Baba. I love her, and I want to marry her...I'm sorry to disappoint you both." He sat with his head bowed.

"Love? What do you know about love? Only because you have been to England for a few years, you talk about love," his father said clenching his jaw.

223

"I've always been an obedient son, but this is my life as well." Saj felt a power enter him as he spoke up to his parents.

"Did you think of us?" his mother said rocking and wailing.

"Mama. Please understand. I don't want to hurt you."

"What will people think? My only son wants to marry a white English girl. It's not acceptable." his father spoke loudly.

His mother softened her tone. "Son, you'll forget her soon. Your life will be better if you marry your own type."

"Please Mama, skin colour or race doesn't mean anything, we're all the same in God's eyes. Isn't that what our religion teaches us?" Saj shuffled.

"Now you are teaching us about our religion," his father yelled.

"No. But we are all human beings no matter where we come from."

"But she is a Christian, not one of ours," his father said.

"So, what?"

"What will your children be, Hindu or Christian?"

"They'll be my children and your grandchildren, and that's all that matters."

"This is outrageous. None of our people will accept it." His father stabbed his finger at Saj.

"I don't care," Saj said meaningfully.

"The priest at the temple will not like this idea."

"She is an incredible girl, and we love each other...If I don't marry Lea, I won't marry anyone. It's my final decision."

"Love is suited more to western culture. No way we should have sent you abroad. It was a terrible mistake."

"But Baba, you wanted me to work in England and earn lots of money. It was your dream."

"You're not living in my house, so pack your bags and leave. I don't want to see you again. You're no longer my son." His father got up, glared at Saj and stormed out.

At that moment, Gita walked in.

"Were you aware of this Gita?" his mother asked.

Gita's head bowed in silence. His mother stared at the wall, motionless for a moment. Wiping her eyes, she stood up and left the room.

"It didn't sound like it went well," Gita said.

"I'm not changing my mind."

Saj could hear his parents having a heated discussion in their room.

"I can't believe how he spoke to us. He has changed since he went to England," his father was saying. "He used to be loyal and obedient. Now he wants to marry some white woman. She'll soon dump him, then he'll come crying back to us."

"Saju has seen the world, his ideas have broadened. He is not your little boy anymore," his mother said.

"Imagine what people are going to say. We won't be able to face them. Our devoted son is a rebel," he said. "Try to convince him; there are many pretty girls here. What's wrong with them?"

"I'll talk to him, but I don't think he's going to change his mind."

Chapter 28

The next morning when everyone had left, Saj phoned Ashok, an old college friend and explained his predicament.

"It's bad at home. Baba is infuriated. But it's my life. Why should I suffer? I love Lea, and I refuse to marry anyone else."

"You are welcome to come and stay with me for a few days," Ashok said.

"I think I will until it has cooled down. Are you on your own?"

"You know me," his friend laughed. "I wish I had your looks. You never talked to any girls in college, you were too shy, but they all liked you."

"That's not helping me much now," Saj said.

"Don't worry. Your parents will come around."

"I hope so."

That afternoon he reluctantly packed a small bag. Feeling sorry for himself, Saj left a note informing his family that he would be staying with his friend. He would never have imagined that one day he would have to leave home under these circumstances.

Saj had spent an anxious week waiting for his parent's response. But the big unanswered question was what he would do if they refused to accept Lea? Would his love for her be strong enough to defy them? His parents would be terribly hurt if he stuck to his decision. But it's his life, he thought.

The next morning Gita phoned. "They have calmed down. Mother wants to talk to you. We all miss you."

His mother came to the phone. "Please come and speak with me after your father has gone to work today." Her voice trembled

"Okay." He breathed in deeply. "But my mind is made up."

His family home had an uncomfortable feel to it as he entered the front door. Gita welcomed him, but her eyes had a worried look.

His mother rushed and went down on her knees gripping his hands tightly.

"Son, don't do this to us," she said. "You are killing your father. Be a good son. We will find a nice girl for you. You will be happy."

Saj drew his mother gently up from the floor.

"Mama, I do understand. Times change. Can't you see?" he said. "You will like Lea. I must make my own decision."

His mother sat on the chair.

"Baba looks well. I thought he would be worse. That's why I rushed to come back."

His mother listened with her head bowed, and occasionally dabbed her eyes.

"What is she like?" she sniffed.

"She is lovely, kind and clever. She is a nurse. Nothing like the distorted image we have here of English girls. If people here don't approve of other races, we're as bad as others who don't like us. What's the difference?"

His mother began to nod imperceptibly.

Saj agreed to move back. His father didn't speak to him that evening. Gita reported next day that she had heard their parents arguing in their room late into the night.

"I heard Mama telling Baba last night; Saj won't change his mind," she said.

"Good."

"They also talked about Ruma taking the overdose. They think she did it because you are not interested in her. Is that true?"

"Yeah, I had to tell her, needed to get it all out in the open. I didn't expect Ruma to react so stupidly though." He took a sip of water.

"But the good bit is she told Baba that you would marry that English girl, whether they agreed or not. And that you would go back to England and wed her. I think they'll talk to you soon."

Saj fell asleep that night more relaxed than he had been for weeks.

"Saju, Saju," his mother was shaking him.

"What's the matter, Mama?" It was midnight.

"It's your Baba." She dragged Saj by his arm to their bedroom.

His father was lying in bed but was very restless.

"What happened Baba," he asked as he sat on the bed.

His father just stared towards the ceiling. He attempted to say something, but his speech was faint and slurred. Saj checked his pulse. He then dashed back to his room and returned with his stethoscope and blood pressure instrument. He listened to his father's chest. His heart was beating fast, and his blood pressure was raised. A couple of minutes passed before his father came around.

"How are you feeling?" Saj asked.

"I am alright, felt a little odd, but I am better now," he replied in a feeble voice.

"Can you lift your legs one at a time." Saj held his leg down to test the power. He then checked his arms and eye movements. It seemed he had recovered completely.

"You rest now."

"What happened to him Saju?" his mother asked.

"It must be a TIA. It is a small stroke with complete recovery. Do you have aspirin?"

"Yes, I'll get it," Gita said and left.

"Baba, you'll be fine. You need to take aspirin daily and maybe you ought to have a couple of tests at the hospital tomorrow."

Saj returned to his room. He sat on his bed holding his head and stared at the floor. Baba could've had a major stroke, he must be extremely stressed out about the whole affair. He played down his father's illness in front of the family so as not to worry them but was aware of the seriousness. Oh, my God. What if this happens again and he died? He rubbed his temples. Would he ever forgive himself? He wondered.

A couple of days passed. There was tension in the air that evening. Not much was said. Gita tried to break the ice. "It's much cooler tonight."

Saj sat in the lounge after his meal, and his parents joined him. He picked up the TV remote.

"Don't turn it on," his mother said and cleared her throat.

Saj put the remote down and turned towards his mother.

"We discussed the whole issue in depth." She paused and looked down. "And reluctantly agreed you could marry this English girl." Then she glanced at his father who sat with a grim face with his arms folded across his chest.

Saj beamed. "Thank you. I needed your blessing." He hugged her.

"But there is a condition," she said.

"What's that?" He shuffled back on the couch.

His father replied, "We want a traditional Indian wedding, among our family and friends. We want them to come here."

I'll need to check with Lea."

First hurdle! He thought.

"Yes!" Saj punched the air with delight, as he entered his room. He couldn't believe his parents had agreed. He was desperate to phone Lea, but it would be early morning in England. He lay wide awake, reflecting on his day. Lea would be so excited when she hears the fabulous news.

Then it occurred to him that he had not actually proposed to her. What if Lea refused! He hoped that she still loves him. Maybe she had given up and found another man.

Saj had a sleepless night, feeling thrilled and apprehensive at the same time. Where would they live? It would be hard for Lea to settle in Bombay. What about her family and friends? And her job? But could he leave his family and go back to England?

The next day was Saturday. He lifted the phone and dialled Lea's mobile. No reply. He rechecked his watch. The time difference was 5 hours. He tried again but still no answer.

Desperate to give Lea the exciting news he rang her home number.

"Hello." Her mother's stern voice.

"IIi Mrs Harding, this is Saj. Is Lea there please?" He took a deep breath.

"Wait a minute." A long empty pause. Saj tapped his fingers on the table. What if Lea didn't want to speak to him?

"How are you Saj? I didn't expect you to phone. Did you receive my letter?"

"Oh, Lea. How wonderful to hear your voice? I'm fine. Yes. I did...I think of you all the time."

Silence.

"Are you still here?" he asked.

"Yes. I thought...you had forgotten me." Her voice sounded shaky.

"How could I?"

"I figured your parents would have married you off by now," she said.

"They nearly did, but I fought them all off." Saj laughed.

"Look. I'm sorry for writing to you. I didn't want to put you under pressure. But I wasn't thinking straight at the time."

"No need to apologise. Do you still love me?"

"I love you with all my heart."

"I talked to my parents about you."

"And?"

Saj paused. "Lea. Will you marry me?"

There was complete silence for a moment.

"Yes, of course. I'll marry you." She sounded ecstatic.

"My parents have insisted on one condition though. I hope it will be alright for you." Saj sounded serious.

"What's that?" Suspicion entered her voice.

"It would be a traditional wedding in Bombay."

Lea kept quiet for a moment, then said, "Wow! I don't know what to say. Bombay! Why not! I just can't believe your parents agreed."

"Me neither. I'll phone you again to confirm details."

"But where are we going to live Saj?"

"We'll talk about it later."

"Saj. You know it will be hard for me to settle in Bombay. It will be easier for us to live here."

"I understand."

"I do love you. I'm thrilled. I can't wait to tell my family." she said.

"I love you too Lea. I'm so happy."

Chapter 29

After the call, Lea danced around the hallway and into the kitchen. Her parents looked up at her.

"What did Saj say?" Chris asked as he put the newspaper down.

Lea fetched a glass of water and took a sip. "He asked me to marry him." She was unsure how they would respond.

"And what did you say?" Margaret sounded unenthusiastic.

"I said...Yes, of course." Lea gulped the water.

"Great news darling. We thought Saj had gone away for good." Chris smiled.

"Oh dear. Are you sure?" Margaret came over to her. "Where would you live? Bombay? I don't think so. Have you thought about what our friends will say?"

"I don't care about your friends. You are so old-fashioned, Mummy. Things are more acceptable now than in your day." Lea frowned.

"What about children?" She snapped back.

"We'll think about that when the time comes."

"So, what are your plans, Lea?" Chris intervened.

"We're going to talk in detail soon, but..."

"But what," Margaret said.

Lea paused for a moment. Then said in a low voice, "His parents want a traditional wedding in Bombay."

"Bombay? His family expects us to go there? Ridiculous." Margaret almost choked on her coffee.

"I've always wanted to go there." Chris tried to lighten the mood. "India is a vibrant land. There is so much history and culture there. It would be a fantastic experience, darling."

The front door slammed shut, and there were quick footsteps on the stairs. Chris called out. "Nicole, is that you? Come in here. We have fantastic news."

Nicole's eyes seemed puffy as if she had been crying.

"What is it, darling?" Margaret asked.

Nicole frowned. "That bastard Mark..." she sobbed.

"Come and sit down. What happened?" Chris asked handing her the box of tissues.

She wiped her tears and sat next to Chris. "You know we've been together for a while now...One of my friend's, Jane told me she saw Mark kiss someone in the pub a few days back. She wouldn't say who it was." Nicole got a tissue out to blow her nose.

"I went to see Mark today at work. He denied it and swore on his mother's life. He said I was the only girl he ever kissed," she said.

"So, what's the problem? You should give him the benefit of the doubt," Lea said sounding confused.

"No Lea... let me finish. I told Mark what Jane said. He asked if she had told me who it was. I said no. Then he came clean and owned up."

"The cheating bastard," Lea said.

"It was a man. Mark is gay," Nicole said wiping her tears. "I liked him a lot, but he said he can't help it. He never feels sexually attracted to women as he does for men. It took him many years to come out. I was shocked."

"Come out from where?" Margaret said.

"Mummy, it means he's finally admitted he is gay," Lea said.

Chris chuckled and smiled but tried to cover it. "Better to be aware now than later," he said.

Margaret moved towards the door. "Oh well, plenty more fish. Tomorrow is a hectic day. Lady Ashby is coming to our charity event and the gala dinner. Come on Nicole. You can help. It will take your mind off it."

Lea gave Nicole a sisterly hug and said, "You'll be okay."

"What was your news?" Nicole asked.

"It'll keep. You go and help Mummy."

"There's never a dull moment in this house," Chris said as he sipped coffee. "I should buy shares in Kleenex." He grinned.

"I know." Lea smiled.

"Listen, you should go with your heart. Do what you think is best."

"A big decision to make, though."

"Don't make the same mistake I made!" Chris said.

"What mistake?"

"I've never told this to anyone. A long time before I met your mother, I was in love with another girl. Her name was Elizabeth. We wanted to get married." Chris said. "She belonged to a poor family. My parents didn't approve. They warned me if I went ahead, they would disown me."

"What happened?"

Chris kept quiet and stared at the wall. Sadness showed on his face.

"Daddy?"

"Being weak, I gave in to my parent's wishes. I wish I had been strong enough to stand up to them...The police found Elizabeth's body in a river nearby. It was reported as a boating accident. She was my first love." Tears shimmered in his eyes.

Lea held his hand. "Oh, Daddy."

"You go for it girl. Don't be concerned about what your mother thinks. Your happiness is what matters."

"Thank you, Daddy." She gave him a kiss on his cheek.

"Do you love Mummy?"

"I think so, but she can be difficult at times."

"I know."

Well, I'm off to make a few calls," he said and left.

Lea pondered the uncertainty of her future. It was a huge decision to make. Was it right to marry Saj? Lea knew little about Indian culture. Her mother's disapproval made her sad. Toby, her brother, was to visit the next day. She wondered what he would make of it all.

Three days went by, but Lea didn't hear from Saj. She wanted to know the wedding date. The family would need to make travel arrangements. That evening she phoned him.

"You must be psychic. I would have called you today. How are you?" Saj asked.

"I'm all right, though nervous. How are you finding life back in Bombay?"

"Chaotic and disorganised as ever. It takes time to settle back into it again."

"Any news on the date?"

"My parents thought that the last week of September would be best for the wedding," he said.

"Oh, my God, only a couple of months away."

"What if I convince them for the end of October...25th? This is a good time of the year here."

"I'll talk to Daddy. Mummy isn't keen."

"That's sad. There will be celebrations and parties for a few days before the actual wedding. So be prepared...that's how things are practised here. I'll book a hotel for you nearer the time if you would prefer?"

"I'm nervous Saj. I've never travelled this far before. I need to make a lot of arrangements, visas, vaccinations."

"I am aware it will be a big challenge, but it will be wonderful. We'll be together forever. I know you can do it...I love you so much," he said.

"Love you too."

Chapter 30

The months went by. Lea was busy with arrangements for
her trip to Bombay. She was lucky to get time off work. Her
father would accompany her, but Margaret decided not to go.
Lea felt disappointed but couldn't change her mind. Nicole
and Toby would also be part of the group which pleased her.
Chris booked the flights and the hotel through a travel agent.
The presence of five-star hotels in Bombay surprised Lea.

The family visited the Indian embassy in London for their
visas. Toby and Nicole were excited about the trip. It would
be different from what they had experienced on holidays
before.

During this time Margaret had a special birthday. A lavish
party was organised. Her aristocratic friends were there plus
Lea invited a few of hers. Champagne flowed, and the guests
were having a great time.

Lea wasn't a party animal. She left the guests and went to
the kitchen to make coffee for herself. Watching the kettle
boil Lea contemplated her trip to Bombay. She hoped she
made the right decision marrying Saj, and it wasn't on
impulse. It would be entirely different there, she was heading
for the unknown. The whistle from the kettle interrupted her
chain of thoughts.

As she came into the hall, she met her friends, they were chatting.

"It's exciting Lea. Saj is a lovely guy, kind, conscientious and handsome. He is a good catch. I am pleased for you," Sophie said. She was a nurse who used to work in the same hospital as Saj.

"I'm not sure," Debbie said. "I've heard stories about these foreign men. They abuse their wives in their society, sorry Lea."

"But that can happen here among English couples. What about Cathy's husband," said Sophie sipping her wine.

"You can't live in Bombay Lea, and besides what about your children?" said Debbie.

"What about them?" Lea asked.

"Their religion and culture. The kids will be confused."

Lea felt invisible. "If you'll excuse me," she said, forced a smile and walked away.

"Leanne!" She heard a man call and turned around.

"Brad. What are you doing here?"

He walked briskly towards her smiled and gave a peck on the cheek. Lea blushed.

"Thought I'd surprise you. You look gorgeous," Brad said.

"I haven't seen you for…"

"Over two years. I met Margaret at the tennis club, she invited me to the party. How are you? You still at the hospital."

"I am good thanks. No, I am working at a GP surgery."

Brad was an old flame of Lea. With long flowing fair hair, blue eyes and sharp features, Lea thought he was the image of Michael Douglas, the famous Hollywood actor. Brad adored Lea, and they had been happy together. Then an opportunity which he couldn't refuse, made Brad move to Edinburgh to train as a solicitor. Lea liked him a lot. He was kind, witty and ambitious but long distance dating didn't work out for them, and they split up.

"I never forgot about you, wasn't interested in anyone else," Brad said as he took a sip of his drink. "The cold weather up north didn't suit me. I have my own firm in London now."

"You've done extremely well Brad. I am pleased for you."

"Doesn't mean much without you Lea." He gazed into her eyes and gently touched her hand.

Lea blushed. She took a deep breath, her heart beating fast.

Looking away, she said, "Have you met anyone in the party you know?"

"I love you, Lea. I want us to try again. It was stupid of me to let you go." His eyes sparkled as he moved closer to her.

"Didn't Mummy tell you that I'm getting married?"

"He doesn't love you as I do. You are a big catch for him. How can you marry a man from such a different background? He is only after your status. You'll be lost."

"You don't know Saj." Lea guessed that her mother had updated Brad with the news. She sipped her coffee, then smiled at a lady who walked past.

"I've got a fantastic job and great prospects. We loved each other. You remember."

"Please excuse me. Nice to see you, Brad." Lea got up, went upstairs and sat in the games room on her own.

Oh, God. What was she going to do? Had she made the right decision to marry Saj? Did she love him enough to go through all this turmoil and hardship? Did Saj really adore her as much as he thought he did? His parents always came first, she would be second best. She couldn't live in Bombay. It would be too hot and dirty. What if his parents didn't allow him to come back to England? They might hate her. If they had children, they wouldn't know where they belonged. Saj was a kind man, but he did have some odd habits. She loved nursing and wanted to pursue a career in midwifery. She had many goals in life. Maybe she would like to work abroad for a charity organisation. What if Saj insisted that she stayed at home as their women do?

At least she knew Brad well over three years. She did like him a lot, and they could have a stable relationship. There would be no conflict about religion or culture. He loved her and was prepared to do anything for her. She never realised he was so hurt when they split up. He had a similar upbringing and a lovely family. Brad was a safer bet, she thought.

Lea had made her decision. She would ring Saj in the morning and call off the wedding. Strolling to her room, she could hear a roar of laughter coming from downstairs. Dance music echoed, and guests were having a fabulous time. When she opened the door, the first thing that caught her eye was a picture of her and Saj from their trip to Wembley stadium. Tears shimmered in her eyes as she picked the frame off the dressing table. She sat on her bed and remembered that happy time.

A couple of minutes later, there was a knock on her door.

Margaret barged in. "So you are here. Brad was asking about you."

"I'll be down in a minute." She avoided eye contact with her mother.

Lea got up closed the door and lay on the bed, contemplating her dilemma. Saj would be devastated if she changed her mind now. She loved him so much and knew he loved her. He must have fought for her with his parents, and that would have taken courage. She could trust life and take a leap of faith. Good things never came easily. It would be a struggle early on, but she could do it. If two people loved each other, they could sort out anything that comes their way, she thought and fell asleep. She missed the rest of the party and had lots of apologising to do the next day.

A week before they were to leave, Margaret changed her mind. She had decided to go for Lea's sake.

Lea was delighted. "Mummy, you're going to behave yourself?"

"I'll be my usual self. I've heard that clothes and jewellery are lovely and cheap in Bombay. It would be a wonderful trip for shopping."

The day of their departure to Bombay arrived. Chris booked a people carrier, and they headed for Heathrow.

"We are carrying so much luggage, it's as if we are emigrating," Chris said.

"At least we'll get warm sunshine. My skin needs the sun. I'm so pale." Toby gazed at the grey sky.

"I won't miss this horrible weather. I am excited about shopping there," said Nicole with a smile.

Lea had mixed emotions. Thrilled that she would see Saj again, but also nervous not knowing what to expect in Bombay. What is Saj's family like and will they like her? What about their house and the area? She hoped her mother wouldn't embarrass her. Fear of the unknown.

The taxi cruised along the motorway as it started to rain.

Margaret screamed. "Oh no!"

"What happened?" Lea jumped.

She rummaged through her handbag. "I forgot to bring my passport. I got the visa late and left it in the drawer."

"Don't panic Margaret. Driver, can we go back? We need to fetch the passport," Chris said.

"You did this on purpose, didn't you?" Lea said.

"Of course, I didn't, darling, I'm so sorry."

"Jesus Christ! We'll miss our flight." Lea checked her boarding pass and then her watch.

The driver turned around at the first exit and headed back. The atmosphere remained tense, and no one spoke. They could hear the rain coming down hard on the roof as they sped along.

"The check-in will close in an hour," Toby said glancing at his watch.

"Driver. Do you think we'll make it in time?" Chris asked.

"It will be touch and go. I'll do my best."

They reached the house. Toby jumped out of the taxi and sprinted. He returned in five minutes with the passport, and they were off again for Heathrow. This was not an ideal start. What would happen next? Lea thought. She held her breath chewing her nails. Everyone appeared tense and kept an eye on their watches, in total silence.

Gathering their luggage, they dashed through the departure lounge. Lea spotted the BA check-in desk. Toby got there first as it was about to shut.

"You guys are late. Let's do this quickly, you need to run," the lady at the desk said.

Lea panted, her heart was racing. She knew it was a strenuous effort getting the whole family together. If they missed this flight, it might not happen again for a long time, she thought.

The luggage was in order which pleased Lea. They all sprinted towards security and went through. Margaret was stopped and searched.

"Why do they always pick on me?" Margaret said, frowning as she rushed to the departure gate. She struggled to keep up with others. Chris glanced at Lea, shook his head and grinned.

The group hurried on. Lea breathed a sigh of relief as her family were the last ones to board. They looked at each other and smiled, as they handed over their boarding passes. God must be on her side. It would be alright from now on, she thought.

Chapter 31

It was late afternoon when the British Airways plane landed at Bombay. As Lea stepped out, the intense heat hit her in the face. She half knew what to expect when she entered the building. Saj had told her so many stories about Bombay. The airport appeared reasonably tidy. The lounge was crowded and noisy, but at least air-conditioned.

"It's so bloody hot and humid here," Margaret said as they queued at the passport control desk.

The officer collected the family passports. He chewed something which stained his teeth red. Lea wondered why?

"Where have you come from?" he asked looking at their passports.

"England," Chris said.

"Are you all together?"

"Yes."

"What is the purpose of your visit here?"

Lea intervened and spoke in a soft voice, "I'm getting married."

The officer looked up then chuckled and said, "You come from London to get married. In Bombay. Why?"

"That's right." Lea was confused.

"Have you been here before?"

"No," Chris answered.

Margaret mopped the sweat from her forehead with a tissue. "This heat is too much," she said and sipped water.

The officer checked their passports and inspected each of them up and down. Both Lea and Nicole were dressed in light cotton long sleeved tops and loose trousers. Saj had advised Lea to wear conservative clothing, because of their culture. Margaret had a long skirt and a blouse on while the men wore short-sleeved shirts and carried their sunglasses.

"Where are you staying?" He sounded stern.

"At the Taj hotel." Chris searched his pockets for the confirmation papers.

"No need." He handed all the passports back.

They had to wait for more than half an hour before their luggage was unloaded. Lea saw a couple of British holidaymakers which pleased her. One by one, they managed to grab their bags from the conveyor belt.

"Look at my suitcase. It's ripped on one side," Margaret shrieked.

Lea's was severely scratched too, but she ignored the damage. After putting her luggage on a trolley, she walked towards the exit. Lea hoped Saj would be waiting. The airport lounge teemed with people as the group strolled through the corridor and came to the arrivals.

A huge crowd was gathered as they waited for loved ones. The scene was chaotic and the noise unbelievable. People shouted and screamed all at the same time. The heat and the stench in the air hit them, as they came out of the air-conditioned lounge. Lea put her sunglasses on and wiped sweat from her face, as the glare of the sunlight was intense.

She looked around for Saj in the crowd. Spotting a person among so many was hard. A couple of men came to them asking to provide a taxi service. The stares from people intimidated Lea. It must be because they were white, she thought.

"Where is he?" Margaret asked Lea.

"Should we take a cab and go to the hotel?" Toby said.

"No. Saj told me to wait for him. There are dodgy characters around here. Keep hold of your luggage," she said glancing at her bags.

Lea waited for ten minutes which seemed like hours. She stood biting her nails and looked around. She remembered Saj telling her, in their culture, they are quite laid back. Timekeeping was not their strength. What if he had forgotten, or got the days mixed up? She couldn't have her mother on her back all the time.

"Do you want a taxi. I won't charge much," a man said. He came from behind and tried to carry her luggage.

"No," Lea shouted shaking her head and stared at the man. She grabbed her suitcase.

"I can take you to a nice cheap hotel," he said.

Lea looked away hoping he would depart, but she kept an eye on her luggage.

"Leave her alone. Go away." A security officer glared at the man and gestured waving his arm. "Madam. Are you waiting for transport?" He turned towards Lea.

"Yes. My friend is picking us up," she said surveying the crowd.

"Madam. You shouldn't be standing here on your own," he said.

Lea pointed towards others. "No, my family are there."

Come on Saj. Where are you? She mopped her forehead and sipped water.

Chapter 32

A tap on her shoulder from behind. "Excuse me."

As she swung around, Saj stood there with a big grin on his face. She smiled back. He wanted to embrace and kiss her, but both controlled themselves. Their society didn't allow them to display affection in public. He had already told Lea.

"How are you? You must be tired," Saj said.

"I'm not too bad. I'll tell you everything later. We need to find the others."

The family stood next to their luggage, away from the crowd.

"Hello. Pleased to see you all. Welcome to Bombay. I apologise for being late. We were stuck in traffic due to an accident." He smiled, sounding like a tour operator.

"Saj. This is Toby," Lea said.

"Nice to meet you, Toby. Lea has told me a lot about you."

"Same here Saj." They shook hands.

"Mr and Mrs Harding. Good to see you again. Thanks for coming," Saj said.

"Please call me Chris." He shook Saj's hand.

Saj tried to greet Lea's mother, but she turned her head away.

"Sorry," Chris said.

"You all must be tired after the long journey. I think we should head straight to the hotel," Saj said. "You're lucky. Today is not too hot."

Lea glanced at Nicole, and both smiled.

"A minibus will take us to the Taj. It will be here any minute. I must warn you. As none of you has been here before. Please be prepared for a few surprises," Saj said with a sarcastic smile.

It was a small, clapped out black vehicle, with numerous dents on the bodywork. The bus had enough space for them to squeeze in.

"We're going to the Taj," he told the driver.

Saj sat in the front seat, like a tour guide. He informed Lea and her family, about life in Bombay. She was fascinated as they left the airport. Small old cars and motorbikes crammed the roads, and people drove like crazy. They jumped lanes all the time in a hurry, without any road sense. Driving appeared disorganised, chaotic, and at times frightening. The air felt humid and polluted. Margaret had her handkerchief on her nose.

"Tell me Saj. What lingo do you speak here?" Chris asked.

"Hindi is the most popular language of the country. But many others are spoken in different regions. Educated people speak English here, so you shouldn't have any problems."

"The Indian culture is one of the oldest and diversified. We have a rich cultural heritage. It is a combination of customs, lifestyle, religion, languages, rituals and cuisine, depending upon the area."

"Sounds interesting," Chris said.

"Guests are considered God here. People welcome them with joined hands and a smile on their face. Not only visitors but people here worship animals, statues, rivers, stones, trees and much more."

"Wow," Toby remarked.

"Watch out," Margaret shrieked as a motorbike swerved right in front of them. The driver honked in anger and muttered a few swear words in his own language.

"Don't worry. This is the way they drive. Road rage is prevalent, and nobody is patient," Saj said with a smile.

"I'll keep my eyes shut, "Margaret said as she wiped the sweat from her face.

They saw modern buildings on one side of the road and a few run-down houses on the other. It was uncomfortable, and they all sweated profusely in the cramped vehicle.

"Are you alright Lea?" Saj turned his head around. He noticed that she was quiet and looking out of the window in a pensive mood.

"Yeah," she said and smiled.

"It's warm in here," Saj said glancing at the driver.

"Sorry, sir. The air conditioner broke down."

"Jesus. Look at that bike. How do they manage? Must be so dangerous." Nicole pointed out to a motorbike riding next to them, with the whole family on it. The couple and their two small children, all sat on it. None of them wore crash helmets.

Saj chuckled. "This is quite common here. Some people carry shopping on their bikes. Bombay is one of the most populated cities in the world. It is overcrowded and is the business hub. People from all over the country come here to work."

"Sounds like London," Toby said.

"Come on, this place is different from London. There is no comparison," Margaret said.

"No Mummy, I meant job seekers." Toby sounded irritated.

Their minibus now cruised in a broader road, heading for the city centre. Tall buildings stood on both sides, some were hotels and offices. They were painted mostly in white, a few in bright colours.

"Another five minutes," the driver said.

"What a relief. I am exhausted. It's too hot," Margaret said.

After an uncomfortable bumpy drive, they finally reached the Taj hotel. Lea gazed at the building as she got out of the car. It was impressive, with beautiful marble work and coloured decoration. When they went inside, she stared in disbelief the grandeur of the hotel. The high ceiling had traditional colours and architecture, with massive, gorgeous golden chandeliers.

"Magnificent," Chris said to Margaret after they had checked in.

"Hmm."

They all got in the elevator, their rooms were located on the 6th floor. As Lea entered her room, she was astounded by its exquisite decor. She hurried to the open balcony. The view was breathtaking. It overlooked the sea, with many sailing and fishing boats in the water. The sun gleamed, and the fresh breeze added to the pleasantness. Lea didn't miss the British weather at all.

After everyone had settled in, Saj came up to Lea's room. For the first time, they had privacy. He sat with her on the couch. They gazed into each other's eyes and caressed with passion.

"Yes! We've done it," Saj said with a grin. He wrapped his arms around her.

"Yeah. I love you," Lea said and smiled.

"I love you too. Tomorrow, we'll visit my parent's house after lunch. I'll pick you all up."

"I'm nervous, what they'll think of me."

"Don't worry. My parents will love you because you are adorable."

"I'll lie down and rest before I unpack," Lea said, then Saj left.

The next day, Saj arrived at the hotel and met them in the lobby. They sat in the restaurant and had tea before they left for his parents' house.

"Have you all settled in? Please ask at the reception if you need anything," Saj said.

"Yes, it's lovely," said Toby.

"My parents have arranged dinner for you all. I hope you'll like it. I'll update you tonight with all the arrangements for the celebration and wedding. Please feel free to ask any questions," Saj said.

"I don't eat spicy food," Margaret scrunched up her face.

"Please don't worry. Mild dishes will be served as well, which I'm sure you'll enjoy," Saj said. "A test match is being played this week, the whole city is buzzing. Maybe you'll be interested." He glanced at Chris.

Saj drove his father's car. It was an old Nissan, they just about managed to fit in. Chris sat in the front seat. Saj had to keep the windows open and locked the rear doors from inside. The car had no air conditioning. Margaret moaned about the heat throughout the trip.

They finally arrived at their destination after a long drive. It was a modest residential street, not as posh as the hotel location. A brick wall stood at the front of the house, all painted white. Saj had the whole place redecorated for the wedding so that it looked respectable.

Lea bit her nails as they entered through the front gate. She glanced at Saj for reassurance. He smiled at her and squeezed her hand gently. His parents waited at the door to welcome the party. They greeted their visitors with joined hands and a smile. Saj introduced everyone, and finally Lea to his parents. They shook her hand, and his mother gave Lea a hug.

"Please be seated. Did you have a pleasant journey?" Saj's father asked.

"Yes, thank you. A long flight but quite comfortable. The hotel is superb," Chris said.

"Not as beautiful as London though," his father said.

Saj's parents struggled to understand their guests' conversation. Their English accent seemed complicated for them to pick. There was an awkward silence for a few moments. Gita came in with a trolley full of sweet and savoury snacks and served the tea.

"Do you have coffee?" Margaret asked. Gita looked towards Saj.

"Sorry. We don't drink coffee, I forgot to mention to get it for you. My fault."

"Try the freshly cooked samosas and pakoras, sweets if you prefer," Saj's father said.

His mother put the snacks on their guests' plates. She insisted they try all the food.

"Mama. They'll take it if they want it." Saj felt embarrassed.

He peeked at Lea, and they both smiled, recalling what he had told her about their culture. Food is served as a sign of hospitality and friendship. Lea and Toby enjoyed the samosas and pakoras. Nicole found them too spicy.

A few flies hovered on the food. "Excuse the flies, the warm weather brings them out." Saj used the newspaper to drive them off.

"Can I use your toilet Saj?" Toby asked.

"Of course. I'll show you where it is." He got up, and Toby followed him. A moment later Saj returned.

"About the arrangements. I can speak on my parent's behalf," Saj said. "The celebration will last two days. The wedding is on Saturday in a big hall. On Friday, the pre-wedding party will be at our house. I think everyone needs to find the right clothes."

"We have to go shopping," Lea said, feeling the excitement growing within her.

"I'll take you all out to the shops tomorrow. You can decide what you want. I'll advise you. Mama will also come with us," Saj said taking a bite of the samosa.

While they chatted, the lights went out, and the whole house plunged into darkness.

"Oh. What happened?" Lea said.

"This is only a power cut. It will come back soon," Saj replied.

Gita brought lit candles. It was spooky. The lights came back after half an hour, they were accustomed to these power cuts.

Saj picked up Lea and her family from the hotel the next day, and they drove to the shopping mall. It was a massive place with many different clothes and jewellery shops. The variety on display excited Lea and Nicole. Beautiful bright and bold colours of dresses struck them most. Margaret was sceptical at first. But even she couldn't resist the glittery garments and picked up more than she needed.

"This really suits you, madam. You appear glamorous in that attire," the shopkeeper said to Lea, as she tried it on. He stood around and encouraged the party to buy more.

Lea smiled and said, "Thank you."

"Please try this on." The girl at the shop passed a saree to Lea. It was a gorgeous glittery blue dress with golden embroidery on it.

"This looks like a sheet of cloth. What do I do with it?" Lea asked Nicole who shrugged.

The shop assistant soon sensed it. "Let me help you."

She took Lea to the changing room and tried wrapping the dress around her. It was difficult. She put a crop top on Lea to go under it which felt too tight around the bust. The girl showed her how to set the dress. Nicole came in and helped her. Lea remembered seeing these clothes in a Bollywood film. She assisted Nicole with hers, they giggled while trying them on.

With Saj and his mother's help, they chose a few traditional dresses for the wedding and the party. Lea got bright red top and baggy trousers. Saj loved the dress. They all bought regular daily light clothes to keep them fresh.

The men tried on long glittery coloured jackets and trousers and loved their new costumes. It was a unique experience for them.

"Look at these beautiful necklaces and earrings. These are real gold." Nicole said.

"How much is this?" Lea pointed at a necklace.

"For you madam, it is ten thousand."

Lea worked it out. It came to only fifty pounds.

When they came to pay for the clothes and jewellery, Lea said, "I can't believe how cheap they are."

"Do you want me to haggle about the price?" Saj asked. "I could get it even cheaper for you." That was a common practice in Bombay.

"No, please don't worry. This isn't much. These people are impoverished."

They finished shopping and came out of the Mall. A few children came to Lea and asked for money. These were destitute, unkempt, and shabbily dressed. Saj politely asked them to go away.

"These are professional beggars. At no time give them any cash otherwise they won't leave you alone," Saj said.

"What's the horrible stench?" Margaret screwed up her face, as they walked to the car.

Saj investigated. "There is a burst sewage pipe."

"The air is so polluted. Look at the thick smoke there." Margaret drew their attention to a double-decker bus.

"There aren't many strict laws here, and people tend to ignore them," Saj spoke.

"I can't wait to try on my new clothes when I get back," Lea said.

"Lea. There will be a few traditional rituals at the wedding. Please don't be concerned because I don't know much about them either. Follow what I'm doing, you'll be alright." Saj said and laughed.

"This is an experience of a lifetime," Lea said as they drove back to the hotel.

"Jesus. Look at that. How do these people manage?" Toby said as a bus overtook them. People were hanging out of the doorway.

"This is dangerous, but it becomes a daily habit for these commuters," Saj said. "The population of Bombay is huge; the public transport can't cope. Most people here work hard more than twelve hours' a day, with only one day off."

"People must get hurt if they fall off those buses?" Chris asked.

"They do, a few of them die every day, but these are desperate poverty-stricken people. Life is cheap here, especially for the poor, unlike England. Maybe because there are too many of us here," Saj said.

Chapter 33

"Look at us." Nicole laughed, as she put on her loose embroidered blue top.

"Which way around do I wear this?" Lea giggled as she tried her baggy trousers. They all had fun with their Indian clothes in Lea's hotel room.

Margaret decided to dress in her own clothes too embarrassed to wear traditional local attire. Chris had his camera out and took pictures of every move they made. Photography came naturally to him.

The party planned to explore the surrounding area that afternoon. Strolling through the streets, they were fascinated to see children playing cricket. The kids used a worn-out bat and a torn, odd-shaped ball but they played with enthusiasm and passion. They shouted and screamed. Chris had always been interested in cricket. He informed them he had been to the Lord's test match in London each year. And could only imagine the excitement in Bombay. The world cup event was to be held soon in Australia.

The afternoon sun lost its intensity to Lea's relief. They walked to a shopping mall and bought a few gift items.

"People are so friendly here. They enjoy their life, always smiling," Lea said as they wandered back to the hotel.

"They don't keep the place clean, though." Margaret pointed at the litter on the street.

"Maybe with a huge population and lack of resources, this isn't easy. These people own fewer material things, but they appear happy," said Lea.

One afternoon, Lea, Nicole and Toby planned to venture out. The management was kind enough to allow one of their employees to accompany them. Saj had advised Lea not to wander outside the hotel on their own. He also told her not to eat or drink food from any stalls, in case they got a tummy bug.

The nearby area was a mix of beautiful tall buildings and poor residential ones. The walls of the houses looked shabby with graffiti on them. The ladies dressed in traditional Indian attire on a glorious sunny day. It was a challenge for Lea and Nicole as they walked down the streets. They received a lot of unwanted attention from men who gawked at them.

Lea thought the colonial buildings looked majestic, especially compared to the haphazard quality of the others. A group of children came and hassled them as they strolled on the pavement. They must be about ten years old, some of them were deformed, which shocked Lea. The beggars wouldn't leave them alone.

"Go away." The guide told them off in Hindi, but they wouldn't leave.

Lea handed them cash, and they left.

"Madam. These are professional," the man said to Lea.

A few cows wandered on the streets. Toby chuckled when he saw a couple of them cross the road on their own. The cars beeped their horns and swerved past the cows, none of them bothered to stop. Few undernourished stray dogs roamed around which surprised Lea.

The guide said to Toby, "Cows are sacred for us so they can go where they want. We must respect them."

Toby screamed and hopped as he stepped in some cow dung. Lea and Nicole couldn't help giggling.

"This place needs a real clean-up operation." He rubbed his foot on the pavement edge to rid the stuff off his shoe.

"What is that foul smell?" Lea scrunched up her face and looked around.

"Madam. The drains are blocked, and sewage overflowed. The heat makes it worse. They take days to unblock them."

"That reminds me," Toby said to Lea. "When I went to the toilet at Saj's house, I couldn't find where to go. Then I spotted a hole in the ground. I couldn't believe it." He laughed.

Lea was dismayed at the degree of poverty, further away from the hotel. They could see slums from a distance but decided to stay away. A few more beggars came their way. This time they walked fast and managed to lose them.

"Shall we go to the beach?" Nicole said.

Lea found crossing the road a hazardous effort. The traffic noise was scary, and there didn't seem to be any road lanes or zebra crossing. People drove at speed, continually honking all in a hurry and not caring for pedestrians. Distinctive old black and yellow cabs and double-decker red buses were on the roads, like 1940s London. After a long wait, they managed to cross.

It was a beautiful sandy beach. The sea was a dark shade of blue. Lea took off her shoes and attempted to walk barefoot on the sand.

"Ah...it's hot." She shrieked, jumped, and put her shoes back on. The guide chuckled.

Lea saw young middle to upper-class locals at the beach. They chatted and laughed with friends. Couples sat and contemplated the sea horizon. Men strolled hand in hand which confused everyone. Toby nudged Lea to draw her attention to the guys.

"Sir, they are not homosexuals. They express their friendship, the Indian way," the guide told them.

Few men swam in the sea, but the women stood knee deep in the water, fully clothed. The beach atmosphere was pleasant as a young man appeared and took a picture of Lea and Nicole. They seemed harmless.

One man came to Lea and asked, "Are you married?"

She laughed and said," Yes."

Hawkers trying to flog cheap jewellery approached them. Lea said no, but they wouldn't accept no for an answer. One of the girls touched Lea's earrings. Toby glared at her annoyed. She stood there for a moment and then walked away.

"We should head back to the hotel. We have been out for a couple of hours now," Lea said and sipped bottled water.

Toby spotted a three-wheeled rickshaw going slowly along the road.

"Look. Let's go for a ride. It will be fun."

"I'm not sure that's a good idea."

"Come on Lea. You need to experience one if you visit Bombay," Nicole said.

Toby waved to the rickshaw. Their guide told them to be careful, and he would wait for them. The three climbed on it. It was cramped, they had to squeeze in tight. Toby asked the man to cycle along for a short distance for a ride. The driver smiled and knew they were tourists. The rickshaw had a hood to protect passengers from the intense sun. He pedalled slowly as he gathered momentum.

"This is exciting," Toby said surveying around.

The driver must be in his fifties, greying, skinny and undernourished. He wore a worn out dirty white t-shirt with many holes in it, and baggy trousers. A piece of cloth covered his head to protect himself from the sun. Sweat poured from his face, as he struggled to pedal in the heat of the day.

Lea felt sorry for the man, it was like forced labour. After a five minutes' ride, she asked him to turn around and go back. He was surprised and smiled at her.

"How can he carry so many people and pedal in this hot weather?" Lea spoke in a soft voice.

They returned to the spot where they left their guide. He was still waiting for them.

"How much?" Lea asked.

"Madam, ten rupees." The man mopped sweat off his face with the cloth.

"Only ten?" She knew that it was worth pennies.

"Take this." Lea handed him a thousand rupees.

The driver stared wide-eyed at the money. "No madam. No, I can't take this," he said and shook his head.

"Please take it," Lea said.

"No," he clasped his hand in a prayer gesture.

Lea couldn't believe it.

"How many children you got," Toby asked.

"Sir, six small ones," the man said.

"How much do you earn?"

"Only a little amount sir.".

Lea handed him the cash. "Buy gifts for your children with this money."

"Thank you." The driver grinned and agreed to take it.

Toby asked the guide to take a picture of them with the driver and his rickshaw.

The man's gesture overwhelmed Lea. She realised how fortunate they were. How they took everything for granted back in England.

"It was a fascinating day out," Lea said as they entered their hotel. Everyone agreed. A revelation and a culture shock for them.

Chapter 34

Saj came to visit Lea and the family the next day. It was the pre-wedding party day.

"What do your parents think of me Saj?"

"They like you of course, just be yourself. My family believe that you're beautiful, and all your family too."

"Your parents are lovely, especially your mother. I expected them to be different," Lea said.

Margaret wore traditional clothes for the first time. They helped each other get dressed.

"Mummy. you look gorgeous," Nicole said.

Lea and Chris agreed.

"Thanks, darling."

The women giggled while they paraded in their colourful dresses. Chris took numerous pictures of them.

"Ladies. You all look stunning." Saj smiled.

A festive atmosphere prevailed when the group arrived. It was boisterous, the house packed with men, women, and children, all in colourful, glittery clothes.

People greeted them warmly, Lea being the centre of attention. Gita put a coloured mark on their foreheads one by one. Guests were fascinated to see an English family among them. Even Toby and Nicole received a lot of interest. Young men and women tried to impress and befriend them.

"You'll have many admirers here," Lea whispered in Nicole's ear, and they giggled.

Saj's parents welcomed them. His mother came to Lea and embraced her. The presence of their guests delighted them.

"I told you. You are already the daughter-in-law," Saj whispered in her ears. Lea smiled and gave him a nudge.

Traditional prayers were offered, followed by rituals. Saj's family were religious, they had many gods and goddesses to pray to. Being the centre of attention made Lea uneasy at first. She became more relaxed as time passed. The warmth and hospitality of their hosts impressed Lea. Toby chatted and laughed with the girls.

"How are you finding Bombay, Mr Chris?" His father asked.

"This is such an incredible city. There's so much going on. Margaret and I are having a fantastic time."

"I'm pleased...And what about you, Mrs Margaret? This dress really suits you."

"Thank you. You are all so kind."

Dinner was served, and they all tucked in. The curries and the starters were mild, and bottled mineral water was present for the guests. Toby enjoyed the food and ate plenty, but Lea wasn't hungry. She tried to absorb everything that went on around her as if it was a dream come true.

There was a superb party atmosphere after dinner. Bollywood music played, and people got up and danced. Nicole and Toby attempted to copy their arm waving moves, which looked hilarious. Everyone laughed. Gita came and dragged Lea by her hand to the dance floor. Chris and Saj also joined in. Finally, Margaret gave in and mingled with the crowd. Saj and Lea held hands. They only had eyes for each other.

The celebration continued until midnight. The group had to preserve their energy for the next day.

"Thanks. We enjoyed the evening tremendously," Chris told Saj's father as they left.

"Thank you, Mr Chris."

It was the Wedding day. At the hotel, that morning, Lea and her family had gathered in her parents' room. A heated discussion went on.

"She can't live here. There is so much poverty although I do accept the people are lovely," Margaret said.

"I would find it hard as well, but the people are so warm," Nicole added.

"It will be up to Lea to decide," Chris said.

Lea listened to the conversation as if she was invisible. Others spoke on her behalf.

"I'll be in my room." Lea stormed out.

272

"How are you?" Nicole asked opening her door.

"Life is so different out here. Mummy's right. I can't live here Nicole, I don't even speak or understand the locals. I'll be isolated," Lea said. "The weather is so hot now, imagine what it will be like in summer. I do love Saj, but then I'd miss you all." Lea's words gushed out.

"I know." Nicole sat next to her and put her arm around her.

"Saj's family are lovely. They have less money but so much warmth. People are so close together. Children here are taught manners and are brought up to respect their elders," Lea said.

"This place is a shopping paradise, though." Nicole tried to lighten the mood.

"I need to talk to Saj."

"Good idea." Nicole left the room.

Lea dialled the house. Saj answered.

"Could you please come to the hotel. I want to have a chat."

"Is everything alright?" Saj sounded concerned.

"I can't talk over the phone."

"I'm busy with preparations, but I can be there in a couple of hours."

Saj sped over to the hotel.

"What's the matter, Lea? Have you changed your mind?" He gave her a hug.

She shook her head.

"Come on darling. What's the problem?"

"Life is so different here. Your family are lovely and kind. I like your parents. They made us so welcome."

"What is it?"

"I love you Saj, but I can't live here."

He didn't know what to say. They were silent for a few moments.

"I do understand how you feel, but we love each other and want to be together. We can think about other issues later. I want to take one step at a time."

They held each other and kissed.

"You fought for me Saj, I'll never forget. I'm sorry, I hope you do understand."

"I'll talk to my parents, convince them that we should live in England. It will be difficult, but nothing has been easy." He gazed at Lea with an ironic smile.

"Okay," she spoke in a soft voice.

"Now let us enjoy today. I'll sort it out. You do want to get married?"

"Of course, I do. I need to get ready soon. Nicole is going to help me."

"A coach will take you all to the wedding venue at 6 pm. I'll be waiting there. How is everyone else?"

"The men tried their clothes on and had fun."

He kissed her and left.

Lea was glad Saj agreed to go back to England. He'll persuade his parents, she thought.

The wedding hall was charmingly decorated with glittery materials and many lighted candles. A colourful stage had been built where the bride and groom would be seated on beautiful velvet couches. Hundreds of chairs were laid out.

It was evening. Soon the hall was full of guests, all dressed in bright and bold colours. Ladies wore exquisite jewellery. People shouted. Children ran around the room excited, as they attempted to catch each other. A few mothers yelled at their kids to calm down as instrumental wedding music played in the background. The aroma of incense burning added to the enchanting atmosphere.

Saj wore a traditional embroidered, dark blue jacket and white trousers. His gaze spanned around all the guests, his family and friends. Who would have thought this day would arrive when his and Lea's marriage would be celebrated with such warmth and happiness? Like most nervous bridegrooms he kept glancing at his watch, hoping she hadn't changed her mind.

He heard the bride's party arriving and went to the door to greet them. All were wearing Indian dress. His eager gaze found Lea. She took his breath away, dressed in a long red dress, embroidered with silver thread, giving a glittery appearance. Saj was surprised that her hands had been painted with henna. She looked radiant.

Lea clasped his hand tightly. "Gosh. Is that you Saj? You look like an Indian prince."

He laughed. "Oh, I've been keeping that from you, in case you were just after me for my throne. And you. There are no words to describe how wonderful you look. I am so lucky to have you."

Lea appeared a little apprehensive as they walked together towards the stage, waving and smiling as people greeted them. A couple of young ladies threw rose petals on them. It was supposed to bring them good luck.

"I hope I don't look silly in this dress." Lea smiled as her eyes focussed on the guests.

"You look gorgeous," said Saj.

"Thank you."

"I like the henna on your hands. It is traditional for Indian brides, but I had no idea you would have it."

Leah grinned, and her eyes lit up. "I wanted it to be a surprise. I knew you would be pleased. Your cousin, Amara kindly offered, and she came to the hotel. She said it was appropriate as her name means eternity.

Saj felt a lump in his throat. Eternity. Yes, he thought. Eternity with this amazing woman.

"It took ages to finish, but that meant we had lots of time to chat. Mostly about you as a little boy. You must have been so sweet."

"Hmm!!"

Saj's father led them to their beautifully decorated golden seats in the centre of the stage. The two families sat on either side of them.

"Why do women wear red on their wedding day?" Lea whispered.

"It has something to do with the rising sun. We believe the planet in charge of marriages, Mars is red in colour and it stands for prosperity and fertility. Does it sound weird?" He smiled.

"No. Just like we wear white in England."

Lea noticed that Gita and Nicole were whispering together. Saj was chatting to one of his friends. Nicole, after some hesitation, sneaked up to him and started taking off one of his shoes. This is a common and fun tradition of Indian weddings. Saj was taken by surprise. To get his shoes back, he had to offer Nicole cash.

"You are a traitor Gita. You were supposed to be on my side." Saj chuckled.

Lea burst out laughing.

"Someone had to tell her about our traditions," Gita said.

"Okay." Saj dug into his pocket and handed Nicole two hundred rupees.

The congregation was hushed as the ceremony began. There were several religious rituals, and then the priest performed the marriage itself in Hindi. There was a translator so that Lea's family could understand the proceedings. There were various responses and actions required, and Lea followed whatever Saj did. Finally, as in England, they signed the marriage register. Both let out a long gasp, almost simultaneously, relieved that all had gone according to plan.

"We did it, Lea," Saj whispered, gazing into her eyes.

She smiled and held his hand tightly.

All the guests wanted to be the first to congratulate the couple.

"What a wonderful ceremony!" Lea said. "I was a bit nervous early on, but I enjoyed it so much. It felt so sincere."

Someone patted Saj on the shoulder. He turned around. One of his oldest friends stood there.

"Congratulations Saj," he said.

Saj got up and embraced him. "I am so pleased to see you after such a long time. Lea, this is Salman. I was at college with him."

"Hello, Lea. I am so pleased to meet you. This is my wife, Keesha. I must say Saj is a lucky man."

Dinner was announced, and the crowd moved towards the extensive buffet. The food looked sumptuous with many vegetarian dishes. The guests queued and waited patiently, which was unusual in India.

Lea and Saj managed to eat something but were constantly bombarded with questions and good wishes. Saj noticed Toby surrounded by young women, all flirting with him. He was tucking into the food with relish, as ever. They moved over to talk with Nicole who was being monopolised by a good-looking young man. He was one of Saj's distant cousins who ran a successful business in Bombay. They overheard a little of the conversation:

"You are beautiful. Are you married?"

"No."

"Will you marry me?"

"No. I don't even know you."

"Would you like me to show you Bombay in my Mercedes? Please give me your phone number. We can explore the original city, not just the tourist areas." He persisted.

Nicole giggled.

"Off you go, and stop worrying her," Saj said.

After the buffet, Lea and Saj led the dancing with their favourite song. Whitney Houston 'I will always love you'. This was an English tradition that Saj had included especially for his new wife. There was lots of clapping and shouting in support.

Then Bollywood music began. The room was filled with singing and laughter. People danced to the hypnotising beats and rhythms of the pumping music; the shaking of the shoulders, the throwing of the arms, the winding of the hips and the flicking of the wrists. All this with no alcohol, so no drunkenness.

After a couple of hours, Rita came up and hugged first her son and then Lea. "I am so pleased for you both. You are so beautiful. What a successful day. You both did so well."

Saj's father and Gita appeared, and it was time for the couple to leave for their hotel. Chris and Margaret added their good wishes. A luxurious car had been hired for Saj and Lea as they climbed in and sank into the leather seats. The waving and goodbyes seemed to go on forever.

Lea was overjoyed with the honeymoon suite at the Taj. Vases of flowers brought a heady fragrance to the rooms and chocolates had been left on the table. The bed was scattered with pink petals.

"Alone at last," she said.

"We've done it." Saj danced her around the room.

"Love you Saj."

"I love you too." Then moved towards the bed.

They gazed into each other eyes for a second. Saj slowly leant forward and brushed his lips against Lea's. She lay down and pulled him on top of her while Saj got intensely aroused and yearned for her. He could smell her sweet perfume on her neck. Lea had her eyes shut as if she was burning with desire. Slowly he slipped his hand under her top and caressed her breasts.

Saj stood up and took off his clothes. Lea stared at his toned, powerful physique. Her dress got tangled with her earrings, while she tried to take it off. She wasn't accustomed to the Indian costume. Both giggled.

Lea had a perfect body, and Saj could only admire it. They lay down and rolled around on the bed, kissing passionately. His body tensed as he could feel the heat from her skin against his own.

Saj turned off the bedside lamp. A beam of light came through the window. He got on top of Lea and caressed and licked every part of her body. She moaned with pleasure and responded as blissfully. As Saj entered her, she cried in elation.

He thrust faster and faster. His heart pounded with the sensation of Lea's naked body pressed against his. She gasped and arched her back, as she neared her climax. His body began to shudder as there were cries of ecstasy.

Saj switched the lamp on and gazed into her beautiful eyes. Then stroked her hair and kissed her on the lip. They both smiled and were lost in the moment.

"What is it?" she asked as Saj kept looking at her.

"Nothing."

"Must be something."

"You are gorgeous," he said in a faint voice.

Lea smiled, blushed and kissed him. They wrapped their arms around each other and cuddled. Both stayed in bed for a while in silence as they gazed into each other eyes.

"Thank you," Lea said

"For what?"

"Everything."

Next day in the afternoon, Saj left Lea at the hotel and went home to his parents. Numerous wedding gifts were at the house to collect.

"Mama, I need to talk to you." He looked grim.

"What's the matter, son?" Rita asked.

"You know this country isn't easy to live in. Life is hard here."

"What do you mean?"

His father and Gita joined.

"Lea would find life too hard in Bombay," Saj said.

"I knew this would happen," his father said.

"So, you're going back and leave us again?" his mother said wiping her eyes.

"I'll be back soon. And you all can come and stay with us whenever you want." Saj said. "I'll still send you money."

"We'll miss you Saju," Gita said as she sobbed.

"You can come and visit us anytime. I can post tickets for you all."

"We understand she'll find it hard to live here. They are nice people. We can't keep you here against your wishes." his mother said with a deep sigh.

The doorbell rang. It was one of Saj's cousins.

After speaking to his parents, Saj felt relieved. He booked his flight back to England with Lea. Fortunately for him, as only a few seats were available on the same plane.

Saj needed to lift his spirits. He asked Lea whether they would like to go on a sightseeing tour of Bombay. They all jumped at the idea. He arranged a minibus and a guide from the hotel, and they drove to the marine drive overlooking the Arabian sea. The beach was beautiful, with clear blue water and golden sand, the waves rippling gently. They stayed there for an hour and had a long walk along the sand dunes. Moving on to the Hanging Gardens, the party had a brief stop at a Bollywood film set.

"Look, Lea. That is Sajan Khan." Saj's eyes gleamed as he pointed to a man stepping out of his flashy sports car. "He is a Bollywood superstar."

The actor was surrounded by his adoring fans asking for autographs, as he made his way through the crowd. Saj had always been fascinated with Bollywood movies.

They finally visited a temple. The architecture was smooth and perfect, and everyone was impressed.

After a long day, the party returned to the hotel and headed for the restaurant on the top floor.

The dreaded day came. Everyone was busy as they packed their bags and did last-minute shopping. At first, Saj wanted to go with his parents to the airport. Then he changed his mind. He couldn't bear to see them upset, so he went with Lea and her family.

During the drive, Saj was in a pensive mood. Others chatted about the events and their experiences.

"I want to come back again, and travel around the country," Toby said. The car sped among the chaotic traffic on the Bombay roads.

"I want to visit Taj Mahal next time," Lea said.

"Me too and Goa. I love the weather here, and the clothes are incredible," Nicole said.

"It was a great trip," Chris added.

"Jesus. Look at that bus. They are on the roof!" Toby pointed.

"This is quite common. People also travel on the roof of trains here."

There was a thud. The car veered to the left and then to the right, screeched and halted. Nicole and Margaret screamed as they were thrown from side to side. They all appeared shaken.

"What the hell happened?" Saj asked the driver.

"I must have hit a dog."

"Everyone's alright?" Saj turned around and asked. They were no seat belts.

The driver stopped the car. It was a stray dog which ran off.

A police officer pulled his motorbike in front of them. He came to the driver and with an air of arrogance said, "You were speeding."

"No. I was within the speed limit," he said looking down.

"Shut up and show me your driving licence."

The driver nervously searched his pockets and then glanced at Saj, who immediately knew he didn't have one.

"We're going to catch a flight to England, we're already delayed," Saj spoke in a soft voice to the police officer.

The policeman glared at Saj.

Saj dug into his pocket, got cash out and handed it to the officer. The man took it and counted the money.

"Don't break the law next time," he said and rode off.

Saj noticed the astounded expression on Lea and the others' faces.

He smiled and shrugged his shoulder. "This happens here all the time, money is king."

They arrived at the airport, well ahead of their departure time. It was crowded and noisy as usual. Saj looked around for his parents.

"Please wait here, I'll go and find them," Saj said to Lea.

Were they too annoyed and upset to come to the airport? He rushed around but couldn't find them. Then he heard someone call out his name. He turned around and spotted Gita.

"Sorry, we're late." Gita panted.

"Where are Mama and Baba."

"They're on their way,"

Saj had no idea what to say. He took them to where the others were seated. They had already checked their baggage at the BA desk, Saj queued up. It was time for them to go.

"Please take care of my son." Rita's voice quivered.

"Of course, I will. Please don't be concerned," Lea said.

His mother hugged Lea, they both shed a few tears.

"Don't worry Mama. I'll come back soon for a visit." Saj mopped his eyes.

He embraced his mother first, and then his father, without looking into their eyes. His father tried hard not to display too much emotion and said, "Look after yourself."

He hugged Gita, who was weeping. "I'll be back for your wedding."

"We'd better hurry; otherwise we may miss the flight," Nicole said.

They all shook hands. Chris thanked his parents for their hospitality. Saj held Lea's hand tight and walked briskly towards security. He didn't want to turn around and see his mother crying. He just couldn't face it.

Chapter 35

The BA 747 landed heavily at Heathrow at midday. Once outside the airport, Toby looked up at the sky. "Here we go."

"I can't believe it." Lea shook her head as she put her coat on.

Chris had booked an executive car to take them home. Saj didn't say much during the car journey, and everybody sensed the mix of happiness and sadness.

"I miss the warm sunny weather," Chris said to diffuse the atmosphere.

"Me too," said Nicole.

The party reached Lea's house. They were all exhausted. The arrangement was that Lea and Saj would live there until he found a job. When he went in, it felt strange. At no time had he dreamt he would be living with her parents. She took him upstairs. The upper floor was huge with numerous rooms. Lea's was large and superbly decorated, which showed her exquisite taste. Saj had never seen her room before. It had an enormous double bed, a small sitting area with a table and chairs and a large leather couch, computer, and television. There was an en-suite bathroom.

Saj put his luggage down and sat on the couch in a pensive mood. Lea went off to fetch tea.

"How are you?" she asked.

Saj held her hand and gestured for her to sit down next to him. Both gazed into each other's eyes, he kissed and hugged her.

Next morning, Saj decided he had to get on with his life. He was keen to move out of Lea's parents' house as soon as possible. He phoned his former consultants in the hospital. They were pleased with his return. No vacancies existed, but they were happy to give him a reference.

He searched online for medical posts. There were a few in medicine, but many available in casualty departments. These jobs seemed unpopular with English doctors. After compiling his CV, he applied for posts around the London area. He rang a few hospitals, one of them asked him to come for an interview. The vacancy was in accident and emergency, and they wanted someone to start soon.

Two days later Saj went for the interview. It was a massive hospital on the outskirts of London, an hour's drive from Lea's. They offered him the job. Saj was delighted. Not an ideal one, but at least a start for him.

Saj started his new post at Victoria General Hospital. He soon realised that he needed expertise in emergency medicine and would need to learn fast. The job was busier than he expected. Shifts were long with only a few days off, so Saj and Lea didn't see much of each other. He had to do nights, while Lea kept busy with her nurse practitioner day work.

One morning on a Saturday, both were off work which was a rare occurrence. They sat in the lounge.

"Mummy and Daddy want to arrange a reception for us next month. We can invite our friends and family. The venue is a Victorian manor house," Lea said.

"My parents can't attend at such short notice."

They would be out of place here, even if they came, Saj thought.

"Would you like to invite any of your friends."

"I'm not sure."

He thought about inviting Dipak. But he would be an embarrassment in front of Lea's family and friends. Especially after he had a few drinks. Better not.

Saj put on a navy suit, white shirt, and a striped red tie for the reception. Lea wore an ivory wedding dress. It was off the shoulder, and the skirt, enormous and puffy.

"You look beautiful," Saj admired Lea in her dress and kissed her.

"Thanks. You look handsome too."

They all sat in the limousine. The large manor house looked magnificent, with beautifully landscaped gardens. Saj had never been to a lavish party such as this before. He felt his stomach fluttery and his heart beating fast when he arrived at the reception. Most of the guests were the elites of society. Barristers, technocrats, investment bankers, business executives mingled. People looked glamorous in designer clothes.

"Try to relax. Most of these people are Mummy's friends. You know what type they are. Smile and don't say much,"

Lea whispered close to his ears. She held his hand tightly, as they mingled.

"I'll try my best." Saj faked a smile.

"Come on. I will introduce you to some of my friends," Lea said.

They walked to a couple of ladies who were chatting.

"This is Debbie…and Sophie."

"Nice to meet you both…I think I have seen you before." He looked towards one of the ladies.

"I work at the General Hospital. We must have come across each other there," Sophie said.

"Oh yes. I remember seeing you there," Saj said with a smile.

"Lea talked a lot about you. She told me..."

"Sophie!" Lea's cheeks turned pink. "Let's mingle Saj." She took him away by his arm.

"Great to meet you both. Sophie, you can tell me later what Lea has been telling you about me." Saj grinned as he was dragged away.

They spotted Margaret in a group of her friends and began making their way towards them. But stopped as the woman in a white hat spoke.

"How did you accept this Indian man, Maggie? I wouldn't allow my daughter."

"Well I tried to advise Lea, but it's her decision in the end which matters."

"How was Bombay? That place is supposed to be dirty, so much poverty," the second woman said.

"Have you been there?" asked Margaret.

"No, but people have told me. I wouldn't like to go there."

"Don't believe everything that you hear. People in Bombay are lovely and warm. If you'll excuse me." Margaret left.

"I read that child marriage is prevalent over in India. It involves underage women and children, many of whom are living in poverty," the first woman whispered.

"That's disgusting," the second woman said sipping her champagne. "I thought that was illegal and banned."

"The legal age of marriage for women is 18, but in some rural areas child marriage is still practised, even though this had been outlawed."

"How come you are so knowledgeable on these matters?"

"Ah. I have been doing my own research since Maggie told me of Leanne getting involved with that coloured man."

"They follow strange customs, don't they?"

"Yes, baby dropping is one of the most shocking and dangerous rituals. Small children are dropped from a temple roof with a crowd standing below to catch the baby. It is believed to bring good health and luck to the child and the family. Crazy."

"Jesus. That sounds barbaric."

"I don't think Leanne's marriage will work...They are different in culture, religion and background," the first woman said.

"True."

"That doctor has it all planned out. He'll benefit financially and gain recognition in society."

"And what about her children. They'll be half-caste."

"I think people should stick to their type."

Saj gritted his teeth and clenched his fist, as he listened to these women talk. How rude and racist, he thought. He could feel Lea stiffen beside him, as she steered him away from the gossips.

The reception buzzed as more guests arrived. A stage had been set up where a live band would play. The buffet was sumptuous, a full carvery with all the trimmings. People laughed and chatted, photographers and media guys took photos and video the event.

The wedding cake was huge. Three tiers on stilts, decorated with hand-crafted icing flowers, flowing down one side like a waterfall. It looked spectacular. Saj and Lea got up on the stage and performed the cake cutting. A big round of applause followed.

"Speech, speech," a few people shouted.

Lea glanced at Saj.

With shaking cold hands, he took the microphone. There was pin-drop silence. Guests were eager to listen to what he had to say. Saj held his breath, his heart beating fast. He stood frozen for a few moments and stared at the crowd.

Clearing his throat, he gazed at Lea for moral support. Then took a deep breath.

"Erm...Lea and I would like to thank you all for coming today." His voice was shaky to start with. "As you will appreciate, this occasion is different from a traditional wedding."

Saj paused and gathered his thoughts. He turned towards Lea's family. "We would like to thank Margaret and Christopher for this reception. Thanks for letting me marry your gorgeous daughter. And for your effort to travel to Bombay. I hope you all had a good time.

"Unfortunately, my parents couldn't come, but they send their best wishes." His lower lip quivered as he remembered them. "I'm sure, it will be a fantastic night. There is live music followed by a disco. Please help yourself to the buffet and the drinks too."

The applause quietened down.

"Please excuse me. I wanted to say something to the two ladies in that corner." Saj pointed at them, so all the guests looked their way. There was a total hush. Lea seemed surprised as to what he intended to say.

"Yes. Those ladies are right. I might not be from a wealthy family. But I'm a professional doctor, and my career has started to prosper. I've great expectations for myself and Lea...So, for the information of the ladies there." He stared at the group of Margaret's friends. "The only reason I married Lea is that I love her."

"Both of us had to struggle and face numerous challenges to be together...I don't want any favours from anyone...yes, I'm from a different background, so what? We're all God's creation...all you need is love...and as far as our likely

children are concerned... that's none of your damn business."
Saj glared at those women. "Thank you all for being so
patient."

The guests were dumbfounded, but everyone cheered and
applauded. Most people stared at those ladies. They
attempted desperately to hide behind others to avoid
humiliation. Murmurs echoed all around the hall.

Saj had surprised himself by speaking out. He hoped he
had done the right thing and not offended any of the other
guests.

Lea looked at him with a twinkle in her eyes, smiled and
kissed him. "I'm so proud of you Saj. You took a stand for
us," she whispered and clutched his hand.

He smiled back and held her hand tight.

When they came down from the stage, many people came
to Saj. They shook hands and congratulated him.

"That was a superb speech," one man said.

"Thank you."

Toby came around. "Bravo. Well done. She is a right old
cow."

Saj and Lea mingled with the guests. Margaret came up to
them.

"I'm so sorry. You overheard those ladies' conversation.
That was Lady Annabel. She is the most significant donor to
our charity. I tried not to antagonise her, but I should have
spoken out. I feel terrible." Margaret looked away.

"We understand Mummy."

"I apologise being blunt to your friends. It worried me you might be offended, I needed to say all that," Saj said.

"No. I'm happy you did. I am not concerned if she pulls out. It was brave of you Saj." Margaret kissed him on the cheek.

"Thank you." He said, quite taken aback.

The lights were dimmed, and an extravagant disco with a fantastic light show commenced. Saj and Lea enjoyed the music.

Later, he approached the DJ and requested to play 'The Way You Make Me Feel.' As the song came on, he took Lea by her hand and lead her to the dance floor. He played his other request, "Angel". Saj loved that song. Gazing into Lea's beautiful eyes, he wrapped his arms around. Both were lost in the moment. Saj forgot all the challenges and hardships he faced, just to be her.

Chapter 36

One day Saj decided to phone his friend Dipak. They met up at the social club that evening. It brought back a lot of old memories for him.

"How are you Dipak? I am sorry I lost touch. So much has happened since we last met."

"I thought of you many times, my friend," Dipak said.

Saj told him about Lea and his parents' initial refusal to accept her. Their marriage in Bombay, and then leaving his family to return to England.

"I can see you have been through a lot of shit, man. I am excited to meet Lea."

"I'm sorry you couldn't come to the wedding. It was a fantastic day."

"You haven't told me how you have been?" Saj asked.

"Not too good."

"What happened?"

"Well, my girlfriend finally dumped me, I'm on an anti-depressant, and in debt. Otherwise, life is excellent." He had a sarcastic laugh and swigged his wine.

"Sorry to hear that. You'll be fine. I'll lend you money? How much do you need?"

"No, I can't take cash off you," Dipak said.

"What are friends for, and you are like a brother to me."

"No."

"I insist." Saj took out his chequebook from his jacket pocket. He wrote a cheque and handed it to him.

"Thanks. I'll return it as soon as I can."

"This is the least I can do for you, my friend."

"You've done well Saj. I am proud of you. How you grew in confidence over the years. You stick up for yourself."

"I had no choice. I am grateful for all your help. One day you will find a nice woman and settle down. Lea is lovely, I am fortunate to have her."

"She is lucky to have you as well. I can't wait to meet her." Dipak gulped his wine.

"I'll invite you for dinner one day. Lea will love to meet you too."

"Remember, we talked about arranged marriages a while ago. Not in my wildest dreams did I think that you would rebel against our society. Good for you."

"Thanks."

"I am so pleased for you."

"Listen Dipak. I need to go. Life changes once you're married." He grinned putting his glass down.

Saj put his jacket on and gave Dipak a hug. "You'll be alright. Call me anytime you want to chat. We should get together soon."

Lea came to their room as Saj was watching cricket on television that evening. Her parents had gone out to a dinner party. He handed her an envelope.

"What's this?" Lea sat next to him.

"Please give this to your mother and ask her if this is enough."

Lea opened it. "Don't be silly. Mummy won't take it." She tried to give the cash back to him.

"No. I insist. I want to pay for our keep. This will be temporary until we find our own place. It will get better, I promise."

Saj held Lea in his arms.

"Don't worry. It will be alright," Lea said.

"I have thought about training in surgery. There are more jobs and career prospects. What do you say?"

"Would it be hard?"

"It won't be easy. I have to sit for a specialist surgical exam. I will need to spend more time with books as I did before."

"But we already don't see much of each other."

"It will be tough for a short while, Lea. In my current job, there are no career prospects. If you don't want me to do surgery I won't."

"You do what you think is best for us." She kissed him on the cheek.

"Tomorrow night, we'll go out for dinner at the Nawab restaurant. Then go to the cinema."

"A Bollywood film?"

"No, an English. You've seen enough of Bollywood dramas for real by now," he said and laughed. "I am going to phone home."

"I'll leave you alone." She left the room.

He called and talked to his mother.

"We all miss you a lot. The house is so quiet without you." She sounded upset.

"I'll visit Bombay when I get my holiday."

"Do you plan to have kids soon?"

"Mama! Give us time. I am in a new job. We'll think about it one day."

"Don't leave it too late. Otherwise, it gets harder. I assume you would like to have a few."

To have children soon after marriage was part of the Indian culture and tradition. People start to gossip about the couple in case they decide not to.

Saj shook his head. "I must go now. I'll phone you again."

Lea returned to the room with a pot of tea.

"How are things at home?" she asked.

"Erm...okay. The family miss me."

Lea hugged him. "This is my fault."

"No, it was my decision in the end." Saj kissed her.

"Your parents love each other, don't they?" Lea said.

"They argue a lot though," Saj replied.

"At least it is not like in the west. The divorce rate is going up at a rapid pace in our society."

"If the divorce wasn't frowned upon in our culture, I'm not sure they would have lasted this long."

"Here nobody cares."

"Unfortunately, in my country, most women feel they have no choice but to accept the harsh realities. Even if they are not happy in their marriage."

After his shift ended, Saj would go to the library and revise for his exams. He travelled all over the country to attend courses for his speciality exam. He was determined to pass the first time.

Because of his hectic schedule, Saj spent even less time with Lea. He tried his best not to take his work home but found it difficult. The travel time to the hospital also added a couple of hours a day. By the time he got home, he was exhausted.

On a rare day off, they went into the town. He never enjoyed shopping but knew Lea loved it. They could spend time together. She bought a few clothes for herself and a shirt for Saj.

After they had finished, they went to a cafe. Lea ordered a cappuccino and Saj had his usual tea.

"You should try this, it's nice." Lea took a sip of coffee.

"I like my tea. It becomes a habit," Saj said smiling.

"Oh, I remembered. Mummy asked me if we want money for the house?"

"Please thank your mother, it's generous of her, I prefer not to borrow."

"But we can give it back to her later?"

Saj was in no mood to borrow money from Lea's parents for the house. It went against his principles. He wished to rely on himself.

"We could rent a place near my hospital. You may have to commute further to work," Saj said.

"I don't mind if we can spend more time together."

"And we'll have more privacy." He smirked.

They found an ideal apartment, not far from his hospital. The surroundings were beautiful countryside, and the location was close to the town. It was situated on the first floor and had three bedrooms. Two of them good sized, one small. Saj was determined to further his career in surgery. He studied hard, it was a challenging exam, so he had to be well prepared.

One evening, Saj and Lea were decorating the sitting room in their new apartment. He had never done any painting work before. In Bombay, it was cheap to hire decorators to do the job.

"Do you like this place, Lea? I know this is a come down from your house." He put the paintbrush down.

"Yes, I do but..."

"What?"

"You're always busy nowadays, I hardly spend any time with you."

"Competing with English doctors isn't easy. I need to work harder. You knew when you married me."

"I know," she said in a soft voice. "I thought we'd have more time though. Now that you're only half an hour from the hospital."

Saj held Lea in his arms, gazed into her eyes and stroked her face. "I'll try my best. Ah...I thought, how about we start a family?" He remembered the conversation with his mother.

"What. Now. But what about my job?" Lea asked.

"You can take time off. I'll look after you."

He suddenly went quiet.

"What's the matter?" she asked.

"I wonder what our children would look like?" Saj appeared pensive.

"What do you mean?"

"Will they be like you, me or...different?"

"Ah, you mean half-caste, so what? They'll be beautiful, with gorgeous colours," she said.

"How would people view our kids. Would they have trouble at school?"

"Don't worry."

"The culture and religion will be confusing for them. How will we bring the children up?"

"We'll think about it when the time comes. Anyway, there are other couples like us. Do you remember Dr Pal who worked at your old hospital? His wife was white, and they had children. We can't be too concerned about the future."

"You are right." Saj looked into her eyes and grinned. "Well...why don't we make a start now?"

"What about the decorating?"

"That can wait." His eyes sparkled.

Lea playfully flicked the paint on Saj.

"I'll get you back for this."

Saj removed his apron and grabbed Lea by her waist. He kissed her on the lips and neck and was intensely aroused. She undressed him, while he took her top off and caressed her. They lay down on the couch, his hand exploring her whole body. She groaned.

Lea pulled Saj on top of her, and as he entered her, she cried in ecstasy. They rubbed against each other bodies, and he thrust faster. She moaned with pleasure as she climaxed. A couple of minutes later he did. Both gazed into each other's eyes, smiled, and kissed.

A week later, he was surprised to receive a cheque from Dipak. This was for the money he had lent him. Dipak must be back to his usual self, he thought. Saj had promised to invite him for dinner and Lea could meet him. It would be good fun.

"Could I speak to Dr Dipak please." He was called by his first name by everyone in the hospital.

There was a moment of silence at the other end.

"Hello."

"I'll put you through to Nick. Wait a moment Dr Saj." The operator said. She recognised his voice.

"But I want..." Saj was puzzled. He didn't want Nick, he wanted Dipak.

A minute later Nick came on the phone.

"Hey, Saj." He sounded grim.

"Hi, Nick. What's up? Where is Dipak? Is he on holiday? I think he needed one."

Nick kept quiet for a moment. Then he said, "You haven't heard the news?"

"What news? I've been busy with work and exams. Not much contact with the outside world."

He hesitated. "About...Dipak."

"No. What about Dipak. Has he quit his job. Has he gone back to India? Come on Nick. You got me worried."

There was another pause. "Dipak...passed away," Nick said in a faint voice.

"What? Is this a joke? It can't be. I met him at the social club a few weeks ago. He was fine, and we had a laugh. I meant to invite him to dinner to meet Lea?" He trembled.

Saj sat with his head in his hands. He loved Dipak. What would he have done without his help, when he first came to England?

"I'm sorry Saj...I know you two were close."

Saj rubbed his forehead.

"How did it happen?" his voice quivered as tears rolled down his cheeks.

"A nurse found his body in the theatre...He committed suicide."

"Oh, my God," Saj said in a quiet voice and put the phone down.

Wiping away his tears, Saj opened a can of lager and slumped on the couch in a daze. He sat motionless contemplating. He gasped for air feeling dizzy and took a sip of his drink.

Was Dipak really dead? During their last time together, he seemed depressed but never thought he would kill himself. How could he take such an extreme step? Why didn't he spend more time with Dipak? He could have helped him. How would he have managed without Dipak?

Back in his college in Bombay, Dipak had always looked out for him. He was like the older brother Saj didn't have. Whenever Saj was short of money which he often was, Dipak would give him some, and he never asked for it back. He remembered a couple of boys were bullying him in college. Once they cornered Saj and threw a few punches at him. Dipak intervened, and the boys let him go. Since that incident, Saj decided that he needed to defend himself and took up martial arts. He remembered once they argued over a trivial matter and fell out. They didn't speak for a week, but finally, Dipak broke the ice.

Saj reminisced his friendship with Dipak. How he panicked when Dipak was nowhere to be seen at Heathrow when he first arrived. His first trip to London and the pub brawl. The Diwali function and Dipak's silliness and his funny dance brought a smile to his face for a second. He chuckled at the memory and then shed a few more tears.

On the outside, Dipak had appeared confident and sometimes arrogant. But in fact, he was despondent and lonely with a heart of gold. Why didn't he recognise Dipak's depression was severe? Maybe because he was fighting his own battle to be with Lea

Chapter 37

It was a rare day off for Saj. He wanted to make the most of that evening with Lea. A couple of weeks had passed since Dipak had died.

"I would have loved to meet Dipak. It's so sad," Lea said.

"If you don't mind, I would prefer not to talk about it," he said putting the pot on the cooker.

"But you need to Saj. It's good for you."

"I know, but we all handle situations differently."

"Will you talk to me if needed?"

"I will, promise." He smiled and kissed her.

"What are you cooking?"

"Chicken curry. I'll show you how to make it," he said pouring the vegetable oil into the pot.

"This will be interesting." Lea gazed at him and grinned.

"My cooking is pretty basic spicy food. Nothing fancy." He laughed.

"Look out! The pot is too hot. It's smoking." She turned down the hob. "What next?"

Saj pulled out a chopping board and got hold of a knife. "You chop an onion, a piece of ginger and garlic." He wiped his eyes. The odour of onion was too much for him.

"This is strong stuff," Lea moved away.

He put the onions in the hot pan, and as he did that, a few droplets of hot oil splashed, making him jump.

Lea giggled.

"Don't worry. Everything is under control," Saj said and chuckled. "Fry the onions and then add the spices." He took a couple of jars of spices out of the cupboard. "Coriander, cumin, turmeric and chilli powders and keep stirring."

"And some salt."

"Yeah." He opened the fridge and got fresh pieces of chicken out. "Then you put the chicken in and fry until it goes brown." Saj kept stirring the pot.

"Wow. It already smells nice." Lea leaned forward and kissed Saj on the cheek.

The phone rang.

"Yes, Mummy I'm fine." Lea sat on the couch. "Okay, I'll ask him. Bye."

"What did she have to say?" Saj said as he chopped tomatoes.

"She wondered if we wanted to go swimming with her."

"Haha. I never told you," he said without looking at Lea as he focussed on frying the chicken.

"What?"

"That I can't swim. It can be embarrassing to admit that. Back in Bombay, most of us don't learn to swim. It's not like over here."

"Why?"

"Swimming is a luxury. There are only a few private pools which are reserved for the elites of society. The majority can't afford to take lessons. It's too dangerous for kids to learn in the sea."

"That's sad. Here most kids learn when they are young."

"It's a matter of priority in our society. And by the time we are grown up, we must think about food and shelter. You've got it easy here."

"But you can learn. Maybe book a few lessons."

"Yes, I've thought about it."

"We can go swimming together."

"It will be fun. Maybe you can teach me, and if I am drowning, you could give me a kiss of life."

Lea laughed. "I think a professional instructor would be better."

"Come and see the dinner. We are more than halfway through the curry. I have put tomatoes, fresh green chillies and coriander and fried it."

"It smells yummy." Lea came from behind and wrapped her arms around Saj's waist as he continued to stir the curry.

He smiled and kissed her.

"Then cover the meat with water and let it simmer for half an hour. It's all done."

"It's not too complicated." Lea poured two glasses of wine and handed one to Saj. They sat close to each other on the couch.

"Are you up for tennis tomorrow?" Lea asked.

"Yeah."

"How did you learn to cook?"

"It's my mother's recipe. I used to watch her. She is an excellent cook."

"I will try to cook it one day. Not sure it will turn out as nice as yours." She smiled.

"You'll be better than me one day, an expert chef."

He gently stroked her hair, leaned towards her and they smooched.

"I love you, Dr Saj," Lea said in a quiet voice.

"Love you too Mrs Saj," he said gazing at her.

They put their glasses on the table, laid on the couch caressing and snuggling. Saj began to unbutton her blouse.

"What about the cooking?" Lea giggled. He didn't stop.

"That can wait," he whispered in her ear.

"What's the problem. You're quiet?" Saj asked as they ate their evening meal, several months later.

"Nothing." Lea looked away.

"Come on. What is it?"

"We've tried, nothing has happened. I'm worried Saj."

"Don't worry, be patient. We'll have children when the time is right. It will happen."

"You don't think we need to get it checked?"

"No. I promise it will be fine." He held Lea's hand.

One morning a week later, there was a significant motorway accident. Many injured people were brought to casualty in critical condition. The hospital was on red alert.

Saj was in the doctors' office for a short break. He had been on his feet all morning.

A nurse came in. "Doctor, there is a call from your wife at the reception."

Saj got up quickly.

"How are you. Is everything alright?"

"I'm fine. Sorry to phone you at work. I couldn't wait until tomorrow." Lea sounded excited.

"Why. What's up?"

"I'm pregnant."

"Fantastic news."

"I know you're busy. I heard about the traffic accident on the radio. See you. Love you," Lea said.

"Love you too," he replied.

Saj had a grin on his face when he returned to the office. But how would his children be treated in society in England? Are they going to bring them up as an Indian or English? He couldn't help wondering.

"Doctor…Mr Roberts. His heart rate is fast," a nurse interrupted his chain of thought. He rushed to check on the patient.

Saj hugged and kissed Lea when he got back home.

"These are for you." He handed her a big bouquet of red roses.

"Oh. These are beautiful, thank you." She kissed him.

He then phoned his parents to give them the good news. They were thrilled.

"We'll pray it's a boy," his mother said, sounding excited.

"It doesn't matter to us, as long as it's healthy."

"Still we hope for a boy,"

"Mama. I need to go."

After the phone call, Lea asked, "Why do your parents want a boy?"

Saj shook his head and grinned. "Because of our culture. Men are the breadwinners. Daughters cost much more to the parents," he said as he ate Bombay mix.

"In your culture, girls are not very well accepted?"

"It's silly, but women are considered a burden in society there, because of the pressure of dowry. And that they might not be pretty or fair enough to be married."

"That's shocking." Lea gasped.

"Sometimes preference for a male child can be so extreme by the family that female infants might be killed," he said. "They may be set afloat in the river or buried alive."

"Jesus!" Lea stared wide-eyed, her hand over her mouth.

"Boys, on the contrary, are the torch-bearers of the family. They carry forward the name and bring dowry. I don't mind either way." He smiled and kissed Lea, as she sat next to him.

"It must be difficult for parents to spend a fortune if they have many daughters," Lea asked.

"My parents are traditional. People give more importance to their society and what they think. These ideas have changed in the last few decades," he said. "Now love marriages are more acceptable. Marriage is a sacred thing. Living together is still an insult to the family."

Chapter 38

It was May 20, 1995. Saj had taken a couple of weeks off. He felt edgy in the hospital and wished his mother was there to support. At two-thirty in the morning, Lea gave birth to a baby girl. Saj held her hand during the delivery. It was all a new experience for him.

Soon after, the doctor looked worried. "Call the intensive care unit." The nurse carried the baby next door in a hurry.

"What's happening?" Saj shouted at the doctor, as their child was whisked away.

"Please stay here with your wife. I'll inform you in a minute."

"Good God. What happened?" Lea began to cry. Saj still held her hand for several moments but could wait no more and rushed next door to investigate.

"What's the problem?" he asked.

"We need to move her to intensive care for observations. She stopped breathing for a moment. I'll let you know soon." The doctor and the nurse left the room, with the baby on a trolley.

Saj seemed frozen to the spot. Lea didn't have any problems during her pregnancy or labour, he thought. At no time had he contemplated that anything could go wrong. Wiping his eyes, Saj slowly walked back to Lea. He knew that he needed to be strong for her.

"What's the matter with my baby?" Lea said and wept.

"Don't worry." He held her hand tightly. "They have taken her for observation. Her breathing was erratic, but she should be okay." Saj faked a smile.

"Look at me Saj. Please tell me the truth."

"I don't know. Honest. That's all the doctor said to me. I'll go and find out. The nurse will be with you."

They had already taken the baby to intensive care. Saj dashed towards the third floor where the unit was. He saw a couple of doctors with their baby, in a side room. The nurse stopped him from proceeding further.

"Please wait here. I'll call the doctor as soon as he's free," she said.

Saj paced up and down the corridor and kept an eye on his watch. It had been half an hour, still no news. He asked the nurse again who went inside and spoke to the doctor. Ten minutes later one of them came out. Saj knew him from his former hospital.

"Hi, Saj. I didn't know it was you. We still don't know what the problem is. She stopped breathing, but it's better now. Her heartbeat is irregular, we'll have to keep her here. The next twenty-four hours are crucial."

"Will she be alright?" he said in a shaky voice.

"We'll do our best. I'll keep you updated. Sorry. I need to go back in." He tapped Saj's shoulder and left.

"Thanks, David," he mumbled.

Saj walked down the stairs to the maternity unit. "Sorry I've been so long." He told Lea what the doctors had said. She sobbed. He felt helpless but gave all his attention to her.

Desperate to see the baby, Saj took Lea to intensive care. The child appeared to be motionless in the cot. She had many tubes and drips connected to her.

Lea mopped her tears. "She is beautiful."

Saj embraced her. "Everything will be all right. She is lovely, like her mother."

"Can I talk to the doctors?" Lea asked the nurse.

"They're busy. If you wait downstairs, I'll let you know as soon as someone is free. It might be a couple of hours," the nurse replied.

Lea went back to the ward for a shower. Saj phoned her family to come in to support her. He hung around hoping to get any information as early as possible.

He hadn't eaten all day. The staff in the unit offered him a sandwich. He sat in the doctors' room on his own, when David walked in.

"Great news Saj. The baby will be alright. We'll transfer her to the ward tonight."

Saj embraced David and cried. "Thank you. Thank you."

"You go and celebrate with your wife."

He wiped his eyes and sprinted downstairs as fast as he could. Lea was sitting in a side room with her parents. Everyone stared at him when he walked in.

He looked at Lea and beamed. "She'll be fine."

Saj stroked her hand and kissed her. Lea shed a few more tears, but they were of joy. The whole family relaxed and smiled broadly.

A couple of hours later, the nurse brought the baby and handed her to Lea. Her complexion was darker, more like Saj, with black hair and brown eyes. She took the baby in her arms.

"She is perfect. What should we call her?" Saj asked.

"You pick a name," Lea said.

He thought for a moment. "How about Nesha?"

"Sounds nice."

"You like it?"

"Yeah."

Saj phoned his parents. His father answered.

"We have a little daughter. You are a grandfather now."

"Marvellous news. I wish it were a boy, but it doesn't matter. Here... talk to your mother."

"We're so happy. You two should keep on. I'm sure it will be a boy next time," she said.

Saj was miffed at his parents. The baby almost died, and all they wanted was a boy!

They took Nesha to her new home and her newly decorated room. Her arrival would change their lives even more than they had anticipated.

Nesha cried a lot at night, and it took its toll on Lea. She appeared exhausted from lack of sleep. On occasion, she was irritable and tearful. Saj tried to help with the housework which was a learning curve for him as well.

One day Saj was playing with Nesha.

"She is beautiful, like her mother," he said.

Lea sat on the couch ready to doze off. She could still afford a smile. "I don't feel beautiful now though."

"It will get easier I promise. Do you want me to do anything else?" Saj asked.

"The flat needs to be tidied."

"I'll hoover around, and then cook a lovely dinner for you."

After cleaning the flat, he gazed at Nesha with love and smiled. Whenever he was home, he spent a lot of time playing with her.

A couple of months passed. One afternoon they were all sitting in the lounge.

"Look, Lea. She smiled, isn't she gorgeous," Saj said with pride. He picked Nesha up from her playpen and kissed her.

"Mummy will be here tomorrow to help out."

"She only comes when I'm on call." He laughed and embraced Lea. "I'm only joking."

Next morning at work, Saj thought about Lea and was worried. He phoned her.

"How are you?"

"Exhausted. Nesha woke me up five times last night."

"Listen, I will ask the hospital if I can take the afternoon off. I can do the housework so you can rest."

"Thanks. That will be nice."

"I love you, Lea."

"Love you too," and she burst into tears.

Chapter 39

Lea's maternity leave sped past. Saj's parents still hadn't seen their granddaughter. She suggested that they come and stay.

"Why don't you visit us?" He phoned his parents. Before they could make any excuse, he said, "I'll send you money for the flight. We have plenty of room."

His parents were thrilled and planned to visit in the next couple of months. Gita wouldn't come because her exams were due.

Saj took the day off to go to Heathrow Airport. Lea was keen to accompany him and asked one of her friends to take care of Nesha. Both waited in anticipation in the arrival area. Saj scrutinised the passengers as they came through the door. There were people from different nationalities, all excited to arrive in England. Once upon a time, he was one of them. How everything had changed for him, he thought.

"There they are," Saj called out. His father pushed the luggage trolley looking bewildered, with his mother ambling behind him wearily. It reminded Saj of the first time he arrived in England.

He couldn't believe how they were dressed. Both wore their own traditional attire. His mother a saree and a blouse, his father a loose long shirt and pyjama like trousers. It embarrassed him.

Saj went forward to greet them and touched their feet. They appeared relieved to see him. His parents said hello to Lea with a big smile and his mother hugged and kissed her on the cheek. Then she embraced Saj. He got hold of their luggage, and they all headed for home.

"Where's Nesha?" his mother asked as they entered the flat.

Lea took them to her room. "She's beautiful," his mother said with a smile holding the baby in her arms.

"This is a lovely place." His father looked around.

"We have decorated this ourselves," Lea said with pride.

"I am surprised Saj does painting work. At home, he did nothing of that sort. We hire people there to do the job," his father said.

"And cleaning and washing sometimes," Saj said grinning. "Men don't do housework in Bombay."

"You have lost weight and look tired. You need to eat well and put on weight," the mother said to Lea.

"The baby keeps me up. "

They all sat in the lounge, Lea served tea. She had made a special effort and bought biscuits, Bombay mix and samosas, ready for their arrival.

"Lea was impressed by the snacks served in Bombay." Saj chuckled pointing towards the tray.

His parents enjoyed the food, they were hungry. They had a lot to talk about.

"The flight tickets were expensive, but your uncle Sina got us a discount," his father said.

"Gita met a boy. She likes him. He has a good job and earns well. His sister studies with Gita at the University," his mother said. "We have seen him, they are a well-respected family."

"If Gita is keen on him," said Saj.

At least they didn't insist on an arranged marriage for Gita, he thought. He was pleased with this transformation in their attitude.

"All our family and friends send their love to you. Ruma is married, she is happy."

"Oh, right," said Saj. "That's wonderful."

He told his parents about his job and his decision to change his speciality.

"Tomorrow after you have rested, we'll go to the shops and buy you some western clothes," he said to his father.

"Sorry, we don't have curry for dinner, but we got fish and chips. All homemade. I hope you enjoy the food," Lea said.

"I'm sure it will be delicious," his mother said.

His parents went to their room to unpack.

"Who is Ruma? Is she one of your old birds back in Bombay?" Lea said as she prepared the meal in the kitchen.

"You are so nosey. No, Ruma is one of my cousins. And yes, she liked me, but nothing happened...it's a long story. You are the only one for me." Saj wrapped his arm around Lea from behind and kissed her.

They all sat at the table for dinner. His parents picked up the spoon to eat the fish because they had never used a knife and fork. As they struggled clumsily, soon they gave up and used their hands. His mother glanced at Saj for reassurance. He nodded and smiled.

"This has a nice flavour," his father said.

"It is," his mother nodded, taking a bite of the fish.

"I'm pleased you like it," said Lea. "But it has no spices."

"Still, delicious," his mother said. "I am Rita, and he is Jaru."

Lea now worked part-time at the doctors' surgery, so she had more time to spend with his parents than Saj. After a couple of days off, he had to go back to work. Rita was outgoing, and always had a smile on her face. She was more relaxed and cheerful than when Lea saw her in Bombay.

His father appeared stern but was gentle. They said their prayers in their room every morning. Jaru didn't demonstrate any affection towards his wife, but Lea noticed the special soft way he looked at her.

Lea cooked a variety of food for them. To her surprise, they enjoyed her meals. They loved the fish and chips even though sometimes she got it from the chip shop. His parents also found her roast dinner delicious. Rita taught her how to cook curries and daal and gave her a few recipes.

They went shopping on a few occasions. Rita was delighted with the unique experience of an all-women trip.

One morning Lea was at home with his parents. Both looked bored watching TV.

His father Jaru heard this beeping sound coming from outside. He was curious.

"What's that noise?" he asked Lea.

"The rubbish collection vehicle. These men come every week."

Standing near the window, he watched the lorry and the garbage being taken away.

"Rita. Come and see. Everything is so organised here."

She got up and walked to the window. "I wish we could do the same in Bombay," she said.

"People throw rubbish in front of their houses and shops. We need to change," Jaru said.

"Shall we all go into town?" Lea asked.

"Yes." Rita smiled.

As they all sat in the car, Lea helped them put their seat belts on. They never used them back in Bombay.

"I am impressed by the roads. They're so clean." Jaru sat on the front passenger seat, as Lea drove.

"People drive with patience here," Rita said, she sat next to Nesha in the back.

"And nobody is honking, so peaceful," Jaru said.

They reached a set of traffic lights on a small road. It was red, so Lea waited.

"You can go now. There's no one coming." Jaru waved his arm.

"No, I can't. It' still red." Lea grinned, she found it funny.

"In Bombay, we'll go."

Lea parked on the roadside in town. The sun was shining, but a chilly breeze was blowing. Jaru saw the sunshine, he left his coat in the car and got out. After he had walked a few steps, he realised how cold it was, even with the sun out.

"I think I'll get my coat," he said as he went back to the car.

Lea chuckled. Both Rita and Jaru were captivated by the high street shops. They stood outside a clothes shop. A young lady dressed in a short tight skirt with beautifully toned legs walked past. That drew Jaru's attention, and he stared at her.

Rita nudged him, annoyed.

"What? I was only curious...she must be so cold."

Lea overheard them and grinned.

"Can we have chips?" Rita asked Lea like a child.

"If you want. There's a shop there." They walked to the shop.

Rita was confused and looked at Lea.

"Do you want chips?" she drew her attention to the food counter.

"No. Potato chips...in a packet."

"Ah, you mean crisps." Lea laughed. She remembered Saj telling her the difference between chips and crisps, like in the USA. It had confused Saj when he came to England for the first time as they didn't eat many chips back in Bombay.

Chapter 40

That night, Lea was fast asleep. A groaning noise from next door woke her up. She glanced at the clock with squinted eyes, two in the morning. At first, she thought it must be a nightmare, then heard it again. Jumping out of bed, she dashed to their room. Saj was away on night duty.

Rita appeared in agony, pale and sweaty and had been sick. She pointed to her tummy to show where the pain was. Jaru stood frozen.

"You should have woken me up," Lea said to him as she checked her pulse. It was fast and weak.

"I didn't want to disturb you," he said.

Lea thought about ringing Saj, then changed her mind. He wouldn't be able to do much over the phone. Without wasting any more time, she called 999 and then sat next to Rita and held her hand.

"It might have been anything you ate. Has she ever had this pain before?" Lea asked Jaru.

"No... No, she never had pain like this."

"The ambulance will be here any minute. I wish Saj were here."

They could hear the siren.

"I'll go with Rita to the hospital," she said to Jaru. "Could you please keep an eye on Nesha. She should be fast asleep. I'll give you my mobile number."

Lea wrote the number down on a piece of paper and handed it to him.

The doorbell rang. It was the paramedics. They came in and examined Rita and gave her a painkilling injection. She was taken away on a trolley.

The ambulance sped along the road with its siren blaring. Lea sat next to Rita, holding her hand. Rita was still in distress. After a quarter of an hour's drive, they reached Casualty. This hospital was closer to where they lived. It was smaller, but they kept the emergency department open. There were plans to close it down and direct all patients to the district hospital where Saj worked.

The paramedics took Rita in on a trolley and left her in a patient bay. They gave all the details over to the nurse in charge. Several patients already waited to be seen.

"How do you feel?" Lea asked Rita.

"Ah...Not so good. It still hurts, I want to be sick."

"The doctor will be here soon." Lea took a deep breath. She reminded herself of her nursing experience with patients, but this was different, she thought.

A nurse came in, asked a few questions and took her observations. They waited for the doctor. Half an hour passed, there was still no sign of him. Lea thought she should let Saj know about his mother. As she dialled, she saw someone hurry past. She rushed out of the bay.

"Saj?" She called the doctor who had walked past. He turned around, and so did other patients waiting there.

"Lea. What are you doing here?" He stared at her.

"Why are you working in this place?"

"They were short of doctors here. What happened? Is Nesha alright?"

"Your mother. She isn't well." Lea took him to the bay.

"What happened Mama?"

"It hurts here." She put her right hand on her tummy.

Saj pressed her stomach and checked her observations. He suggested a few tests and talked to the nurse. They found an empty bed, and she was transferred to the ward. The doctor gave her another injection, the pain slowly improved.

Lea rang home to check on Nesha, but the phone kept ringing. She was concerned and redialled the number. After a long wait, Jaru answered.

"Is everything alright? You didn't respond," she asked.

"I'm sorry...Yes, she is asleep," he stuttered.

"Rita will be okay. I will come and tell you more."

Lea got a taxi home. Saj meant to finish his shift soon. Daylight was breaking when she arrived. After attending to Nesha, she phoned a friend, who came to stay with the baby. After a quick cup of coffee, Lea headed straight back to the hospital. She knew Rita was petrified being on her own in an alien surrounding.

Rita had x-rays and blood tests later in the morning. Saj went around seeing other patients while Lea stayed by her side.

"Thank you," Rita said as she looked fondly at Lea.

"For what?"

"For looking after me. I couldn't have wished for a nicer daughter-in-law," Rita said. "We all have pre-conceived ideas about other races. We feel safe with our own people. There are good and bad individuals in every race. Some of us think we're better than others. I now understand it's not right. We are all the same...different colours, but the same heart beats inside."

"I know." Lea squeezed her hand and returned the gaze with affection.

"We wanted Saj to marry someone like us...but we were wrong."

"My mother was the same."

Rita paused, looked at Lea and said, "You'll take care of Saj. You won't hurt him. He's my only son. We love him so much." Tears shimmered in her eyes.

"I love him. I'll always take care of him, please don't worry."

Rita sat up and embraced Lea. A few minutes later Saj walked into the ward.

"Excellent news. All the tests are negative. You must have been allergic to something you ate. You can go home soon." Everyone was delighted.

"I'm off now. Heidi is looking after Nesha, and I must let her go." Lea kissed Saj, hugged Rita and left.

Saj came back towards the end of his shift.

"How are you feeling Mama?" Saj asked.

"Much better now. Listen. I wanted to talk to you. Can you pull up a chair and sit down?"

"Sure." He sat next to his mother.

"We always want what's right for you. I know your father has been hard on you at times. When you were a child, he wanted you to do better in life than he did. Your father used to say, one day my son will be a top doctor." She wiped her eyes. "Your Baba was too strict, and we argued about it. He didn't mean it. He loves you, though has a funny way to show it."

"I know."

"We made sacrifices, so you could get the best education. We were unaware of your wishes. You never expressed your feelings since you were a kid."

"I should have spoken out."

"Lea's a lovely girl, and we're so pleased you married her. We are so proud of you both."

"Oh, Mama. I felt so despondent to leave you all." Saj held her hand.

"Both of us are sorry if we hurt you anytime. We always thought we are right as parents, but we were not. You have done so well." Her eyes glistened.

"No point to dwell on the past."

A nurse came in. "Sorry to interrupt Dr Saj. Mr Wiley is not well."

"Mama, I have to go."

A couple of weeks later, Saj had a weekend off work. They all went on a sightseeing tour of London. Nesha came too. The trip was the highlight of his parent's visit to England. Both were thrilled to view the historical landmarks. Saj drove around central London, and he and Lea pointed out many of the tourist attractions. It brought back memories for him when he visited the city with Dipak, about seven years back.

"Look, Rita. That is Buckingham Palace, where the Queen lives." Jaru drew her attention. It was rare for him to be excited about anything. Both had known about the Queen and the Palace all their lives. They also visited Westminster, St Pauls' and Madame Tussauds', then stopped on the way home and had dinner in a restaurant. Everyone had a fantastic day out.

The day of Saj's parent's departure to Bombay was filled with sadness. Lea wished his parents could stay longer. Rita wanted to prolong their visit, but his father had to get back to work. They had stayed with them for more than a month. Lea had developed a special bond with Rita.

Saj drove them to Heathrow on his own. It was a quiet drive with extended periods of silence.

Rita said, "Lea is a wonderful girl. Are you happy?"

"Yes Mama, I am."

"You've been subdued lately."

"I get exhausted at my job. Nothing to worry about."

There were emotional scenes at Heathrow, as Saj bid them farewell.

"I'll come and visit again soon and send money," Saj said. "And remember to take your tablets," he told his father as they walked away.

Unfortunately, Saj had had to say goodbye to his parents so many times. That made him sad, though he couldn't do much. He wished they lived closer.

Chapter 41

With a cup of tea in his hand, Saj sat in the doctors' office contemplating. He had just seen an Asian couple; the husband came in with chest pains. They reminded him of his parents. Two months had passed since they had returned to Bombay, he still missed them.

"Dr Saj. A girl has come in with burns. She doesn't look well." A nurse informed him.

"Why didn't she go to the burns unit?"

"I don't know. Maybe because the patient has further to go."

Saj left his drink and got up. What he saw distressed him. There was a beautiful, eighteen-year-old Asian girl with one side of her face scalded lying on the bed. The incidence happened in the kitchen while she cooked. She winced with pain while he examined her.

He contacted the burns unit in another hospital for advice. The plastic surgeon on duty gave Saj few instructions and advised him to transfer her to their department the next morning. He treated her with painkilling injections and tablets, and gradually her discomfort eased.

"It didn't happen in the kitchen, did it?" Saj stared at her.

The girl remained silent with her head bowed.

"You need to tell me what really happened. Why are you here on your own? Where are your parents?"

She hesitated for a few moments and avoided his gaze. "You wouldn't understand." Her voice quivered. Tears shone in her eyes.

"Try me, what happened? I know it wasn't from cooking."

The girl paused, looked down and away and said, "I like this man, but he's white...my parents were furious when they discovered. They tried to get me to marry my cousin. This man is on the dole and drinks a lot. I don't want to be with him." Saj handed her a tissue.

"Last week, he found out I liked a white man." She became quiet and mopped her eyes.

"Today, as I walked back home from the shop, my cousin stopped me in the street. It was only minutes away from home. He appeared drunk and told me he knew I didn't want him. And if he can't have me, nobody can."

Saj leaned forward.

"He took out a bottle and squirted liquid on my face and ran away. I screamed. It hurt so much. I shouted for help, a kind man who drove past stopped. He said I needed to go to the hospital, brought me here and left. Maybe he didn't want to get involved." She sobbed.

Saj had heard enough. "And where is your cousin?" he asked with his forehead creased.

"I don't know."

"We need to inform the police, and your parents must be told. That villain can't run away."

"Please don't. The honour of my family is at stake. You must know what it's like in our culture," the girl said wiping her tears.

"I'm sorry, but as a doctor, I am not allowed to conceal the truth. A nurse will come and sit with you." He stood up and left.

This brought back the reality of his own traditions. Many Asians who live in England face similar misfortunes, the clash of cultures, he thought.

Saj was determined that this evil man must be brought to justice. He informed the nurse in charge, who contacted the police. She also rang the girl's parents, who were worried about her welfare. Saj spoke to the doctor in the burns unit again with the new information. The specialist suggested he transfer the girl to them straight away.

Driving back home late that night, Saj yawned as he reflected on the incident about the girl. This tragic event would be detrimental to her psychologically and ruin her matrimonial prospects. He thought about the effects that facial scarring had and realised that he would like to specialise in plastic surgery.

He tiptoed into the house at 11 pm. Nesha was fast asleep, but Lea was watching TV. He had dinner, poured himself a glass of wine, and sat in the lounge to unwind.

"What's the matter? You're quiet," he asked as he sipped his drink.

"We don't spend enough time together, you don't see Nesha either," she said.

"I don't know what to do Lea. Work is hectic and so is my surgical training. I'll try to find more time, I promise." He kissed her. "Oh yes. I would like to specialise in plastic surgery. What do you think?"

Saj told Lea about the girl with burns, and how upset he had been. He dozed off on the couch. She nudged him, turned the lights off and they headed to their bedroom.

Chapter 42

The years had flown by. It was 2003. Saj completed his training and became a consultant in plastic surgery at a London hospital. Lea had another baby, a son Jake. She changed her job and now worked part-time as a district nurse. Nesha was eight and had grown to be a beautiful girl. Jake was five. Saj's parents were happier, now they also had a boy.

The family had moved to a big house in a quiet suburb in Surrey. Saj's new home was modern and elegant, with views overlooking the fields. It boasted of three bedrooms, a big lounge area and an average sized landscaped garden.

"Children. We are going to Disneyland Paris," Saj announced one day.

"Yeah." Both jumped up and down. Lea overheard him in the kitchen and came in the room.

"Are we going away?" Lea sounded excited.

"We're all due for a holiday. I've heard Disneyland is not just for kids." He kissed Lea.

The family had a superb holiday. Lea and the kids enjoyed quality time with him.

Saj had been to Bombay on a couple of occasions to visit his parents. Lea went with him once and took the children with her. Rita sang Lea's praises to all her friends and family. She told them, Lea was the best daughter-in-law anyone could wish for. Wherever she went, they treated her like a queen. Both also attended his sister Gita's wedding on that trip.

His father had been sick after he retired from his job. Saj paid his medical expenses. At times, Lea had the impression he still carried guilt on his shoulders. These sentiments were stirred up each time he spoke to his parents on the phone.

It was Saj and Lea's tenth wedding anniversary, and they had organised a celebratory party at home. Guests packed the house. He enjoyed socialising whenever he got the opportunity. Many doctors and their partners were invited. Music played in the background and champagne flowed while Saj chatted and laughed surrounded by his friends.

Lea's mother, Margaret came with her new husband. Her parents had been divorced for three years, but she had remarried. Chris was still on his own and didn't turn up. Nicole had gone abroad volunteering for a charity organisation. Toby lived with his girlfriend in London, and they had a son.

After the buffet, there was a disco. Saj had too much alcohol and displayed his silly Bollywood moves by throwing both arms up in the air and hopping on one leg. Everyone laughed. He grabbed Lea's hand and tried to get her to join him, but she didn't find it amusing. He presumed she didn't approve of him being too familiar with a few of the women.

Lea juggled her time between her nursing career and taking care of the kids. It was hard work for her. Saj suggested giving up her job, but she enjoyed her nursing.

The children had moved to a new private school, four months back. Since then Nesha appeared subdued. One morning the school telephoned and informed Lea that Nesha's work had slipped. She didn't seem interested in her studies. Lea couldn't understand the reason.

She sat with Nesha in the lounge one evening when Saj was at the hospital.

"You've been quiet lately and disinterested in school. What's the matter? You can talk to Mummy."

Nesha kept silent and looked away.

"I won't be annoyed."

"This girl in my class, Kate," She said looking at her hands.

"Yes."

"She doesn't like me, she calls me names."

"What names?"

"Paki...Is it because I'm dark skinned?"

Lea tried not to show her horror.

"Don't listen to her. You're beautiful, and she's jealous."

"And... another girl sometimes takes her side and taunts me, Mummy." Her lips quivered.

"Come here." Lea gave her a hug and kissed her. "I'll go and talk to them and sort it out. Now let's go to bed."

Lea made an appointment to meet the Headmistress who seemed a sweet lady. She listened to what Lea had to say. The Headmistress called the mother of the girl and arranged a meeting the next day.

They sat at the headmistress' office waiting for Kate's mum. She was half an hour late. They all gathered around the table, and the headmistress explained the situation.

"My daughter hasn't done anything wrong," the mother frowned. She sat with her arms crossed over her chest.

"But why would Nesha make it up?" Lea asked.

"You'll have to ask her," she said looking away.

The headmistress intervened and addressed both the girls. "This type of behaviour is not tolerated in my school. We treat each other with respect. If I hear or witness anything of this sort again, there will be severe consequences. Do you understand me?" She stared at Kate, who shrank back in her seat with her head bowed.

"I won't stand for this," Kate's mother said. "You have no evidence. That girl lied." She pointed at Nesha.

"I did not," Nesha said and cried.

"Nesha. You come to me if anyone says anything racist to you," the headmistress said.

They all left the office, with nothing resolved. But at least it was on record and would be monitored from now on.

It was Bonfire Night. Wild celebrations took place all over the country with firework displays everywhere. People came to hospitals with injuries, despite all the warnings given to the public.

Saj had a full day at his plastic surgery unit. He was on call that night. Since he had become a consultant a couple of years back, his responsibilities had multiplied. He hated all the managerial work and budget cuts in the National Health Service. Sitting in committee meetings for hours frustrated Saj, not much was ever achieved.

He had finished a grand ward round and felt his stomach churning after his long shift. As he wandered to the canteen, he met a doctor in the corridor.

"Dr Saj, another burns victim has come in. We want your assistance."

"Sure," he said with a sigh. "Food has to wait."

Saj always obliged and cared for his patients. He accompanied the junior doctor to the unit. A young girl lay on the bed, crying in pain. The nasty burn on her right arm horrified him. This girl was ten years old, long blonde hair and blue eyes. Her parents were there with her. The mother was distraught.

"How did this happen?" Saj glanced at the mother, as he examined her arm. There were significant blisters on her forearm, and the superficial skin discoloured.

"Erm...She attempted to light one of the fireworks. It exploded," her mother said in a shaky voice.

"What the hell was she doing with the fireworks at her age?"

"I don't know." She sobbed. Her husband put his arm around to comfort her.

"Can you all wait outside please."

Saj stayed with the girl for more than half an hour, along with the other doctor and a nurse. He gave treatment orders and came out of the room.

"This is a deep burn. Healing will take time, maybe several weeks or months. I hope it wouldn't leave too many scars, only time will tell."

"Thank you, doctor," her mother said.

Saj noted the time and hurried for the canteen.

The young girl who was admitted with burns was going home that day. Saj worked hard for more than three weeks to treat her. She underwent minor surgery and was fortunate that there were no complications. The girl had become part of the unit and had grown fond of Saj.

He finished work early as he had promised to take Lea and Nesha shopping. Lea had dropped Jake at his friend's party. It was Nesha's birthday soon. He had arranged to meet them in the hospital.

They all walked to the car park. Near the hospital entrance, Saj came across the girl who came in with burns. Her parents were with her as they headed home.

"We never got a chance to thank you for all your hard work. We're very grateful," her mother said.

"All part of the job." Saj shook hands with the girl. "You be careful with fireworks next time, don't go near them."

"I won't," the girl said.

"Ah, this is my daughter Nesha, and this is Kate, a special patient of mine." He introduced them to each other.

Lea and Nesha stood next to Saj, but neither spoke. The atmosphere had suddenly changed.

"We had better make a move. Thanks again," the mother said, and they left.

"Do you know Kate's mother?" He asked Lea as he drove into town.

"Yes. We know both the mother and the daughter."

"We?"

"Well, it's a long story. Nesha was bullied by Kate at school. I met her mother, and she didn't want to take any responsibility. She said Nesha lied."

"Why didn't you tell me this before?" He stared at Lea.

"How could I? You're never at home," she shouted.

After a moment of silence, Lea calmed down. "You're always at work. I don't get time to sit down with you for a proper conversation."

"What can I do? You knew that when you married a doctor."

Nobody spoke for the rest of the drive.

Lea had returned home after she picked up the children from school. She sat in the kitchen with a cup of coffee. The doorbell rang.

It was Kate and her mother. The mother smiled sheepishly at Lea.

"Please come in," Lea said.

They all sat in the lounge.

"Erm…We've come here to apologise," the mother stammered.

"No worries."

"I am ashamed the way I spoke to you at school. Kate admitted everything. We're both sorry. Your husband was so good to us."

"Don't worry, all in the past." Lea smiled.

"We're not racist. I don't know why Kate said those things. Please forgive us."

"All is forgotten, it's probably a phase. So, no more apologies," Lea said. "I can't remember your name. I'm Leanne."

"Sally...and you know Kate."

Kate sat in silence looking embarrassed.

Sally turned towards Kate. "You have something to say to Nesha."

"I'm sorry. Can we be friends," Kate said in a quiet voice.

Nesha looked at her mum for reassurance, then smiled and said. "Yeah."

Chapter 43

One Friday morning, Saj had arranged an appointment with
the Chief Executive of his hospital. Lack of funds affected
patients' care, and he was unhappy about the state of affairs
in the NHS.

"We are short staffed in the unit. No new appointments
are being made. There is a shortage of beds in the surgical
units. It appears patients' well-being isn't the main priority of
the health service," Saj said.

"Our resources are limited."

"I'm astonished, we have enough funds to spend on
managers, but none for the patients."

"If you're not happy, you know what you can do." He
sounded abrupt.

Saj had had enough. He got up and left the meeting.

He went for a long walk to clear his head. And to think
about his long-term future. Would he like to carry on like
this for the next twenty-five years of his life? He would end
up hating his job, he thought.

After Saj returned home that evening, he slumped on the couch. Opening a bottle of wine, he pondered about his career. He spent most of his time at work which lead to arguments with Lea. His goal was to have more quality time with his family.

He turned the television on to unwind. He didn't want to concern Lea about his job issues. She came and sat with him.

"That lady came to the house with her daughter Kate and apologised. I invited them to Nesha's birthday party," Lea said.

"Good." His thoughts were elsewhere.

"You're not listening. I don't know why I bother."

"I am. Sorry, there is too much on my mind right now."

Saj dozed off with the glass in his hand. The phone rang, that made him jump. He spilt the wine on the couch. "Oh shit."

Lea answered it.

"Saj. It's your mother." Lea sounded worried and gazed at him.

"Late for them! Must be two in the morning there," Saj muttered as he walked to the phone.

"Hello." The colour drained from his face.

Lea held close and stared at him. "What's happened?"

"So, he doesn't have any chance?" he spoke in a quiet voice.

"Mama. I'll come as soon as I can," he said and put the phone down.

Saj gulped his wine.

"What happened Saj?"

"Baba...He had chest pain, they took him to the hospital, he has passed away," Saj said in a shaky voice.

"Oh, my God." Lea embraced him.

Saj wiped his eyes. "He was only sixty-seven. I can't believe it." He put his head in his hands.

They hugged each other and wept.

The next day, Saj asked the Chief Executive for compassionate leave to attend his father's funeral. The hospital administrator first refused, citing short staffing as the reason. Saj was furious at his attitude and insisted, so he eventually agreed.

Saj departed for Bombay the day after. He stayed with his mother for five days.

Lea waited for Saj in the arrival area at Heathrow Airport. It was midday. She was apprehensive, unsure of what to expect. When he came out, he was quieter than usual, that was to be expected.

"How is Rita?" she asked.

Saj shrugged his shoulders. "Not too good."

"My fault you stayed in this country. I'm sorry."

He kept quiet for a moment and then said, "But it was my decision, though, I take full responsibility. It's not your fault." He kissed her on the cheek.

Neither said much during their drive home. There was still an hour before Lea had to pick the children up from school.

"I want to talk to you about my ideas for our future," Saj said. She sat down next to him.

"While I was away, I had time to think."

He looked at her. "I've been stressed out about my job for a long time."

"Nobody gives a damn about the patients in the Health Service. They only want to save money, and have their priorities wrong," Saj said sipping his tea. "I'm sick and tired no one will listen. The hospital authorities wouldn't give a damn if I quit my job. Those bastards wouldn't even allow me to leave for Baba's funeral."

"A friend of mine who is also a consultant plastic surgeon left the NHS. He took up cosmetic surgery because there is a growing demand for such treatment from private patients. I have considered it as the best option. I can carry on with my work and do aesthetics on a Saturday. If it works well, I can open my own clinic. What do you think?"

"Will it be as rewarding? Plastic surgery helps victims, whereas cosmetic treatments are for vanity."

"It would be. It's not all vanity. Most of these people suffer from low self-esteem, depressed by their appearance. They are happier and gain confidence after their treatment."

"I didn't think of that. You'll make it work anyway. You always do," Lea said. "I've to pick the children up." She kissed him and got up.

"We could all go for a walk, beautiful day," Saj said with a smile.

They held hands as they left the house.

Chapter 44

A year later, Saj sat in his cosmetic clinic in Harley Street, London. He had done exceptionally well in his practice, as he was a talented surgeon and a perfectionist. Cosmetic surgery was in high demand and Saj was a busy man. Patients loved him. He achieved excellent results without any complications.

With his dashing looks, Saj was popular amongst the ladies. Well-groomed and dressed in designer clothes, he attended cosmetic conferences all over the world. He devised his own technique for face-lifts, which was well received by his colleagues. Demands for delivering lectures and training surgeons were huge.

Soon, he mixed with celebrities, who were his clients. National television and fashion magazines interviewed him regularly. They couldn't get enough of him. At no time had he expected his practice to take off in such a spectacular manner. Work took over his whole life. He enjoyed fame and fortune and felt on top of the world.

That evening, as usual, Saj returned home at around 10 pm. Lea was watching television, the children were in bed. He sat down with a glass of wine.

Lea focussed on the television and was quiet.

"Is everything alright?" he asked.

She paused, looked at him and said, "Do you remember you were supposed to be at the parents evening today?"

"Oh shit, I forgot. This interview distracted me."

"I was the only one there on my own. You never see your children, I'm sick and tired of making excuses for you!" Lea pointedly poured herself a glass too.

"I'm sorry, but I'm doing all this for us, and for the children's future." He gulped down his wine.

"We don't need an extravagant lifestyle. We want you to be around. When was the last time we went out together as a family, or even on holiday?"

"I have asked you to come with me to the conferences abroad, but you never want to," Saj said.

"That is your work, not a proper vacation."

"Okay. I'll take time off soon, and we'll go away, I promise."

"How many times have you told me before?"

"I struggled to set up my practice, it was tough. What if we move to a bigger house. We'll have spare rooms for guests to stay. Maybe with a swimming pool and a games room. What do you think?"

Lea turned her face away. "Whatever...Oh, your mother phoned earlier. She said you don't speak to her nowadays and wants you to ring her back."

"I'll call her tomorrow." He poured another glass.

She left the room and went to bed. Saj had a few more glasses, then came to the bedroom. As he lay down, he kissed her on the face and neck and wanted to make love.

"I need sleep. My head hurts" She turned away from him.

"You have these headaches too often," he said in a sarcastic tone.

Another year had passed. Saj moved to a more prestigious clinic in Harley Street. He also travelled to LA to operate on wealthy clients, offering facelifts, liposuction, breast augmentation, injectable treatments, and lasers. The rich and the famous all wanted a piece of him. He considered himself indispensable.

One day, a famous film actress came in for a consultation in his Harley Street practice. She had requested he visit her at her home, Saj refused. She would have paid him whatever he asked for, but he wasn't interested. The actress came through the back entrance with two bodyguards, to avoid the paparazzi. They waited in a separate room.

Other clients recognised her, as she walked through the corridor with her minders.

"Jesus Christ! That's Elizabeth Bailey. Did you see her go past?" one woman whispered to another.

"I should get her autograph," the other said.

"I'll phone my daughter and tell her. I've bought this amazing iPhone which has just come out. It gives me an excuse to use it." She took the phone out of her handbag.

"Wow. I need to get one," the other woman said.

It was Saj's 40th birthday. He threw a lavish dinner party at a plush five-star hotel in Kensington, London. The event was held in an exquisitely decorated hall, and he invited many of his celebrity clients. Saj had developed a noteworthy social circle. The buffet was sumptuous including caviar and oysters.

Lea didn't feel comfortable. Saj was surrounded by women, and he bragged about his achievements. Celebrities didn't impress her. She preferred her real friends.

"Great party." A beautiful blonde lady came over to Saj.

"Thanks. And you are?"

"Vanessa." She smiled and shook his hand. "I'm the director of Aesthetic Pharmaceutical, which supplies your clinics."

"Oh yes. I must be your best client."

"Absolutely. You're an asset to us, Dr Saj. Thanks for all your business over the years. This place is buzzing. You're very popular." She looked around.

"I had to work hard to get where I am. It hasn't always been a smooth ride. You have to be good at what you do, and I deserve it."

"And despite the stock market crash and global recession this year, your cosmetic surgery business is doing extremely well."

"I'm lucky." Saj smiled.

"You're a genius in your field," Vanessa gazed into his eyes fluttering her lashes.

They chatted for a while. Saj excused himself to greet other guests.

"Richard."

"Hey, Saj. Fantastic party." They shook hands. Richard was a consultant in Harley Street.

"Thanks. I'm glad you are enjoying it."

"You know me. I always have fun," Richard said.

"Sorry to hear about you and Melissa. How are you coping?"

"Okay. I have good and bad days. You knew it wasn't working for us. She was seeing this other doctor behind my back."

"I have no idea what she saw in Adam."

"He is fat and ugly. I gave Melissa everything." Richard gulped his drink.

"You'll be fine." Saj touched his arm. "If you need to chat, do come around."

"Thanks."

"Perhaps we should go for a game of tennis sometime," Saj said as he walked away.

When Saj and Lea got back home, both were exhausted. Lea paid the babysitter, and she left. Saj had had too much to drink and lay on the couch. She perched next to him.

"Awesome party. What did you think?" He glanced at Lea.

"Most of the people there were shallow. They're not my cup of tea."

"But they are rich and famous?"

"Money and fame don't impress me. You must enjoy the company of all those pretty ladies," Lea said.

"Are you jealous?" Saj grinned. "They mean nothing. You're the only one for me." He embraced and kissed her.

Chapter 45

She was a princess of a middle eastern country in her sixties. Her armed bodyguards stood outside the theatre door. Saj was performing a facelift on her, but it didn't go to plan. The patient bled excessively in surgery. Everyone looked worried, she was a valued client. Saj struggled to stop the bleeding. The theatre assistant mopped sweat off his forehead.

"Blood pressure is dropping Saj," the anaesthetist said. He perspired even behind his face mask.

"Why is she bleeding so much?" he mumbled. "We need to give her more blood."

The assistant went out.

"Dr Saj. No blood had been ordered." She stuttered.

"What?" he yelled.

"I don't know, it must have been missed," she said looking at her feet.

"How did it happen? I don't believe it. Order now." He said with a frown.

"Hope this will work." Saj used another instrument.

Eventually, the bleeding stopped.

"Her blood pressure is stable now," the anaesthetist said wiping sweat from his brows.

It was touch and go at one stage. Saj couldn't imagine the consequences if the patient died on the table which would have ruined his reputation. He threw his mask and gown away and took off his gloves.

He stormed out of the theatre, still furious about the mistake the nurse had made.

"Can you please come to my office now?"

When the nurse entered, she remained near the door.

"How could you miss that? She could have died!" Saj glared at her pointing his finger.

"I'm sorry Dr Saj. It won't happen again, I promise," she said in a shaky voice.

"I delegate people to do simple jobs, and they mess it up. In future, I will check it myself." He took a few deep breaths.

"I didn't concentrate. I'm very sorry. My husband left me a couple of days back." The nurse broke down and sobbed. Saj handed her a tissue.

"I'll give you one last chance. You can go now."

"Thanks, Dr Saj, this won't happen again." She hurried out.

The family had moved to a luxurious house deep in the countryside on the outskirts of London. It boasted five bedrooms, an outdoor swimming pool and a tennis court.

"Darling, I'm home" Saj announced one evening, as he closed the front door. He heard nothing back. Walking around the house, he couldn't find anyone. He went to the kitchen and saw Lea with a bottle of whisky.

"Have you been drinking?" he asked.

"What does it matter to you?"

"I don't want an argument. What happened?"

Lea kept silent for a few moments, then stared at Saj. "Do you know what day it is today?"

"Erm."

"Our 15th wedding anniversary. Oh. You do remember the year we got married…1992?" She said with sarcasm.

"Oh shit. I'm sorry, I forgot. There is too much pressure at work. I'll make it up to you, promise." Saj tried to kiss her, but Lea turned her face away

"You love your status, fame and money. These are the most important thing in your life; we don't matter much. I don't even know where you are or...who are you with, most of the time."

"That's not true." He poured himself a glass of wine.

As Jake walked into the kitchen, there was an uneasy silence. He was eleven but appeared older than his age. Tall with a dark complexion, black hair, and brown eyes, Jake had the handsome looks of his father.

"Hi Dad," he said as he filled a glass with water.

Jake had a black eye with a few scratch marks on his face. He tried his best to avoid looking at Saj but couldn't get away.

"What the hell happened to your face?"

Jake kept silent and glanced at his mother.

"Come on. what happened?" Saj said sternly.

"He had a fight with a boy at school...Oh, I forgot, you haven't seen Jake for three days."

"What was it about?"

"A boy called him a Paki," she said taking a sip.

Saj took a deep breath.

"Sit down Jake. Tell me what happened?"

"This boy. I tried not to react and ignored him. But he kept on teasing me," Jake said.

"And."

"Then I grabbed his shirt and threw him to the floor...I hit one of the chairs and hurt my face."

"What about the boy?"

"He also had bruises on his face. I pinned him down. The teacher came in and separated us."

Saj smiled. "At least he learnt a lesson and won't do it again."

"I had to go and talk to the headmaster yesterday. He wasn't impressed with Jake's aggression. He did tell the other boy off," Lea said.

"You need to ignore them. These kids are jealous," Saj said. "I'll teach you Tae Kwon Do."

"What's that?" Jake asked.

"A form of martial arts. Maybe you can join a class and take lessons."

"Yes, Dad...that would be cool."

After Jake had left, Lea said, "Saj, listen to me. I'm going to live with Mummy for a while. The children will come with me."

"Please don't go. I will take time off for you all. I do love you." He came and sat next to Lea and tried to hold her hand. She pushed him away.

"I'm lonely Saj. You had better change your ways. No more broken promises."

"I swear I will change." This time she let him hold her hand.

Chapter 46

One afternoon, Saj was sitting in his office in Harley Street. He was replying to some of the hundreds of emails he received. One was an enquiry from a man who wanted operations for a sex change. The phone buzzed.

"Hi. It's Vanessa from Aesthetic Pharmaceutical. You remember we met at your birthday party?"

He paused for a moment. "Erm...Oh yes."

"How are you?" she asked.

"Great and you?"

"Not too bad. Do you plan to attend the Cosmetic Surgery Conference in Las Vegas in September? My company would love to sponsor you, all inclusive."

"I need to check my diary if I'm free, but it sounds good. I'll ask my secretary to phone you and confirm."

"We'll be honoured if you could come. I'll ring tomorrow."

"Bye."

Saj leaned back in his chair. He remembered Vanessa was the blonde, slim, attractive woman he had briefly spoken to at his party.

He had been in theatre all morning and decided to go shopping. It was a rare opportunity for him to venture out and relax. The afternoon was sunny and warm.

At Harrods, he tried on an elegant navy Versace suit; it fitted well. He also bought a bottle of Calvin Klein perfume for Lea. As he strolled around the tastefully decorated counter, he passed a woman. She glanced at him and smiled.

"Hello, Dr Saj." She was an attractive lady, with an unusually large bust. He always noticed being a cosmetic surgeon.

Saj stopped and gazed at her, confused. "I'm sorry I don't recognise you."

"Michelle...Michael Dempsey. You operated on me several months ago."

"Oh yes, I remember. You look amazing, different. Are you pleased?"

"Yes. I am so much happier now. Thank you."

A few years ago, Michael had come to see him. He was 50, balding and overweight; one of the top lawyers in the country. Although Michael had been married for many years and had 4 children. He had always felt uncomfortable in his male body and dressed in women's clothes whenever he could. But still shared the same house with his wife and they had a supportive relationship.

Michael wished to take things a stage further. He was already on hormone therapy and wanted to book the necessary surgical procedures with Saj. After studying his psychiatric report, Saj over time performed various operations to turn Michael into Michelle.

"Good to see you again, Michelle. I must go."

Although Saj had seen her after the final operation, he was amazed at the transformation. He felt rewarded he could have been able to help.

When he got into his car, he grinned and couldn't believe it was the same man.

Saj and Lea were relaxing in reclining chairs on the patio looking at their beautiful garden. It was a gorgeous summer evening. Butterflies clung to the purple buddleia, and perfume from the roses filled the warm air. He watched the birds hop in and out of the flower beds looking for food. They conversed, and she giggled. Lea hadn't laughed for a long time, and that made him happy. He told her about Michelle. She was proud of him.

Saj's mobile phone rang.

"It's Vanessa. I checked with your secretary. She told me you're free to go to the Vegas conference."

"Sure. I'll speak to you later. Bye."

"Who was that?" Lea asked.

"A pharmaceutical rep about a conference in Las Vegas. Why don't you come? You'll love it there. We can take the children."

"When is it?"

"The first week in September. I can't remember the exact date."

"Oh no. Jake's in a sports event. Sorry I can't go."

"I got something for you." He handed her the perfume he bought at Harrods.

"Thanks." Lea didn't show much interest. "You asked me to remind you to phone your mother."

"Oh yes. I will call her later."

Nesha came out to the garden. She was a beautiful young lady of fourteen. You could see a lot of Saj and little of Lea in her.

"How are you, my angel?" He hugged her. She sat next to him.

"Daddy, I don't see you much," she said in a soft tone.

"I promise I'll take time off soon."

"But you always say that."

"I know. My work is so busy, but soon we'll go to London together."

"Promise."

"I promise darling." He kissed her on the cheek.

Chapter 47

Barack Obama was all over in the news as the first African American to serve as the President, when Saj landed in the United States. The year was 2009.

The spectacular show of water fountains timed to music, greeted him at the beautiful Bellagio Hotel. Las Vegas glistened in the hot desert sun. Not a cloud in the sky. The city that never sleeps.

Saj lectured to a vast audience of renowned international medical professionals. He gave a slick and stimulating presentation on his new face-lift technique. The audience was fascinated, and he basked in the glory. The doctor from Bombay had done well for himself, he thought and smiled.

After the extended applause, many surgeons came to speak with him and offer their congratulations. Some of them wanted to form professional liaisons with his clinic in Los Angeles and Hollywood.

Saj was on his way to his room.

"Excellent lecture." He turned around. Vanessa stood there. She wore a low-cut blouse and a short skirt.

"I didn't know you were here," he said.

"Oh yes. I wouldn't miss this. You were wonderful."

"Thanks."

"Are you enjoying your stay in Vegas?" she asked fluttering her long dark eyelashes.

"It's alright. My wife and children couldn't come. I miss them."

"A few of us are going on a tour to the Vegas Strip this evening. Just to have a look around and visit a couple of casinos. Would you like to join us?"

"I'm not the gambling type, thanks. I'll have an early night."

"Come on, there's a lot here to see at night. You don't have to gamble if you don't want to." Vanessa smiled.

He thought for a moment. "Okay, but I won't stay out too long."

"Super. I'll meet you in the lobby at nine." She walked away.

Saj had a long phone call with Lea and the children.

"This is an amazing place, Lea. You should have come."

"Definitely next time."

"Yes. We will take the children. They will love this place. I miss you."

"We all miss you too Saj."

He had dinner sent to his room.

Saj dressed casually in jeans and a white shirt. As he exited the lift, Vanessa was waiting for him. She looked stunning in a short black, red and silver sleeveless and backless dress.

"You're late." She glanced at her watch.

"It's only just past nine." He was surprised at her abrupt comment.

Vanessa introduced him to four others. As they left the main entrance, the spectacular fountain show started again. A large crowd gathered to watch. The display of water, music, and lights, on an enormous man-made reservoir, danced to 'Billy Jean'. It was magical. Saj thought that Lea and the children would have loved it. He must come again with the family.

The group boarded a stretch limo and headed to the city. Vanessa sat next to Saj. In one of the casinos, he was tempted to play like everyone else. Saj had never gambled before. It was like a giant flashing noisy hall, with line upon line of people putting coins into slot machines. The place dazzled but felt chilly with the air conditioning.

"What's the time?"

"Ten past eleven," Vanessa said.

"Strange, there are no clocks here."

She laughed. "The idea is for people to keep gambling, and not know the hours that pass."

There was a wide range of individuals in the casino. Saj spotted holidaymakers from many different countries, and of all ages. There were even a few brides in their white dresses who had just married Elvis-style in the white chapel. The buzz there was infectious. He observed people with fascination.

"Come on. You should try your luck, you never know," Vanessa said, interrupting his thoughts.

First, he risked only a hundred dollars, and couldn't believe it when he doubled it at the roulette wheel. This was exciting; he had never won anything before. He put five hundred on red. Again, he made a profit. There was no stopping him now.

"Today is your lucky day." Vanessa laughed as she sat next to him and quietly looped her arm in his.

"I'll try a grand." The wheel spun, but luck had deserted him this time.

"Oh dear, never mind. You have to put it down to experience," Vanessa said. "Let's go and have a drink."

But Saj wouldn't give up. Competitiveness came naturally to him. Desperate to win the money back, he put ten thousand down.

"Are you sure?" Vanessa sounded awe-struck.

Saj nodded and played for ten thousand. A crowd had gathered. There was tension as the silver ball rolled around and around.

"Oh no."

"Black 23," said the croupier.

Saj had now lost ten thousand dollars.

"Let's go for that drink now." He tried not to display the shock and shame he felt inside.

They went to a few bars and tried many different cocktails. The lights dazzled, and people crowded the streets. The group returned to the hotel at 2 am. He saw Vanessa to her room.

"Sorry, about losing all that money, I feel responsible," she said, opening the door.

"It was only a few day's work," he slurred, waving an arm dismissively.

Vanessa gazed at him with her big blue eyes. "Do you want to come in…for a coffee?"

"I need to go to bed. I'm lecturing again tomorrow. Damn it. I forgot to phone Lea."

"Only for five minutes?"

"Thanks for the offer. Good night." Saj weaved his way towards his room on the 15th floor.

The next evening after dinner, Saj went for a stroll along the Las Vegas Strip. Many hotels depicted famous cities in the world. 'New York New York' hotel with its tall, imposing skyscrapers, Paris hotel with the Eiffel Tower and the Venitian with its superb canals and gondolas. Neon signs flashed all around making it look magical. The children would have loved the lights, he thought.

Pedestrians had to cross the busy roads on bridges. Homeless people and street musicians peppered the walkways. They tried to get handouts from the passers-by. Saj was fascinated by observing everything around him. As he wandered, a man approached him and handed him a card. It was a prostitute contact card.

"Do you want one of these women?" the man asked flicking a big pile of cards.

"No." Saj smiled. The man was persistent. These cards littered the sidewalks, but none were there during the day. He wondered who cleared them all up and at what time.

People stood in doorways attempting to draw attention with offers of discounts on shows, food, and casinos. They were dressed in a variety of costumes. Showgirls, robots and Star Wars characters, all offered to let you take pictures of them for a fee. Saj didn't know that. As soon as he tried to take a photo, the man turned away from him.

A truck drove up and down the Strip with a large sign. It read "Girls Direct to You!" and a phone number. Saj chuckled. Men sold tickets for musical shows on the streets.

It was the grand gala evening on the last day of the conference. Guests crowded the hall dressed in their best attire. Saj wore his designer dinner suit and looked handsome. Champagne flowed in the elegant ballroom, and people conversed and laughed.

While Saj waited for a drink at the bar, Vanessa appeared at his side. She wore a tight, short red dress with matching high heeled shoes.

"Hey." She beamed and gave him a peck on the cheek.

"Hello."

"You handsome brute." Vanessa gazed into his eyes.

"You're not too bad yourself." He tried to be polite.

"Would you like to sit down?"

"Sure." They sat with their drinks.

"So how is the conference?"

"Good, but I'm ready to go back. I miss Lea. I've two...."

"The audience seemed impressed by your presentations. They think you are the perfect cosmetic surgeon. You have everything anyone could wish for."

Saj grinned and said, "As they say, don't always judge a book by its cover."

"What do you mean?" She twirled her hair.

He paused for a moment. "Well, people may think I've everything...an ideal career, a lovely family, confidence, fame and fortune...At times I don't feel good." Saj stared at his glass. He had had a few drinks by now.

Vanessa gave him her full attention. "Go on."

"I come from an ordinary background from Bombay in India. My achievements are like a dream. People think I'm so confident or even arrogant. Deep down I'm not." His speech became slurred as he gulped champagne.

"I'm surprised."

"I had to prove myself, and that was difficult. Everyone is afraid, and I'm no exception. Fear that something may go wrong with my surgery. Trying to impress others, to appear confident even when you're not." Saj had an ironic smile.

"I'll get us another drink. Do you want the same?"
Vanessa asked.

He nodded.

She got up and came back a few minutes later with the
drinks.

"What if an operation goes wrong? My patients'
livelihood and career depend on my surgical skills,
especially for celebrities. They can sue me and ruin my
reputation."

"Your work is vital to these people."

"And today…one of the surgeons got up and challenged
me during my lecture...that the facelift technique I presented
was originally his idea. I swear at no time I knew this
existed. Never been so humiliated." His voice trembled as he
sipped the drink.

After a moment of silence, Vanessa asked, "You were
born in Bombay. Do your parents live there?"

Saj hesitated and took another sip. "My father died not
long ago."

"I'm sorry. You poor thing." Vanessa stroked his hand.
Saj moved it away.

"My mother and sister still live there." He stared down at
his glass.

"Do you miss them? I'm sorry, I shouldn't ask." She took a
sip of champagne.

He remained quiet for a minute and glanced around. Then
said, "Yes, I do feel guilty. I abandoned them in Bombay
when they needed me, but I adore my wife and my children.

I have a wonderful family. Shame I don't get to spend more time with them. I hate the fact my work has taken over of my life."

"Enough of this. Shall I get you another drink?"

"Hmm," he said in a faint voice.

A man tapped him on the shoulder. "That was an impressive lecture, Dr Saj."

"Thanks." He looked at him and gave a half smile.

"And don't worry what Dr Longford said."

Saj nodded.

A few guests got on the dance floor. Vanessa returned with the drinks.

"I don't normally booze like this. Enough of me. What about you?"

"Would you like to dance?" she asked.

"No... I don't." He was incoherent

"Come on." Vanessa dragged him by his arm.

She was a fantastic dancer and had a wild and erotic technique. Saj tried a few silly moves of his own which made her giggle. After a few fast songs, the lights dimmed. The tempo of the music slowed down.

He wobbled as he turned around to leave the dance floor. Vanessa put her arms around his neck and held him back. At first, he resisted, then gave in. Keeping each other close, they moved to the music. Saj enjoyed the sweet scent on her neck, and he could hear her breathe. Vanessa's breasts were squeezed on his body. He was getting aroused. She became naughtier and rubbed her lower body against his while they danced, and stroked his hair.

Saj thought about Lea and tried to move away again, but Vanessa was strong and held him tight. His head was fuzzy, his legs weak. She gazed into his eyes and kissed him. Saj was turned on, and he grasped her bottom. They were lost in their world, completely oblivious to the surroundings.

Vanessa stopped, took his hand and guided him towards the lift. The elevator was empty, and they started caressing. The gentle ding announced her floor.

They kissed with passion as they entered her room. Saj kicked the door closed. Vanessa hurriedly took his jacket and tie off, and instead of unbuttoning, tore his shirt open.

"Sorry...I can't do this. I'm married, and I love Lea." Saj attempted to push her away.

Vanessa was persistent, kissing his neck and fondling him with expertise. An acute surge of desire took over Saj. She pulled his trousers down, giggling and pushed him on her luxurious queen-sized bed and got on top of him. Then caressed and licked every part of his body she could reach.

"I shouldn't be doing this." His voice was incomprehensible. He tried to resist the arousal he felt, as he gazed into her eyes.

Vanessa hurried to take her clothes off. Her body trembled with desire. Saj yearned for her as both rolled on the bed, their naked bodies pressed against each other. She put his manhood inside her and cried with ecstasy. Then she clutched his hair and pulled him deeper inside her. Their body movements were rhythmic. Vanessa gasped and moaned, and then Saj groaned with pleasure. Afterwards, they lay on the bed, their bodies glistening even in the air-conditioned room.

"Are these...?" he mumbled, as he fondled her breast.

"Real?" She giggled. "You did these a few years back. Don't you remember?"

"I do too many of them, and it becomes a blur."

Saj stretched and yawned and soon fell asleep.

When Saj woke up the next morning, he looked around with squinted eyes, unaware of where he was. He thought his head would explode and he felt sick. Then he glanced at his watch. It was 11 am. A beam of sunlight entered the room past the partly opened curtains. Rubbing his eyes, he yawned. He saw Vanessa sat in front of the mirror as she put on her make-up.

"Good morning." She turned around and smiled. "Did you enjoy it last night?"

Saj kept quiet for a minute. "Erm...I don't remember much, my head hurts." He sat up on the bed and rubbed his forehead.

"You had a splendid time."

"Oh, my God. What have I done?" Saj jumped to his feet, looked around, and found his clothes spread out on the shiny marble floor. He hurriedly put them on, carried the jacket and bow tie in his hand, and left. Walking towards his room, he met a couple of doctors in the corridor.

"Good morning Dr Saj," one of them said.

"Morning," he spoke in a low inarticulate voice.

He got to his room and struggled to open the door. His hand trembled.

He hoped it was all a nightmare. But his bed was still made up. He looked up at the mirror as tears rolled down his cheeks. He held his head in his hands with shame.

Saj wiped his eyes. How could he do this to Lea? He loved her. How would he face her now? He had betrayed her trust. Why did he drink so much? Vanessa? What did she want from him? He thought about phoning Lea and tell her the truth, then changed his mind.

For half an hour he sat with his shoulders slumped staring at the wall. Then he got up for a glass of water. He remembered he had to catch the flight back home that afternoon. Dragging himself to the shower in a daze, he was appalled by what he had done.

Chapter 48

Back in London, Saj was working late at his clinic one evening. He had returned from Las Vegas a couple of days before. His workload always increased when he came back from a trip. Lea got annoyed as he spent even less time with her. He made an effort to take the kids to Madame Tussauds, which they enjoyed.

He sat at his desk contemplating his night with Vanessa. He felt horrified and guilty, undecided whether to tell Lea his secret. Why did he let himself get in that situation? Why couldn't he say no? He sipped water.

His mobile phone buzzed.

"Hi darling, I'll be home soon," Saj said.

"It's Vanessa."

His tone altered. "Ah."

"How are you? I haven't heard from you since we got back."

"Been busy."

"You sound serious."

"Lot of work to do."

"Do you want to meet for lunch? I'm in your area tomorrow."

"I can't."

"When are you free. I need to see you?"

"What happened in Vegas was a huge mistake?"

She kept silent for a few moments.

"Do you like me? Am I not pretty and sexy enough?"

"For God's sake, I'm married, and I love my wife."

"It didn't stop you before...and nobody needs to know about us."

"I had too much to drink that night, no idea what I did." Rubbing his forehead, he leaned back in his chair

"Yes, you did."

"I regretted the whole thing later. I love Lea and my children." He scribbled on a piece of paper.

"They don't need to know. We can still have fun."

There was a knock at his door.

"You have to forget what happened. I must go. " Saj put the phone down, rested back and took a deep breath. "Come in."

His secretary entered.

"I wanted to confirm your appointments for next week."

"Erm."

"Are you okay?"

"Yeah." He avoided her gaze. She left the office.

Saj needed to talk to someone and share his feelings; otherwise, he'd go crazy. He bowed his head. But who? Whom can he trust? Richard. He is experienced in worldly matters and a trustworthy guy. He worked as a consultant cardiologist in Harley street, divorced with two children. Saj had known him for five years.

He dialled his number and waited. The phone kept ringing. He was about to put it down when Richard answered.

"Hi Richard," he said in a faint voice.

"Hey, Saj. Haven't heard from you in a while." There was silence.

"Are you there. What's up?"

"Erm. I need to talk to you. Have you got a minute?"

"Yes. Sure."

"You know I went to Vegas for the conference."

"How did it go? Did you lose at the casinos?"

"It was very successful until the Gala night. I felt a bit lonely without Lea."

"And?"

Saj hesitated for a few seconds, bit his lips and said in a muffled voice, "I slept with someone." He shut his eyes, his lips quivered.

"What?"

"I had a one-night stand in Vegas." His eyes glistened.

"Bloody hell. Someone, I know?"

"I'm so ashamed Richard. It was a mistake. I don't know what to do."He mopped his eyes.

"Does Leanne know?

"No. I feel so guilty. I love Lea so much, can't imagine losing her."

There was a pause. "You don't need to tell Lea. She will never know."

"I feel horrible. I am tense, can't focus on my work. I'm worried about making a mess with my patients."

"Better not tell her."

"But I can't look in her eyes. She'll guess something is wrong. The thought of her leaving me…."

"My advice will be to keep quiet. The Lea I know will take it very badly. What came over you in Vegas?"

"Too much to drink. But I need to take responsibility, it was my fault."

"Come to my place tomorrow, and we'll have a chat. I have my daughter staying with me today, so I need to spend time with her."

"Thanks for listening, Richard. See you tomorrow evening. And thanks!"

The next morning, Saj was at a meeting in Knightsbridge. A renowned company offered to expand his cosmetic surgery business. He would open a chain of clinics all over the country. It was a tremendous opportunity for him, which would make him millions.

While he sat there, his mobile rang. The call was from an unrecognised number. Saj thought it might be a patient, so he excused himself.

"When are you free for a coffee?"

Saj gasped. It was Vanessa again.

He clenched his jaw but tried to stay calm. "I'm busy. Please don't phone me again. I'm sorry. It was only a one-night thing. Forget about it!" He hung up. When he returned to his seat, he had a frown on his face

"Is everything alright?" his colleague asked.

"Yeah," he said as he wiped a few drops of sweat from his forehead.

In his lunch break, Saj went to his car to collect some papers. It was cold and drizzling, so he put his overcoat on. His phone rang. He knew it would be Vanessa, so he blocked the number. It buzzed again as he walked back, it came up as an unknown caller. He was fed up and turned it off.

Why didn't she leave him alone. What a blunder he had committed? Saj desperately hoped Vanessa would get the message.

The sun was shining with clear blue skies. It was a Saturday afternoon. Saj had a rare day off and was spending time with Lea and the children. The family sat in their dining room for tea, with biscuits and Bombay mix.

"So how is school?" Saj asked.

"Cool, I still have a lot to do for my exams," Jake replied.

"Jake has done well. He is top of his class," Lea said.

"Excellent." Saj smiled as he looked towards Jake. "Like father like son."

"And I'm captain of my school hockey team," Nesha said trying to prove a point.

"Fantastic. I am so proud of you both," Saj said. "Who wants to go to Pizza Hut, and later to a movie?"

"Yeah." The children screamed.

Lea got up to answer the phone.

"Saj...it's your secretary." She called out.

"What does she want on a Saturday? She knows I am off today," he grumbled, as he walked to the hall.

"Hi, Linda. What's the problem?"

"This is Vanessa."

Saj's face dropped, and his colour drained away. He sat on the chair, his head was spinning, and his heart beating fast. He never imagined she would phone him at home. How did she get his number? He knew Lea would hear his conversation from the dining room.

"Are you there," Vanessa asked.

Saj recovered and said in a stuttering voice, "Yes."

"You ignored me. Nobody does that," Vanessa sounded agitated. He could only listen to her speak.

Then she turned sweet. "Saj, I want to see you. Your wife wouldn't know. I want us to be friends. Please come to mine on Wednesday evening...25 Regent court, Bridgend. Will you remember?"

"Yeah."

"I'll make it worthwhile for you." She changed her tone. "Because if you don't, it will get nasty for you. You have your lovely family, and your excellent reputation to think of."

"Bye." Saj put the phone down and stood motionless. His mouth was dry, and he breathed deeply, as he went through emotions of anger, fear, guilt, and hopelessness.

Clearing his throat, he shouted from the hall. "I'll be a minute."

"Why did she phone on a Saturday?" Lea asked as he walked back in.

Saj avoided eye contact and thought for a moment. "Erm...One of my patients had problems."

"Is it serious?"

"No, she'll be alright." He sat down and turned to the children. "Now, where were we?"

Later that week, Lea was cooking curry for dinner. It was 5 pm but still bright outside. Saj promised to come home early that evening. She had learnt to cook Indian food over the years. A few of them from recipe books and others from Saj's mother. The children loved her meals.

While she cooked, Jake sat in the kitchen reading a book. Nesha was upstairs in her room. Lea heard a car on the gravel drive and was pleased Saj had come home. The doorbell rang. She left the saucepan and went to the door. A woman dressed in a smart suit stood there.

"Can I help you?" Lea asked.

"I'm here to meet Dr Saj on a business matter," the woman said with a smile.

"He's at work; he'll be here in half an hour. Would you like to come in?"

"Thank you."

"You have a beautiful house," the woman said looking around.

"Thanks. By the way, I'm Leanne."

"I'm Charlotte." They shook hands.

"Please take a seat. What can I get you?"

"Coffee please, white no sugar."

Lea got up to make the coffee and checked on the curry. The children came into the lounge.

"These are my children, Nesha and Jake. They're waiting for Saj to get back for dinner."

"Lovely kids," Charlotte said.

She took a sip of her coffee and stood up.

"I'd better leave now." She picked up her handbag.

"You can finish your coffee. Saj should be home soon," Lea said.

"I've got another appointment to go to. I'll catch up with Dr Saj another time," Charlotte said and walked to the door. Lea followed her. She said goodbye and left.

Half an hour later, Saj arrived home. He kissed Lea and hugged the children. The family enjoyed their meal together.

"This is delicious. You cook great curries, Lea." Saj took another spoonful of rice.

"Yummy," Jake said.

"Which one is your favourite," he asked Jake.

"Chicken stew."

"I like daal," Nesha said.

The children finished their dinner and left the room. Lea tidied up the kitchen.

"How was your day?" he asked.

"It was okay. The usual stuff. Tracy will babysit when we go to the party. I'm looking forward to it. It will be fun." She wiped the kitchen surface.

"I'm exhausted and fed up. This company offered me huge incentives to open a chain of clinics. But I refused. I want to spend more time with you and the children."

"Oh...there was a lady here to see you, must be from that firm. She had to leave."

"Who was it?"

"Her name was Charlotte. She said she had a business proposal for you."

Saj shrugged and sipped wine.

"What did she look like?" He picked up the newspaper.

"Well, she must be in her early thirties, attractive, slim, blonde with blue eyes. She seemed strange though," Lea said as she put the plates in the dishwasher.

It must be Vanessa! Lea was clearing up and fortunate for him, didn't notice his worried facial expression. Saj was alarmed she had been to his house. Why would she go this far? What should he do now?

"I'll watch the cricket," he said and left the room in a hurry.

He lay awake that night contemplating. He loved Lea, and the thought of losing her was inconceivable. How could he do this to her? This whole incident with Vanessa could ruin his life and his career. How foolish of him. He should have stayed away from her. Why did she chase him? The bitch seemed hell-bent on destroying him. He wished he hadn't drunk so much that night. When he first came to England, he criticised the drinking culture here. But he was no better. What a hypocrite he had become, he thought.

Saj decided to pay Vanessa a visit the next day. He told Lea he would be late home that evening. He had a meeting to attend.

Her apartment was situated in an expensive suburb of the city. It was raining hard. He pressed the intercom button at the entrance, his hand shaking. She answered.

"What a pleasant surprise. Come in."

She wore a revealing black dress. "Please sit down. What can I get you?"

"Nothing."

Her apartment was huge and elegantly furnished. Saj could see a balcony which overlooked the green. Vanessa got herself a glass.

There was an awkward moment of silence as he looked around.

"Nice place. You seem to have done well for yourself." He sat on the dark leather couch.

"Yeah...with help from my two ex-husbands," she said sipping wine.

Was Vanessa married twice before? He was astonished, alarm bells rang. She must be only thirty, he thought.

"I'll get to the point. Why did you come to my house yesterday?" He took a deep breath and wanted to take control of the situation.

"You avoided my calls." She gazed at him and played with her hair.

"What do you want from me?"

"I want to spend time with you."

"It was my mistake. I love my wife. I had too much to drink that night and couldn't say no. I wish I had." Saj yelled as he shuffled on the couch.

"You have a beautiful house and a lovely family."

"Stay away from my house and my family." He glowered at her.

"I will, but we can still see each other. Leanne would never know."

Saj's gritted his teeth when she called Lea by her name. He took a deep breath.

"If you want money, I can give it to you. How much do you want?"

Vanessa paused for a moment, then said, "Being with you is what I want. We would be good for each other."

"You don't understand. I'm married. I adore my wife and my children, and there is no...we. I don't love you."

"You should have thought about it that night." Vanessa got up for another drink. "Do you want wine?"

He didn't answer and looked the other way. She poured another glass and sat next to him. Then stroked his arm. He moved away.

"All I want is to spend time with you."

Saj thought he wasn't getting through to her at all.

"I've been thinking about you for two years, then I got close to you in Vegas."

Vanessa had planned all this!

"We can have fun together, you and me. As we did in Vegas." She moved closer to him again.

"This is bloody well not going to happen. It was an error of judgement. Why don't you get it through your head?" Saj shouted and stood up.

"I want you."

"You're crazy, delusional. You need psychiatric help." He glared wagging his finger at her.

"I have seen them all. The psychiatrists can't do anything for me."

What!

"If Leanne finds out about our night of passion in Vegas, you'll lose everything." Vanessa was spiteful as if she hated him.

Saj had enough. He grabbed her by the neck that sent her drink flying. He scowled at her, his face close to hers. There was fear in her eyes, her pupils were huge as she gasped for air.

"If you come anywhere near my house or my family again...I'll kill you...and nobody will miss you." He held her down for a minute, and then let her go. She went white and was trembling.

Giving her a final wrathful look, he walked to the door.

"If I can't have you, nobody can," Vanessa shrieked.

A large glass vase crashed into the door just as he reached it.

Saj spun around. Vanessa's lips trembled.

"I feel pity for you." His hands tightened into fists as he walked briskly out, leaving her front door wide open.

Next morning, Saj was operating in the theatre. He forced himself to concentrate on his work but felt his head would explode. How would Vanessa react to his aggressive outburst? Should he tell Lea the truth before Vanessa does? Maybe she'll be too scared to say anything now after he had threatened her. How stupid he had been? What if he lost Lea and the children? He couldn't live without them.

"Mr Saj. There!" The theatre assistant pointed towards the patient's neck. Blood was oozing.

"Okay." He realised he forgot to clamp a few blood vessels. Quickly he repaired the leak.

"Are you alright?" she asked.

Saj nodded his head. His nurse mopped beads of sweat off his brows.

Sitting in his office that afternoon, he still contemplated the situation with Vanessa. Saj felt frustrated. There wasn't a soul in whom he could confide. He cancelled his meetings for the day. Why was Vanessa trying to destroy him? He had done her no harm. He felt ashamed to hurt Lea.

How did she get hold of his home telephone number and address? It must be Linda. He went straight to her office.

"Did you give a lady my home address?"

"She phoned me and asked your number and address...I tried not to, but she was insistent," Linda said in a shaky voice.

"And?"

"The lady told me that she had a business proposal for you. She couldn't discuss it at the clinic. She wouldn't take no for an answer."

"How could you do that?"

"I'm sorry Doctor. I know I shouldn't have."

"At no time ever give my personal details to anyone. You should know about confidentiality." He stormed out of the room.

Linda was shaken. One of the nurses had heard him shouting and came in. She put her hand on Linda's shoulder. "Something is bothering Dr Saj. His behaviour was odd in the theatre today."

By the end of the day, Saj had made up his mind. He would tell Lea the truth.

It was a gloomy evening. Saj sprinted towards his silver BMW and was drenched when he got to the car, even with his coat on. He sat deliberating for more than ten minutes as rain pelted on the windows. Then he started his car and drove off. It rained relentlessly, and the visibility was poor.

. When he got home, his heart was pounding. The thought of breaking Lea's heart sent shivers down his spine. He took a deep breath and stepped out of his car.

Lea seemed in a pleasant mood and kissed him. "You're back early. Are you okay?"

"Erm. Yes. I am tired, had a busy day."

"Jake's exam results came in. He passed. An "A" grade student like his Dad."

"Good." He put his briefcase down avoiding eye contact with Lea.

"He wants to be a doctor like you."

"Hmm." Saj walked to the lounge and turned on the television.

"Aren't you pleased?"

"Sorry...Yes...great." He gave a half-smile.

"Dinner will be ready in fifteen minutes." Lea went to the kitchen.

Saj was quiet at the table, as he pondered his next move. Nesha and Jake were full of life as usual. They spoke about school and messed around, which kept Lea occupied.

"Teresa has invited us next Saturday. They are a lovely couple."

"Hmm."

After the meal, he paced around the lounge. Fear, uncertainty, regret, guilt, and sadness. He felt them all. The children went upstairs to their rooms, while Lea cleared the kitchen. Then she came and sat with him.

It was showdown time. Saj pretended to focus on the TV, but he gathered his thoughts in the meantime. The mood in the room was sombre. Perhaps Lea sensed there were issues.

After a few minutes' he glanced at her and said, "I need to talk to you."

Lea nodded.

Saj paused for a moment, held his breath and said, "You know that woman...who came to the house the other day." He sounded serious.

"What about her?" She gazed at him biting her nails.

"Lea. Please listen to everything I tell you...before you make up your mind."

By now she was entirely focussed on him.

"You know...when I went to Vegas for the conference. She was also there. She runs a cosmetic business." His lower lip trembled.

"You're worrying me Saj." Lea stared at him.

"Something happened...between her and me. I'm very sorry." His eyes glistened as he attempted to hold back the tears. "It was only one night. She meant nothing...I love you, Lea...I had too much to drink on the gala evening. Don't know why. She has become obsessed with me and will not take no for an answer."

Lea sat there frozen, staring at the TV. She looked pale even in the dim light of the room. Tears rolled down her cheeks.

"Please believe me. That woman means nothing to me. It was a huge mistake, and I take full responsibility. I'm sorry. You're the most precious thing in my life," he said in a quivering voice.

She kept silent.

"That woman is determined ● destroy us. She wants to be my mistress. I told her it would never happen. I love my wife...she is a psychiatric patient and crazy...she has planned all this for a long time. She is spiteful and feels rejected."

There was a hush in the room which seemed like an eternity to Saj. The TV was on in the background, but inaudible.

"What made you overindulge in drinks?" Lea spoke in a monotonous voice turning her face away and wiped her eyes.

"I don't want to make excuses. I missed you in Vegas. I wished you were there. I never told you this before, but I'm not as confident as I appear. I have this fear that something may go wrong, my patient may develop complications and sue me... these are wealthy and influential people, perhaps because I'm still...the doctor from Bombay."

"Poor you." Lea spat.

"An American surgeon humiliated me in front of the whole audience. He said I copied his surgical technique, which was totally untrue." Saj paused. "And maybe at times, I feel guilty that I left my parents. Not being there when Baba passed away."

"All for this shallow life of luxury and fame, forgetting the real essence of life...your loved ones...perhaps I assumed this crazy lifestyle would hide the scars inside me." He shuffled on the couch.

"I don't expect any sympathy from you. You may think these are all excuses. I know I made a terrible mistake, but I'll never do this again. I'm sorry. I love you so much." He took her hand. Lea snatched it away. "You mean everything to me, Lea. I can't apologise enough. Could you please forgive me?" He mopped his eyes.

There was pin-drop silence in the room.

"What's her real name?" Lea asked.

"Vanessa...She owns Aesthetic Pharmaceuticals, a supplier for my clinic." Saj hung his head.

"Does she live locally?"

"She lives in Bricksend."

"She is pretty. No wonder you fell for her."

"It wasn't like that. You're beautiful. I hate that woman. I love you, Lea."

Wiping her tears, she stood up. "I'm going to Mummy...the children will come with me."

"Please don't go. I love you."

"You betrayed my trust."

Lea slowly walked upstairs. Saj sat with his shoulders slumped staring at the wall.

After half an hour she came down with her bags followed by the children.

"I want to stay with Dad," Nesha said as she wept.

"You need to come with me, darling. I'll explain it on the way."

"Please don't go, Lea. I made a terrible mistake. It will never happen again," Saj said his eyes flooded with tears.

The children came to him, and he hugged and kissed them. They cried and then they were gone.

Half an hour later, Saj stood and surveyed the house. He went to pour a glass of wine but stopped himself. Instead, he fetched water from the kitchen and sat down feeling numb.

Is this what he had struggled for all his life? He felt empty inside. Life without Lea meant nothing for Saj. He had taken it all for granted. A beautiful house, money and fame he had it all. But now the most precious possession in his life was gone...his family. He believed he deserved what he got.

The truth was finally out in the open which gave him some sense of relief. Resting his head back, he dozed off on the couch. The mobile sat on the table buzzed which woke him up. He rushed to get it, in the hope Lea texted him. Rubbing his eyes, he glanced at his phone.

"Go to hell you bastard. I'll stay away from you."

Oh no. Lea hated him.

He put on his reading glasses and reread the text. It was from Vanessa. He wondered whether to laugh or cry more.

Chapter 49

A couple of weeks had passed since Lea left home with the kids. Saj missed them desperately and had no interest at work. He had been to his clinic only a few times. Linda had to cancel most of his appointments except the urgent ones.

One evening he returned home, put his briefcase on the floor and stood there motionless for a minute. He sauntered to the kitchen and got a glass of water. A pile of dirty dishes lay on the side. There were used cups on the table, old tea bags in the sink and curry was spilt on the cooker. A couple of open cans sat on the draining board which he had forgotten to put in the fridge. He sniffed them. They stank. He opened the bin and forced the cans into the already overflowing bag. He gulped water, took his jacket off, rolled his sleeves up and got on with clearing up the mess.

What had he done? He would never see his family again.

The phone buzzed.

"Hello," he said in a quiet voice.

"It's Richard. How is it going, man?"

"Okay." He lied.

"You need to get out of that depressing place. I'm going out with my friends to Sasha bar on Saturday night. Would you like to join us?"

"I'm busy on Saturday."

"Come on. I know you're not. It will be good for you. I'll see you there at about 8 pm."

"But I am…"

Richard put the phone down before Saj could make any more excuses.

He strolled back to the kitchen and surveyed the place. Opening the fridge, he picked up the milk carton and examined it. It was out of date. He put it in the bin. As he lifted the bag, it burst open and the waste scattered all over the kitchen floor. He broke down and sobbed.

What was Lea doing now? She must hate him. He couldn't change what had happened. Soon she would be asking for a divorce, he thought and grabbed a tissue and wiped away the tears.

Saj sat at the table in Sasha bar, staring at his glass. It was teeming with trendy punters. Richard was Saj's age, chubby with short, sparse blonde hair and wore designer glasses.

"Come on old fella. Get a grip on yourself. You've lost weight. Are you growing a beard?" Richard asked.

"I'm alright though I haven't been eating much. I can't be bothered to shave."

Saj took his phone out from his jacket pocket, paused for a minute and dialled Lea's mobile. It kept ringing. No answer.

"Listen, I have been through the same shit, but I am happier now being single. I can do what I want. No responsibility, not answerable to anyone." He leaned back in his chair and gulped his beer.

"I'm not like you, Richard." He took a sip of orange juice.

"There are beautiful women around. You are wealthy and famous. It's her loss."

"I miss Lea. I can't live without her and my kids."

"Hey, Sally." Richard turned around and called out to a woman standing near the bar. She was chatting with her girlfriend. "She is single and great fun."

"Please don't start Richard. I'm not interested. I love Lea, and nobody can replace her." Saj shook his head and took another sip.

"I was only trying to help."

"I know, thanks." He forced a smile.

Sally walked over to the table. "What's up, Richard?"

"This is my friend Saj," Richard pointed towards him.

"So, you are the famous Dr Saj. I have heard a lot about you," Sally said as she sat close to him.

She was a slim, dark, attractive lady in her early thirties. Saj almost choked with the whiff of her strong perfume.

"I'll get some drinks. Would you like a pint, Saj?"
Richard got up.

"Lemonade for me please."

"We are going clubbing from here. Would you like to join
us?" Sally gazed at him and batted her lashes.

Saj held his breath and turned his face away. He took a
final sip of his juice and jumped to his feet.

"I need to go. Could you please apologise to Richard," he
stuttered.

Before she could reply, he grabbed his coat and walked
briskly towards the door. It must not happen again. He
needed to stay away from all temptations, he thought.

Saj moved a couple of steps forward and stood right at the
edge of the pavement. A lorry whizzed past at speed and
honked. It couldn't be more than a foot away as Saj felt the
force of the wind on his face.

But what if Lea changed her mind. He should tell her it
was a big mistake and would never happen again. He loved
her. She might forgive him.

"Excuse me. Are you alright?" A man tapped him on the
shoulder from behind.

"Yeah, I'm okay," he said in a trembling voice. Then
slowly walked in the direction of the car park.

It was dark, and only a few cars were parked. Saj sank his
head back on the leather headrest. He was convinced that
Lea would ask for a divorce. Losing her would be
unbearable. He rubbed his neck muscles which felt tight and
gently moved his head around.

He closed his eyes for a couple of minutes. Then picked up his phone, took a deep breath and dialled Lea. He knew she wouldn't answer. It continued to ring as he waited and waited. To his surprise, she responded. He sat up.

"Hello," she said in a faint voice and sounded serious.

"Hi, Lea. How are you?" He cleared his throat.

There was silence from the other end.

"Nice to hear your voice," Saj said.

After a pause, Lea said, "You betrayed my trust. I loved you with all my heart."

"I am really sorry. Please forgive me. It will never happen again I promise." His voice quivered. Tears filled his eyes.

"How could you do this? You really hurt me."

"I know it was my mistake. I love you," Saj said.

"You should have thought about that when you had sex with that slut. It's too late. All this fame and power has gone into your head."

"Now they don't mean anything. I miss you so much."

Silence.

"I've given up drinking. Would you like to meet up and talk?" Saj said.

"No."

A pause.

"How are the children? Can I speak to them?"

Another pause.

"Hello Daddy," Nesha said.

"How are you, my angel?"

"I miss you, Daddy. I want to come home."

Wiping his eyes, he said, "I miss you all so much. How is Jake?"

"He doesn't want to come to the phone," Nesha said.

"Put Mummy on the phone."

"I have to go now."

The phone went dead.

Saj stared at the phone. Lea didn't want to see him. It was the end of his marriage.

The headlight of a passing car shone in his eyes. It distracted him. A police car sped by with its siren blaring. He regained his poise started his car and drove off.

Three more weeks passed as reality was beginning to sink in that Lea had gone forever. Saj ignored his clinic and didn't even bother to phone. When his secretary contacted him, he told her he was unwell. It seemed he had lost interest in life.

He was desperate to talk to Lea. But she ignored him. It was a stormy evening; the high wind threw him off balance as he got in his car. He sat there for a few minutes deliberating before driving off. When he arrived at Margaret's house, he was drenched. Margaret had recently undergone a hip operation and walked with a stick.

"How are you?" she asked at the door.

"Not too good." He looked away.

"Lea is distraught. Sorry."

"I wish to explain a few things to her. It was a mistake. I love her so much."

It seemed to him that Margaret had attempted to persuade her to talk to him. Lea would not come down to see him that night either.

"You've soaked Saj. You need to get out of those wet clothes. Come and sit down."

"Thanks, I'm fine. I had better go." What else could he do?

With a heavy heart, Saj trudged to the front door. He turned around hoping Lea might come down. She didn't.

It was still pouring, and the wind had picked up, as he hurried to his car. Lightning flashed, followed by low rumbling thunder. Saj shuddered as he got into the car and drove off.

Chapter 50

Lea came downstairs ten minutes after Saj had left.

"He is distraught. I don't want to interfere darling, but you should have listened to him," Margaret said.

Wiping her tears, Lea said, "Work had taken over his life Mummy. We don't matter anymore."

"Well, that happens with men. They lose sight of what's crucial to life. It doesn't mean they don't love you."

"He betrayed my trust with that woman. Good luck to him. He'll never find a better wife."

"I know darling but…"

"I sacrificed so much for him."

"But he does love you."

Lea's mobile which lay on the table buzzed.

"It must be Saj again. I won't answer." She allowed it to ring off and turned it into silent mode.

Margaret sat next to Lea. "Darling. Why don't you have a word with him?"

"I don't want to tonight."

Five minutes later, the home phone rang.

"He doesn't give up. Tell him I don't want to talk to him," Lea said, her brows drew together.

Margaret got up and answered.

"There has been an accident...I swear I didn't see him." The man sounded hysterical.

"Jesus! What accident?" Margaret gasped.

Lea jumped up and grabbed the phone. "What accident, who is this?"

"I think it's a silver BMW. It came from nowhere...He attempted to avoid me, and the car rolled over. I found this mobile next to the car. He looks hurt and is trapped. I tried to pull him out, but I couldn't...I phoned 999, and they're on their way. I'm sorry." His voice trembled, he sounded terrified.

"Where are you?" Lea's voice quivered.

"On Andover Road...I don't know exactly where. It's too dark."

Lea could hear the ambulance siren in the background.

"They're here. I must go. I'm sorry."

"Oh, my God, Mummy." Lea hugged her mother.

Nesha came downstairs, followed by Jake. "What's happened?" she said.

"There has been an accident...It might be to do with your Daddy. We don't know yet." Margaret's had tears in her eyes.

Lea trembled, she seemed unsure what to do.

"I never wanted to leave Daddy. It's all your fault Mummy. I hate you," Nesha said and ran out of the room.

"I think we should head for Andover road." Margaret tried to stay calm.

"Yeah. Let's go." Lea picked up her car keys.

"Children, we'll go and investigate what happened. We'll be back soon. I will ask Anita next door to stay with you while we're gone," Margaret said.

After a short drive, they reached the site of the crash. The visibility was poor, but Lea could see the lights of the emergency services flashing. A policeman waved her to stop. She parked the car, and they got out. As she hurried to the crash site, the full extent of the accident was evident. Lea screamed when she saw Saj's car on the side of the road overturned. She ran towards the car, but the policeman held her back.

"That's my husband in there." Lea was frantic as rain pelted down.

"Madam, he has been taken to the hospital," the officer said.

"Which hospital?" Margaret asked.

"The General."

"Was he ...?" Lea's voice trembled and she looked down.

"He was conscious. I can't tell you any more," the policeman said.

Lea broke down and wept. Margaret embraced her, and they hurried back to the car.

"I should have listened to him, Mummy. I still love him...This is my fault."

"Don't blame yourself, darling." Margaret choked with emotions.

Lea drove to the hospital. They hurried to the reception.

"I'm Mr Saj's wife. He was in a car crash earlier." She mumbled.

It was past midnight; there were only a few people around.

"He'd been transferred to Intensive Care."

Lea shuddered. They dashed to ICU on the opposite side of the hospital. Lea was shaking when they arrived there. Margaret followed her but struggled to keep up. The receptionist asked them to wait in the adjacent room, while she got someone to talk to them.

Nobody came. After half an hour which seemed like two hours to Lea, a nurse approached them.

"How is he?" Lea asked.

"Three doctors are with him now. He suffered multiple injuries, and is on a ventilator," the nurse said.

"Jesus Christ." Lea gasped. Margaret held her hand.

"Am I allowed to see him?" she asked.

"Sorry, not now. The doctors are busy with him. They'll come and talk to you when they're finished. Would you like a drink?

"Glass of water please?" Lea wiped her eyes.

Margaret phoned home to check the welfare of the children. She told them she would be back soon after speaking to the doctor. Lea sat in the waiting room chewing her nails and checking her watch frequently. Each passing minute was agony for her.

"It's all my fault Mummy. I should have listened to Saj and believed what he said. I was too hard on him. What if he dies? I love him so much, and I know that he loves me." She sobbed.

After an hour's wait, one of the doctors came in.

"I'm Mr Roberts, the consultant. I'm afraid your husband has suffered severe internal injuries, both to his chest and abdomen."

"Jesus!"

"Fortunately, it seems that there hasn't been any damage to his brain. He has been assessed for the full extent of his injury. After a few more scans, we'll operate on him as soon as he is stable."

"Is he going to live?" Lea asked in a stuttering voice.

"It's too early to say. The next forty-eight hours are crucial. We'll do our best. You go home and get rest. We'll keep in touch and update you," the consultant said and left.

Lea decided to stay. It was three thirty in the morning.

"Are you sure? You can't do much here," Margaret said.

"No, I want to, Mummy."

Margaret gave her a hug and a kiss. They ordered a taxi to take her home. After she left, Lea slumped in the chair in the waiting room.

"Would you like a drink?" Lea must have dozed off. She opened her eyes, looked up and saw a nurse standing in front of her holding a cup of coffee.

"Thanks. What time is it?" Lea rubbed her eyes and glanced around.

"Ten past eight," the nurse said.

"How is my husband?"

"He is stable. The doctors will tell you later."

"Thanks." Lea sipped her coffee.

"I used to work with Mr Saj at the Royal Beacon. It must be 1989," the nurse said. "My name is Lucy. I remember him. He was a very kind doctor, and his patients loved him."

"I am Leanne. I worked on another ward in that hospital." They shook hands.

"He was new in this country at that time. He has done so well in his career. I hope and pray that he pulls through."

"Thank you."

"If you need anything, please ask." Lucy left to attend to a patient.

Lea paced around the room for the next hour and was relieved when Margaret arrived.

"Anita is at home with the children. I phoned the school and told them they won't come in today. How is Saj?"

"They think he is stable, the doctors will tell us later."

"Have you informed his mother in Bombay?"

"No. I need to do that."

Rita was alarmed and cried on the phone. Lea was brief and told her she would let her know more soon.

Lea and Margaret went to the hospital canteen for breakfast. Lea only had coffee. At midday, she saw the consultant in his office.

"Your husband is stable, though still not out of danger. We're monitoring him closely," the doctor said.

"Can I see him?" Lea asked. Her eyes glistened.

"Yes, you can. I'll get a nurse to go with you."

Lea felt terrified not knowing what to expect. She slowly walked towards his room accompanied by the nurse, hesitating for a moment before she entered. Lea was alarmed at the sight of Saj, in the dim light. What she saw was worse than she had ever imagined. She gasped for air and felt dizzy. The nurse helped her to the chair.

Saj lay in bed, unrecognisable. His face was swollen and had numerous cuts and bruises. It could have been anyone other than him. Tubes came out of his nose and mouth, and many drips going in. He had bandages wrapped around his head, and his body was covered with a sheet.

"Oh, Saj, my love, what have you done?" Lea sobbed as she sat next to his bed. "I forgive you for everything. I should have heard you out. You left your parents to be with me...I never told you how grateful I was." She wiped her tears.

Lea wanted to hold his hand, the nurse advised not to touch him. She left to give her privacy.

Forty-eight hours had passed since the accident. Word got around. Many of his friends and a few reporters came to visit him. Lea received numerous phone calls about his welfare. Several of Saj's high-profile clients and celebrities sent their representatives with flowers and their best wishes. The side room seemed like a florist's shop.

Lea realised for the first time, how popular and loved Saj was. She felt exhausted but stayed by his side most of the time. He was taken to the operating theatre a couple of times during this period.

One morning as she held his hand, Lea felt Saj move his right fingers. Then after a few minutes, his eyes half opened. He turned his head and gave a half-smile. She smiled back, squeezed, and kissed his hand as tears ran down her cheeks.

Later that afternoon, the doctors gave Lea the brilliant news. Saj was out of danger, but it would be a slow recovery. Lea embraced her mother with delight. She was now prepared to do whatever it took, to keep her marriage and her family.

After a week in intensive care, Saj was transferred to a private room. A long month of painful rehabilitation followed. During this period, Saj, Lea and the children had the opportunity to rebuild their relationship.

Chapter 51

It was a cold sunny afternoon, coming up to Christmas. A festive feeling was all around town. Lea's car pulled up in their gravel drive. Saj got out, stood and stared at his beautiful home. He slowly walked to the front door. Nesha and Jake were already waiting for him with the door open. Both ran and embraced him.

He sat in the lounge in silence. Lea brought him tea with biscuits, and of course Bombay mix.

"We missed you, Dad." Nesha mopped her eyes.

"I missed you all so much." He kissed both of them.

"We're the school cricket champions. I am the captain of the team," Jake said with pride.

"Well done."

After a while, the children left to go to their rooms.

Saj and Lea sat close together. He held her hand.

"You know Lea. I reflected a lot while in the hospital. I vividly remember the moments before the crash. I thought my time was up and I didn't care." He looked into her eyes.

"Please don't..."

"Let me say…I've been given a second chance, I want to make the most of it. I lost sight of what is meaningful in life.... money, fame, fortune...to be liked by people as a foreigner in this country...never be short of cash like my father...that is all I focused on."

"I realised these only give a temporary satisfaction, they don't mean much. I missed spending time with you all. I'm sorry for all my ignorance and stupidity." Tears shimmered in his eyes.

Lea gazed at him with affection and squeezed his hand.

Saj regained his poise. "Ah, but now I have made my decision."

He paused for a moment. "I plan to change my work...sell my business and go part-time. I'll cut down on my lavish lifestyle. Then I can spend more time with you."

"You love your career and your job."

"But I adore my family." He smiled and kissed her.

"Please don't make your decision in haste."

"Oh no, this isn't an impulse. These ideas have been in my head for more than a month, and there is more...I intend to go abroad for short visits. And help poor people who can't afford treatments. I'll start with Bombay and work at charity hospitals. Treat patients with burns and cleft palate, which are major issues over there. What do you think? Would you like to accompany me?"

"What about the children?"

"We shall go during school holiday times and take them with us."

"Sounds marvellous. I would love to." Lea smiled.

Jake walked in and showed Saj his school report. He had excellent grades.

"And when I've fully recovered, Jake and I will join martial arts classes together. What do you think?"

"Awesome." Jake sounded excited. "Mum got me a play station, Dad."

"That's great. Perhaps we can play together later. I'll buy a cricket world cup game for you."

"Cool, Dad."

"And more exciting news. Your mother, sister and her husband are coming to visit us after Christmas," Lea said.

"It's getting better by the minute." He grinned and kissed her.

"I'll make you another cup of tea. I've made some samosas and onion bhaji's." Lea left the room along with Jake.

Saj stood and surveyed the lovely lounge. There was an air of serenity in the room. He glanced at a picture frame of him and Lea from their wedding in Bombay which rested on the mantelpiece. A tall beautifully decorated Christmas tree with dazzling lights stood at the corner of the room. He picked up one of the Christmas cards. It read 'Merry Christmas to a wonderful family'. He beamed. Saj knew that he had been handed a second opportunity in life. He was probably the luckiest man in the world. This time he wouldn't mess it up.

As he looked up, lost in his thoughts, he saw a big colourful poster on the wall which read, 'Welcome Home. We all Love you.' He sat on the couch, leaned back and smiled to himself knowing that his nightmare was finally over.

ABOUT THE AUTHOR

Gos Jilani is a perfectionist. This debut novel cleverly combines his experiences and expertise as a doctor within the National Health Service, and his successful private cosmetic clinic on the Isle of Wight in United Kingdom. The latter demands high levels of creativity and an interest in people and their motives, as does his second career as singer and DJ. Gos has performed as an artist at major music events throughout the UK, including Glastonbury and the Isle of Wight Festivals. His cultural heritage allows a subtle yet colourful blending of both Indian and Western cultures.

ACKNOWLEDGEMENTS

Thanks to Glenys Williams for her proof reading and encouragement and Stacey McCourt for her help in publishing the novel. Also, thanks to anyone else who crossed my path during this journey.

Printed in Great Britain
by Amazon

87618579R00241